DR. SINGLE DAD

LOUISE BAY

Published by Louise Bay 2024

ISBN – 978-1-80456-025-9

BOOKS BY LOUISE BAY

The Boss + The Maid = Chemistry

<u>The Doctors Series</u>

Dr. Off Limits

Dr. Perfect

Dr. CEO

Dr. Fake Fiancé

Dr. Single Dad

<u>The Mister Series</u>

Mr. Mayfair

Mr. Knightsbridge

Mr. Smithfield

Mr. Park Lane

Mr. Bloomsbury

Mr. Notting Hill

<u>The Christmas Collection</u>

The 14 Days of Christmas

<u>The Player Series</u>

International Player

Private Player

Dr. Off Limits

Sign up to the Louise Bay mailing list at
www.louisebay/mailinglist

Read more at www.louisebay.com

ONE

Dax

I'm a lucky bastard, and more than happy to admit it.

There's nothing I'd change about my life, not even this January cold that seems particularly bitter this morning.

I live in the most vibrant area in the best city in the world: London. Just beyond my doorstep lies everything I'll ever need, from handmade suits to some of the most beautiful women on the planet.

Most of all, I love my work. Except I don't *just* love it and it's not *just* work. It's more than a passion—it's a calling. It's what I was put on this planet to do.

Because of my work as a research doctor, life will be better for millions of people. The work I go into the lab to do is my legacy. Not many people can claim they'll be remembered long after they're gone, but given my team is on the edge of an early breakthrough in endocrinal research, there's no doubt I will be.

The thought always gives me energy as I make my way to University College Hospital from my flat in Marylebone.

It's early, not even six and still dark, or as dark as it ever gets in central London. Most of the others on my team don't start arriving until nine, but there are a few of us who like to get a head start on the day. Or the year, as it's the second of January.

The automatic sliding doors at the hospital's main entrance jump apart just as I feel my phone vibrate in my pocket. That's gotta be one of my brothers. For a second I consider ignoring it—I'm in the zone and don't want to deal with one of their so-called emergencies. They've all got wives or girlfriends now. They don't need me. But I give a two-fingered salute to Mason, one of the security guards sitting at reception, and pull out my phone.

A US number I don't recognize flashes on the screen.

The lift doors open, but I don't step inside. Instead I accept the call.

"Dax, hi there, it's Kelly," a woman says.

Kelly...Kelly...Kelly?

I try and make the connection in my hippocampus. Who the fuck is Kelly? Luckily, she makes it easy for me.

"From Santorini."

She doesn't mean the island, but the restaurant at the end of my road. Things start to slot into place. When I'm late back from the lab, I sometimes stop at Santorini for a plate of the tomato keftedes, which are spectacular. Kelly was a waitress there. American with jet-black hair, olive-green eyes and one of those voices that sounded like she should sing jazz for a living.

More memories filter back. A few months ago, I stumbled across her leaving party when I'd met Vincent for a quick beer after work. She recognized me. We had a good night together. Shots. Sex. A great breakfast the morning after. From what I remember she was heading home to the US the week after.

It was probably more than a few months ago. More like...almost a year. I've not heard from her since. As far as I can remember, we never exchanged a message, let alone talked on the phone. Did we even swap numbers?

I guess we did.

"Hi, Kelly."

"How are you, Dax? Long time no speak."

She can't be calling to catch up. What does she want? I just don't understand why she's calling. "I've just arrived at work. How can I help?"

"I need you to sign some papers. To finalize a few things."

"I think you have the wrong number, Kelly. This is Dax Cove. I haven't seen you in nearly a year."

I'm about to hang up, convinced she's mixed me up with someone else, when she says, "Actually, I last saw you nine months ago."

That sounds about right, if oddly specific.

"It was a wonderful night," she says. "And when I landed back home in the States, I found out I was pregnant."

Heat twists through my chest and I fight for breath. "Right." I push out the syllable like it's a rock I'm heaving over a cliff.

Nine months.

"It's nothing you need to worry about. I've dealt with it." She lets out a laugh. "I'm not ready to be a mother."

Dealt with it? What does that mean? I'm certainly not ready to be a father. Not now, not ever. That's not what I'm here to do. Unlike my brothers, who all saw themselves as fathers at some point, I've never wanted to be someone's dad.

"Like I said, I just need you to sign some paperwork. You're down as the baby's father on the birth certificate, so you need to sign the adoption agreement."

More heat pushes down my body and across my limbs. For a second or two or three, I can't speak. I can barely form a thought. "You had a baby?"

"I did," she says, her voice a little pinched. "I haven't asked you for anything. I did it all through my dad's health insurance."

There's a buzz in my ears, and I can't tell if the sound is coming over the line or from inside my head. I try and swallow, try to push it away, but it remains. "You...had a baby?" I ask, trying to clarify what exactly has happened.

"Yes. She was born about an hour ago."

She.

She.

She.

"And you were planning on telling me when, exactly?"

"Never!" she says. "I found a family willing to adopt her. I did everything. I just didn't realize you'd need to sign the paperwork in person. It's adoption agency policy or something. I'm a little fuzzy on the details. I just gave birth."

"The adoption paperwork," I say, trying to sort through the quagmire of information being lobbed at me. "So, you got pregnant, had the child today, and you're trying to sign the baby over for adoption as we speak."

I have a child. In this world. Right now.

I'm trying to be logical. To organize the information and figure out what I'm meant to do, how I'm supposed to respond. My knees buckle as the realization of what's happening starts to sink in. I stagger to the wall for support, before I fall down. The buzzing gets louder and louder and I cover my free ear with my hand.

I don't know what to say or do or think. It's like I've lost executive brain function or something.

"Right," she says. "I need you to join a video call with your passport in hand so this guy at the adoption agency knows you're consenting. Then you need to sign the agreement. That's all you have to do."

I have a kid.

A daughter.

I don't want a child. Ever. Kids aren't part of my plan. I have no interest in doing what my brothers have done—settling down, popping out babies. It's not that I don't love my nieces. I do. I just don't understand my brothers' desire to cloud their focus. To create a distraction when it's not necessary. To wipe bottoms and blow raspberries rather than do the important work I know they're all capable of. I don't understand why they would want to sacrifice so much for so little reward.

It's their decision. It was my parents' decision. It's definitely not my decision.

I have work to do—work that's going to change millions of lives. Raising one life can't matter more than the many others at stake.

None of that changes the fact that at this moment in time, I'm a father. I have a child who's about to be adopted... and despite the fact that I absolutely don't want a daughter, there's something about having someone else raise her that doesn't sit easily with me.

I was brought up by doctors who were accustomed to taking responsibility for people's lives, and they instilled the same sense of duty and responsibility in me and all my brothers. Leaving someone else to care for a child that I brought into the world goes against everything I believe in—everything I know.

At the same time, this wasn't my choice. Yes, I chose to have sex with Kelly. Yes, consenting to sex is implicit consent to accept the consequences of that action. But I took steps to mitigate those consequences, just like I always have. This was an accident. A mistake. And it doesn't change the fact that I don't want to be a father. I have bigger, more important things to do.

All I have to do is sign some papers and my life will be as it was less than five minutes ago.

So that's what I'm going to do. Sign the papers. Forget this ever happened. Get on with the work changing a million lives, rather than just one.

TWO

Dax

I punch Vincent's name into the phone and he answers before it rings.

"I need to borrow your jet. I have to fly to Washington, DC," I say.

"Nice to hear from you, Dax. How are you? Keeping well? How's work?" He's mocking me. It's nice to know some things never change, even when my world is being turned upside-down.

"Is it available?" I ask, ignoring him.

"You want the jet *now*?" he asks. "It's not even light out."

"Yes. Is that possible?" Maybe I should have looked at getting a commercial flight first. I could have avoided any questions from Vincent.

As if on cue, he says. "What's going on? What's on fire?"

"Is the jet available?" I ask. "That's all I need to know. If it's not, let me hang up so I can find an alternative." I've never hired a jet before, but it can't be hard. I check the time. Five to six. Nothing is going to open for at least a couple of hours.

"I have no idea. I know I'm not using it, but in terms of a pilot..."

Vincent trails off, and I start to wonder how I'll bring this baby back to the UK without a passport. And nappies. Fuck. What else haven't I thought about? My plans haven't gone beyond: one, bring baby back; two, hire a nanny; three, get on with my life.

I don't know if it was my upbringing, something in my DNA, or just gut instinct that had me telling Kelly to cancel the adoption. Whatever it was, the decision is made. I can't shirk my responsibility to the child. I participated in her conception, and now it's my duty to participate in her...existence, I guess.

It's my *duty* to go and collect this child and ensure she's looked after.

"The plane is at City Airport. It will be ready in thirty minutes." Vincent's announcement brings me out of my thought spiral.

"It will?"

"Listen, I don't know what the fuck is going on, but I want to help. You need a lift?"

"I can get a cab." I keep my passport in my desk drawer, so I don't even have to go home first.

"What about a travel companion?"

"What?"

"I have a spare few hours. I can get to City in an hour. We can travel together."

I nod before I speak. "Yeah, actually that would be good." I find some strength in my legs and head back into the hospital lobby, where there's a twenty-four-hour shop stocking a weird assortment of things, from dental floss to slippers. It's just what I need, given I'm about to fly to the US to pick up my daughter.

"Anything else you need?" he asks.

I almost ask him if he has nappies and maybe some baby clothes, but that would create more questions than answers. I can pick up what I need when we get there. How much can a newborn need for a quick transatlantic trip within forty-eight hours of birth? "Not at the moment."

"I'll see you in an hour."

He didn't once ask me why I need a jet. I appreciate it more than he'll ever know.

———

THE STEWARDESS OFFERS us champagne as if it's a perfectly reasonable thing to do before eight in the morning. Vincent and Jacob shake their heads without looking away from me. They've been steadily staring since we boarded the jet.

"No, thank you," I say, trying to pull my mouth into a smile.

"Now I know something's wrong," Jacob says, jabbing his finger at me. "You just tried to fake a smile. It's freaking me the fuck out. You rarely smile, but you *never* fake a smile. Not for anyone. What the hell is going on?"

He's right. I'm trying to act normally even though normal is the last thing I feel. My insides are churning, like I know my life's about to change and I'm not ready for it. It's not that I think I've made the wrong decision by resolving to keep the baby. Rather, I'm not quite sure what the consequences of my decision might be. If I'd had some notice, I could have hired a nanny and she could have come with us to pick up the baby and everything would have been just fine. But it's likely that I'll have to deal with this child personally, at least until I'm back in the UK. And I haven't got a clue where to start.

I pull out my phone, ready to search "newborn care how??" Food, bed, nappies. There can't be much else, surely?

"Dax, did you hear me?" Jacob asks. "What's going on? Why are the three of us headed to the US, when I was expected to spend the day eating Weetabix in my pajamas because I have two days off in a row." He sounds like he used to when Nathan beat him at table football—like a whiny teenager.

Vincent pats him on the arm, trying to calm him.

"I don't know why you're here," I reply, sliding my finger up my phone screen, unclear what I need to focus on first. "I didn't ask you to come."

"He offered," Vincent says. "We want to help with... whatever this is."

"I don't need help."

"That's usually the case," Vincent says. "Normally, you're Mr. Self-sufficient, Mr. Got-it-together. Mr. I-don't-need-you-peasants. But today, you called me before six and asked to borrow my jet." I look up and we make eye contact. He holds his hands up in surrender. "It's not a problem. My jet is your jet. I'm just saying you've never once asked me for anything. Ever. And you never do anything that isn't planned to within an inch of its life. All of a sudden you're taking unplanned trips to the US and asking for jet-sized favors."

"It's a little out of character," Jacob says, his voice slightly less frantic than it was before.

I shrug, trying to focus on my phone. "Today is not a

typical day." After a few beats of heavy silence, I continue, "Typically, I don't get phone calls telling me I'm a father."

I finally look up to find Jacob and Vincent gaping at me. Vincent's mouth is hanging open and Jacob's eyes are so wide, there's a thirty-two percent chance his eyeballs will pop from their sockets.

"Wanna put some meat on that bone?" Vincent asks.

I slide my phone onto the table in front of me and tell them what I know, which isn't a lot.

"You've never wanted kids," Jacob says. "Are you sure you're making the right decision?"

My dad gave me some advice when I was sixteen and trying to decide which area of medicine to specialize in. I wanted to get a head start researching universities. He told me if I was struggling to make a decision, I should decide one way or another but not tell anyone or take any steps to cement my decision. Then for the next day or so, I should try the decision on like a new pair of shoes. Did it fit? How did it feel? Did I regret anything?

I haven't had one hour, let alone twenty-four, to try out my decision to cancel the adoption process, but I know I'm doing the right thing. Though the choice is hardly simple, it wasn't difficult. I feel the rightness of it in my bones.

"All I know is I couldn't have a child of mine out there with someone else as its parent. It's my responsibility."

"She," Jacob says quietly.

"She what?" I ask.

"*She's* your responsibility. Not 'it'."

Right. *She.* A specific baby-person. I give a short, sharp nod to acknowledge the correction but don't say anything else.

"I'm going to be an asshole for a second," Vincent says. "But have you checked that—"

"I've asked the hospital to take some blood. I'll do the same when I arrive. But come on, guys. Kelly wasn't ever going to tell me. There's no upside for her to pretend I'm the father. And it's not like she asked for financial support. Calling me was very obviously a last resort."

"That's true," Jacob says. "So what about when you get this baby home to London? How can we help then? We're your brothers, Dax. You can ask for help, you know."

"I've got to arrange a nanny who can arrange everything else. It shouldn't be too disruptive."

Jacob snorts. "Okay then. Back to business as usual as soon as you're home."

I shrug, a little defensive. "Yeah. Pretty much. I'll have to turn one of the two spare bedrooms I have into a nursery, but—"

"You don't think you'll move?" Vincent interrupts.

"I can walk to work. Why would I move?"

"More space. Is your nanny going to live in?"

I haven't thought about that. The nanny is definitely going to live in, and I suppose she can't share a room with the child. The third and final bedroom will have to be the nanny's. But that doesn't leave any room for my study. Maybe I should get a bigger flat at some point.

"The kid is going to be a foot and a half long," I say. "They're not going to need much space."

"*She's* going to need more than you think," Vincent says. "A name to start with."

"I know," I say, although I've not thought about names at all. Naming a child isn't on any of the newborn checklists I've glanced through since boarding the flight.

"Maybe you should make it a D-name," Jacob says. "To match yours."

I recoil in horror. "Are you serious?" I shake my head,

trying to rid myself of the thought. "Maybe *you* should try therapy. There are so many questions I have about your relationship with Mum and Dad right now. And your ego. Just no."

"Do you have something else in mind?" Vincent asks. "We had the name picked out months in advance."

"I haven't met—" I'm about to say "it" and realize Jacob and Vincent will probably give me a lecture, so I change tack. "I haven't met her yet. I don't want to pick a name and have it be...wrong."

"How very unpractical of you," Jacob says.

"This is just the beginning," says Vincent. He beams like he's got a secret. "I've got a feeling we're going to see an entirely new Dax, now he's a father."

I resist the urge to groan. "There will be no new Dax. I've ordered a cot, some milk and some babygrow sleepsuits things, bottles and nappies. I've been very practical. I just don't have a name." Now that I think about it, I'll have to pick a name in order to get a passport. Maybe I should come up with some options. How on earth do I go about naming another human being? It seems...bizarre.

"Wait until she shits all over you," Vincent says and chuckles. "It will be an amazing journey. I can't wait to share it with you."

She won't be shitting on me, I think to myself. The nanny will be dealing with all the shitting. I'm not saying I won't ever touch the child, and when she's older, of course we'll have conversations and see each other. But my research has to come first. My life is full already, and I plan to maintain my priorities even after it—*she* comes to live with me.

I'll ensure her nanny is kind and capable. I'll make sure she goes to the best schools and has every opportunity. But I won't be the father cleaning up drool and dirty nappies. I won't be cooing or singing lullabies.

"You're going to be a great dad," Vincent says. "Things will...rearrange when you see her. Take it from me."

I'm not going to challenge his assertion because it will lead to far too much conversation. Nothing needs to change aside from the arrangement of my flat. It's just a tiny human who will have a full-time caregiver. If the nanny does her job right, I'll probably forget the child is even in the house.

THREE

Dax

I feel like I'm being interrogated by the FBI. Since they brought me the results of the blood test, confirming I'm the biological father of the child Kelly gave birth to, I've spent two hours talking to people from the hospital and the adoption agency. I've been trying to convince them that no, I don't want to put the baby up for adoption, and no, I won't change my mind.

"I'd like to see the child, please," I say, standing. They've run out of questions and concerns and I've been as patient as I'm prepared to be. I've got things to do, a job to get back to. I can't sit around until these people—who have no claim over my child—get over themselves.

"I'm going to give you my card," the short blonde woman with the red nails from the adoption agency says. "I'm not sure how adoption works in the UK, but we could help you navigate the process of bringing your child back to the US and—"

"Which way is out? Where is the baby?" I start testing the doors lining the small room we're in.

"If you wait here, we can bring your daughter through to meet you," the older woman says.

"I want to see her immediately," I say. "Or I want to see whoever's in charge."

"We won't be a moment," the older woman says, shooting me a smile that says she gets it and will keep the other woman in check.

"You okay there?" Vincent asks, from where he's been sitting on a sofa at the back of the room.

"Yeah, I just want to get on with it. I need to get a passport so we can get out of here."

"There's no rush, mate. Seriously, we're here until whenever."

It's not like Vincent and Jacob don't have better places to be. I'm sure they do. But I appreciate him acting like he's some kind of jobless aristo who doesn't have an inbox that's blowing up or a wife at home who wants him back.

The door opens and the older lady from the hospital returns. "Mr. Cove, I have the pleasure of introducing your daughter." The word *daughter* echoes around my head like a handful of marbles thrown into a cave. I try to shake off the noise. The nurse wheels in a transparent tray on wheels, just like the one I saw when I went to visit Madison and Nathan in hospital.

I swallow. "Right," I say. "Thanks."

She wheels the cot beside me and when I glance down, there's a bundle of blankets and a hat and a small section of human face.

My daughter.

My knees weaken—something I never experienced before today but now is becoming alarmingly familiar. I grasp the edge of the bassinet to make sure I don't fall over. Maybe I'm dehydrated. Or perhaps I'm coming down with a virus.

"I'll leave you two for a few minutes and then I'll send one of the nurses through to discharge her."

I nod, taking in the weird-looking creature in the bassinet.

"Oh, I forgot," I say. "Is Kelly here? Can I speak to her?"

The woman winces. "She was discharged. She left a few hours ago." She flips through the papers in her arms. "But she left this for you."

It's a sealed brown envelope. When the woman leaves, I sit back into the chair and pull out the papers, checking everything's been signed properly. While we were traveling, I had my lawyers draw up some paperwork. She's signed everything, renouncing all her rights to the child and giving me all legal and moral responsibility. I don't want any muddy waters. Kelly wanted the baby adopted and the outcome will be the same. She doesn't have to have anything to do with the child. That's my job now.

I push the papers back in the envelope and stuff them into my backpack. There's no note or forwarding address. Makes things much easier.

When I clip my backpack closed, Vincent is standing over the bassinet and I go over to join him.

"She's sleeping," I say.

"They do a lot of that in the first few weeks," Vincent says.

I don't know where the thought comes from, but before I have the chance to think, I blurt out, "How do we know she's actually sleeping and not..." I can't actually say the word *dead*, but that's what I mean.

"You can get monitors that clip on to the diaper," Vincent says. "It detects if there's a lack of movement."

My heart squeezes a little. After Sutton and Jacob's miscarriage, some of the excitement for Vincent and Kate's baby turned to fear. Hopefully, the fact that Sutton announced at Christmas she was four months pregnant will make life easier for everyone. But I can feel his anxiety.

"Maybe I should get one of those," I say.

"You going to pick her up?" he asks.

I reach behind my neck and scratch. "I don't want to disturb her. Not until I've signed all the discharge paperwork and we're leaving."

Vincent's grinning like an idiot at the baby. "You told your parents yet?" he asks, not taking his gaze from the bassinet.

I shake my head. "I'll tell them on the way back."

"You know they're going to be fine with it." He laughs. "Who'd have thought you'd be a father before me?"

Considering this was a race I never thought to enter, it's safe to say the answer is "no one."

I sigh. I'm not worried about my parents' approval. I know they'll be thrilled—even if the circumstances are a bit unconventional. I just want life to get back to normal. I wish we could speed through this bit where I have to have family members come round to meet her and coo over her and ask me a thousand questions I don't have the answers to. I want the nanny in place and for us all to be in a routine. Then life can get back to normal.

Jacob crashes through the door, looking slightly disheveled. "I got one." He holds up a car seat. "It fits on to this pushchair I got. You can wheel it around."

"Thanks," I say, and I glance at the baby. "Let's leave her in that cot thing until I have the discharge paperwork."

Jacob follows my eyeline and his expression instantly melts. "Oh, that's her. He crouches over her. "Hey, baby Cove. I'm your uncle Jacob," he coos. "I'm going to have a daughter soon. You two are going to be best friends."

"She's going to like me better," Vincent says.

"Impossible, I'm brilliant with kids. It's my job." He goes to the other side of the room and washes his hands in the sink I hadn't even noticed. "Have you picked her up?" he asks. With clean hands, he strokes her cheek, and she turns her head towards his finger.

"Hello, sweet girl," he says.

Her eyes are closed, but in her sleep she moves her mouth so it forms a perfect 'O', and the corners of my mouth twitch. I reach out and touch her forehead with my fingertips and sharply pull my hand back.

The door opens again and a nurse and someone in scrubs comes in. We go through the discharge paperwork while Vincent and Jacob compete over my daughter's attention.

"That's it," I tell them. "We're free to go."

"Are you going to put her in the car seat?" Vincent asks.

"Sure." I go over to the sink and wash my hands. It's not like I've never handled a newborn before. Of course I have —I had an obstetrics residency. But I've never handled someone who...I'm responsible for. I feel like I'm about to fuck it up and drop her or something.

I slide my hand under her head and the other under her bottom and lift. Are babies always this light? I feel like I could easily squeeze her too tight or trip and toss her to the other side of the room. She's so delicate. Fragile. I have to resist putting my cheek to the top of her head. I don't know who I'm trying to comfort—her or me.

I nod at Jacob. "How much does she weigh?" I ask. "Can you check that booklet thing they gave me?"

"Seven pounds, two ounces," he says. "About three kilos. She's just perfect."

I clip her into the car seat and test the straps to make sure they're fully fastened. Her socked feet are sticking out of the blanket, her bare, scrawny legs on show.

"I need another blanket," I say and make a mental note to do some online shopping on the plane ride back. We're going to need some blankets. And socks.

"There's one in the car," Jacob says. "I bought some other things along with the seat. Just bits and pieces you're going to need before we get home."

"Good," I say. "Things will get back to normal when we're home with a nanny and there's a routine."

Jacob smirks as he punches the call button for the lift. "Things aren't ever getting back to normal, let me tell you."

I glance down at the baby lying peacefully in her car seat—and suddenly I know what I'm going to call her. "Her name's Guinevere."

"Of course it is," Jacob groans.

Jacob always teased me about my obsession with Arthurian legend growing up. But the name makes sense. It's unusual yet recognizable. Neve and Gwen are both nice shortened versions, and it goes nicely with Cove.

"Her middle name can be mum's name. That's that ticked off the list. We can get the passport now."

The sooner we have the passport, the sooner we can get home, the sooner I can employ a nanny and get back to life before Kelly's phone call. Within a couple of days, everything will be back to normal.

FOUR

Dax

Each of the CVs I've seen are excellent, but the nanny candidates I'm interviewing just don't match up.

"Did you see the way she kept touching her hair?" I ask as I shut the door to the apartment. "She's dealing with a newborn. She can't be touching her hair like that. It's unsanitary." I rip up the CV and toss it in the bin as I head back into the sitting room. "She might have nannied for the Beckhams back in the day, but she's not nannying for me."

"I didn't notice her touch her hair," Nathan says.

Of course he didn't. Nathan isn't known for his attention to detail.

"You're meant to look out for this stuff so I can focus on what they're saying."

"Right," he says. "Who's next?" He yawns and lays back on the sofa like he's about to watch the football. Doesn't he realize? This is an emergency. I need to find a nanny. The temporary nanny who's been here the last three days is due to start with another family tomorrow. I need to find someone *today*.

There's a knock at the door. "No one is due for thirty minutes," I say.

Nathan has a guilty look on his face.

"What have you done?" I ask as I stand and head out to answer the door.

On the doorstep I find Jacob and Vincent. "What are you two doing here?"

"Here to see our niece," Jacob replies.

"We have uncle visitation," Vincent says.

"Thank God you're here," Nathan says. "He's driving me crackers. I've sat through six interviews, all with perfectly good nannies he's found spurious reasons to reject."

"Hygiene is not spurious," I reply.

"She didn't touch her hair, mate," Nathan says. "Any one of the nannies that we've interviewed today would be perfectly fine."

"This is my one job when it comes to Guinevere. I have to find a decent nanny." I know I'm going to be a terrible father. The least I can do is make sure she has an excellent nanny.

Jacob shoots me a grin. "You have more than one job. And you're going to make a ton of mistakes. I know the prospect doesn't sit easy for you, but you'll get used to it."

"You've got to shit or get off the pot," Vincent says. "Who's next on your list?"

Nathan picks up his jacket. "I'm out of here. I have my own nanny to worry about. Good luck, guys. Maybe you'll have found someone by the time dear, sweet Guinevere has reached eighteen."

"Thanks for your support," I say as Nathan passes me on the way to the front door. I can't hide my sarcasm.

"Dax, I've sat here for five hours trying to support you while you've been fucking around playing with your dick. Make a decision, man."

"He's right," Jacob says. "No one is going to be good enough to care for your daughter, but unless you're going to give up work and do it yourself, you need someone."

The hairs on the back of my neck prickle as he says the word *daughter*. That's not how she feels to me. To me, she's just Guinevere, a child I'm responsible for ensuring she's— fed and clothed and educated.

He pulls the paper from my hand. "Now who's this? The next candidate?"

The doorbell goes.

"Be nice to her," Jacob hisses.

I'm nice to all of them. I can't help it if they don't fulfil the job requirements. This one is twenty minutes early. Does she have a problem telling the time?

I throw open the front door and am greeted by the back of someone's head, her almost-black hair piled up on top of her head like she's tried to stuff too much hay into a binbag.

She spins around and her smile seems to take up half of her face. "Good afternoon. Dax Cove? I'm Eira Cadogan."

She's wearing a burgundy coat with small black buttons up the front. She carries an umbrella in one hand and a huge bag on the opposite shoulder, as if she already has the job and is ready to move in. There's something vague familiar about her, but I can't put my finger on wher might have seen her before.

"Excuse me." She glances down at herself. "I'm cov in mud."

She's right. There are splashes of mud all over her coat. She looks up at me and grins conspiratorially, as if we're in on the same joke. Except we're not. I don't want my child looked after by someone who can't get to an interview without looking like she came out the worse for wear after a fight with a pig in a sty.

"I think you have some on your face," I say, inching forward to check. Is there any point in even letting this one through the front door? It's a waste of my time. She's quite literally *covered in mud.*

She rolls her eyes as if the mud is a pesky child who needs to be dealt with. "Do you mind if I just have five minutes to clean myself up? It's always the same in January. Mud and puddles. You can't avoid them."

We're in the center of London. It's not hard to avoid mud. In fact, I'd say it's pretty difficult to *find* mud.

"I suppose, I just—"

She brushes past me and heads toward the back of the house. "Is it just through here?"

"Yeah, as far as you can go, on your right." I tip my head back and groan. I just want to find someone good. This process is such a ball ache.

Jacob and Vincent pull me into the sitting room. "This resume is excellent," Vincent says. "These Portland nannies are the best," he says. "Royalty all over the world use them."

"The thing I've learned this morning is the CV doesn't mean anything. I just met this one and she's not going to cut it. She's covered in mud for crying out loud. How can she look after a child if she can't even sort herself out?"

"Anyone can get covered in mud in this weather," Jacob says. "You can't write someone off because of that." Guinevere starts to cry, and I try not to show that I find it intensely irritating. She has everything she needs. Why is she crying?

It's completely irrational. I try to zone her out. The temporary nanny will see to it.

"This CV is really great," Jacob says. "Some of the high-profile placements she's had are really impressive. I bet she's expensive though."

"This girl won't work. She looks like the kind of person who *attracts* mud. She's..." I wince. "Messy."

Vincent takes me by the shoulders. "You need to get a grip. Nathan's told us what's going on. Unless this woman whips out a lizard and asks to bring her baby-eating reptile to live with you, you need to offer her a job."

"I do not."

"Then you're going to be left on your own with a three-day-old baby."

Frankly, I'll take a baby-eating lizard looking after Guinevere over doing the job myself. "I agree, I need to find someone today, but this woman isn't it. The next one will be better."

"There isn't a next one," Jacob says. "Nathan said you'd seen six out of seven."

I scan the coffee table and start going through the CVs I printed out. "I'm sure there are a couple more." I grab the ranking table I devised last night, listing the candidates in the left-hand column and the fifteen qualities I'm looking for along the top. Each candidate is given a score out of ten in each category, leading to an overall possible score of one hundred and fifty. Six candidates in, and no one's scored above a twenty-five. There's only one space left.

Jacob is right—the pig wrestler is the last candidate of the day.

"Of course you have a spreadsheet." Jacob snatches the paper out of my hand. "Twenty-five?! That's ridiculous." He shakes his head. "*I'm* going to score the candidate who just arrived. If she gets over one hundred, you have to hire her. You can't just interview nannies for the rest of your life."

"You're not picking Guinevere's nanny. That's my job."

"A job you're not doing, to be fair," Vincent says.

"High standards aren't a bad thing." The woman who just arrived—I check my table to confirm it's Eira Cadogan —is an absolute no-go as far as I'm concerned. If she's prepared to turn up to an interview covered in mud, how on earth am I going to be able to live with her?

"High standards are fine," Vincent says. "Impossible standards aren't."

I push my hands into my pockets, uncomfortable with how familiar this conversation feels. Over the years I've had it with teachers, my father, professors. Most of the time it's been entirely hypocritical, coming from people who are just as perfectionistic as me.

"Come on," Jacob says. "We're here to help you get a sense of perspective. I promise we're not going to put our niece in danger. We want what's best for her." He gives a sideways nod at the door. "Let's see this woman. Give her a chance. She might be great for you and little Gwinnie."

I resist the urge I have to growl at the nickname.

I poke my head into the hallway, but there's no sign of her. "Where is she?" I ask. Vincent and Jacob just look at each other.

"Maybe she overheard us and left. Probably thinks you'd be a nightmare to work for," Vincent says. "Not sure how she got that idea."

She can't still be in the loo. Covered in mud and suffering digestive distress? That's a bridge too far. I head down the corridor and find the loo door closed. Bowel issues, *of course.* I roll my eyes. That's it. There's absolutely no point in even having a conversation with this woman.

A sweet singing voice trills down the corridor. I've never heard the temporary nanny sing, but I think I remember that music is supposed to be good for babies' brain development. I follow the sound to Guinevere's makeshift nursery, determined to ask whether it might be prudent to switch from a jaunty lullaby to Mozart, only to find a no-longer-mud-caked Ms. Cadogan holding Guinevere over her shoulder, singing to her.

She catches sight of me and her already wide smile deepens.

"You have the most beautiful daughter." The mud has gone from her cheek and she's taken off her coat. Her hair isn't exactly tidy, but she's less disheveled than she looked when she came to the door. "She's just precious." She lays Guinevere back in her cot, now fast asleep, the crying stopped.

The temporary nanny bustles back into the room. "Sorry, sir, just had to go to the toilet." She peers at the baby. "She's sleeping?"

Eira smiles. "Of course. That song will put any child to sleep." She narrows her eyes, but they still...kinda...sparkle. "It's my secret weapon." She winks at me. "Shall we?"

For a split second I wonder what's she's talking about, and then I remember she's here for an interview.

"I hope you don't mind, but my brothers are going to join us. They have more experience with this kind of thing."

"It's not a problem," she says, floating past me as if this is her house and she knows exactly where she's going.

THE FOUR OF us settle in the sitting room, Eira by the window on the Barcelona chair, while the three of us sit opposite her on the sofa. Eira is handling the questions well. She doesn't seem intimidated by the three of us and volleys the answers to our questions back to us like she's Markéta Vondroušová.

"Your background is very impressive," Vincent says. "What's been your favorite job?"

She smiles. "There hasn't been a job I haven't enjoyed, but I suppose I like the ones where I feel I'm helping the most. I've been in some positions where I'm one of four nannies working around the clock, seven days a week, and I never feel like I have the same impact as when I'm the only nanny."

"Four nannies?" A slither of panic lodges itself in my chest. Should I have more than one nanny for Guinevere? A weekend nanny sounds like a good idea. I haven't thought that far ahead.

Vincent reaches for his coffee and manages to send mine flying all over the coffee table.

"Shit," he says, holding his hand under the table, waiting to catch any drips on the carpet.

I look around, trying to find a cloth or something. "I'll get some kitchen roll."

Out of the corner of my eye, I see Eira stand, but I dash out of the room.

When I return with a roll of kitchen towel, Eira is on her hands and knees at the coffee table. "There now—crisis averted. That's the best kind of crisis." She laughs and stands. "Let me find a bin for these tissues."

"I'll take them," I offer, but she brushes past me to the kitchen. "The bin is under the sink," I call after her.

She returns to the living room, and I can detect the

scent of my handwash. Maybe she's not as messy as I first thought. "There." She grins as she retakes her seat. Her cheeks are flushed as if she's just come in from the cold and her eyes are full of mischief. "Nannies always have tissues in their handbags. Along with a thousand other things."

"A regular Mary Poppins," Jacob says, and finally the sense of familiarity clicks. The coat, the umbrella, the bag, the...eye sparkle.

"Our patron saint," Eira says, not missing a beat.

Jacob is clearly delighted, evidenced by his next question. "When would you be able to start?"

I clear my throat, trying to wrestle back control of the interview. Despite what Jacob thinks, this isn't his decision. "We're obviously seeing other candidates."

"I'm available immediately," she responds. "When are you looking for someone to begin?"

"Is today too soon?" Vincent asks.

"Vincent!" I growl under my breath.

Eira laughs, but I don't feel she's laughing at me—more like she thinks we're incorrigible. "Why don't I leave you to have a chat amongst yourselves and you can call the agency. I'll see myself out."

Maybe it's because she lives in other people's houses, but she seems so comfortable. As if there's nothing she could come across that would ruffle her feathers. She beams at the three of us as she stands, and I watch her, trying to figure her out.

I'm still trying by the time it occurs to me that I should have seen Eira to the door, but by then, she's already gone.

FIVE

Eira

I've only taken three steps outside little Guinevere's building when my phone rings. I know it's my sister before I answer it. Not because I've assigned a distinctive ringtone to her call, but because she's gotten used to me not being at work for the last three months and as a result, she calls me throughout the day. I don't mind. In fact, I quite like hearing her voice and knowing she's safe. I just worry that she's not enjoying where she is if she's constantly calling me.

"Are you okay?" I ask.

"Sure," Eddie replies. "I'm just home from lectures and about to start some work, then I realized I need to go to the library."

Scintillating. "Okay, well I'll let you get on with it." I glance back at the building I've just exited.

Usually I have an instant connection with a family. Or not. Ordinarily, I leave an interview knowing whether or not I'm going to be offered the position. But with Guinevere, I'm not sure either way and...I don't know if I want it.

Not because Guinevere isn't an absolute dot. She is. And not because it's not in a great part of town—it is. But the flat's small and Dax, the father... Well, he could be a problem for me.

The first rule they teach you at nanny school is about the line between you and the family and specifically, how not to cross it. I've always found it easy to stay professional —to look the other way when I see something I shouldn't, or overhear a row that should be kept private. But there's something about Dax that makes those boundaries seem... blurry. Maybe it's the size of the flat. Maybe it's because the agency told me Guinevere's mother isn't involved.

Maybe it's the fact that Dax is completely and utterly, one hundred percent gorgeous.

From what the agency said, the position offers good money, which means I'm unlikely to turn it down. The economic conditions at the moment mean high-paying roles are few and far between. Nannies aren't moving from well-paid positions, and there are fewer foreign wealthy families coming to London than ever before. For the last three months, I've been holding out for a plum role—something I've always managed to secure—but if something doesn't come up soon, I'm going to have to compromise. My savings are dwindling and Eddie's next three-month rent instalment is due next month.

"What about you? Are you okay?" she asks.

"Of course I'm okay," I say. "I'm always okay."

"How did the interview go? Do you think you got it?"

"No idea," I say. Looking into Dax's eyes was unsteady-ing. It was as if he could see me through to my bones. I felt a pull towards him as if I already know him, or somehow know I *will* know him. I can't quite make sense of it.

Finding your charge's father attractive is never going to

end well, and I've been lucky to have dodged that dilemma for my entire career. In most of the positions I've held, the fathers haven't been particularly involved with the children. They're traveling or working and I have limited time with them. But that's clearly not going to be the case with Guinevere's father. Sharing a house with a man so disarming, so very attractive, might be...distracting. Probably better if I don't get offered.

"I've got another one tomorrow. Something will come up."

"Something with a Saudi prince whose wife died in a tragic accident, and he falls in love with you as he sees you care so well for his son and heir."

I don't even try not to roll my eyes. "Do you actually study any computer stuff, or are you curled up in bed reading romance novels?"

"There's room for both," she says defensively. "But seriously, I see a hot single dad in your future. A rich one."

I glance back over my shoulder. There's no doubt Dax is hot, even if he's not my usual type. And anyway, if I saw him again, he'd be my boss. I'm not about to start any kind of flirtation with someone who's responsible for my pay packet. I don't even know if he's single.

Not that it matters either way. He'll be my boss and off-limits, or I'll never see him again. It's really that simple.

"I see you failing your exams in the future if you don't stop thinking up plots about my love life."

"I just want you to have a little fun. Shoot me."

"I know. But I just want you to pass your exams. You're going to keep me in the manner to which I want to become accustomed in my old age." The fact is, once Eddie is out of full-time education and able to stand on her own two feet financially, I'll be able to think about planning for my own future. Though I joke with her about funding my retirement, I don't actually expect anything from her. Looking after me isn't what I want for her. I just want her to be independent and happy.

She laughs. "That's absolutely going to happen. I'm pretty sure I'm going to launch a successful tech start-up and make millions."

"Okay. Well you get busy with that. I'm about to head into the underground, so got to go."

We say our love-yous, which we never miss—it's unspoken between us, but we both know that if anything ever happens to either of us, the last thing we want to have said to each other is *I love you*. There's never any doubt when you say it at the end of every conversation.

Before my phone is back in my pocket, it starts to ring.

It's the agency.

"It's not-so-great news," Felicity shrieks, as if she's some kind of wailing Italian widow. "I'm so sorry. He wants someone older. I told him I think he's a fool."

Dax's face dissolves in my head. Even though I'm relieved, there's something lodged in my chest that won't shift.

This is for the best, I tell myself. I've avoided any kind of silly crush on my boss.

But it means I'm on Callie's sofa for the foreseeable future. Maybe I need a bar job for a few weeks, just to keep my savings topped up.

The thing about being a live-in nanny is that your home is completely dependent on your job. No job equals no place to sleep at night. Since my last assignment ended three months ago, I've been on my best friend's sofa. Callie and I met at Portland, but she went the daytime nanny route—no live-in assignments.

"Thanks for letting me know," I say. "I still have the interview tomorrow with the family in Holland Park?"

"Oh, they just called. They want to move it to Tuesday next week."

My heart sinks. Rescheduling an interview is rarely good news. It either means the family is thinking of moving abroad, or they're looking at options such as live-out nannies or nurseries.

"Anything else coming up?" I ask.

"It's quiet. Never seen anything like it. It's like twenty oh-eight. But things will pick up in February. I'm sure of it."

She said the same thing about January.

"Okay, let me know if anything new comes in."

I take a seat on a low wall outside a restaurant that's not open yet and bring up a job site on my phone. If I'm going to find a temp job, it needs to be flexible enough that I can go to interviews at short notice. Maybe bar work that only requires evening shifts? Although, if parents work, they often want an interview in the evening. I should sign up with a temp agency. I just don't have any experience doing anything other than looking after children.

A harried mother pushing a buggy with a toddler in front and an older child on a buggy board at the back comes toward me. The older child has her school uniform on and is singing at the top of her lungs, "I like to move it move it." From the look on the mother's face, she's sick of the song. And who can blame her?

I smile, and then notice a navy kid's rucksack working free of where it's shoved under the buggy. It lands on the curb, just about to fall into the road.

"Excuse me," I call, leaping to my feet.

The woman doesn't hear me over the dulcet screeching. I grab the rucksack and call again, "Your rucksack!"

I run after her and tap her on the shoulder. She stops and snaps her head around, ready to rip my head off if I'm any kind of threat to her kids.

"Your rucksack." I hold it up by the strap.

Her body slumps and her eyes fill with tears. "Thank you."

"It's okay," I tell her.

"I didn't feel it fall off." Her voice rises at the end of the sentence, as if she's on the brink of tears. She's not upset about the backpack. She's upset because she's had a broken night's sleep, she's been up for four hours, cleaned a pooey nappy, negotiated with a five-year-old over breakfast cereals, socks and hairstyles, wrestled a toddler into its coat, while she's not brushed her own hair or teeth.

"It's okay. You've got a lot to do in the mornings. And you've got two happy kids. That's the most important thing."

The child in the pushchair is clapping along to, *"You've got to move it move it,"* which the older kid hasn't stopped singing. Over. And over. And over.

"Thank you," she says.

"You've got this," I say and nod at her.

She takes a deep breath. "I got this."

I smile and wave at the older kid as she peers at me from behind her mum as they charge toward a nursery. A warm feeling settles in my stomach at the thought I made that mother's morning a little better.

I've got this, I say to myself.

I carry on toward the tube station, past a churchyard where I spot the beginnings of a crocus pushing its head out of the soil on the other side of the railings. I stop and bend over. "You're early," I whisper. "Keep safe under the soil for a few more weeks. That way you won't get bitten by the frost." I look up to the sky. "The problem is that beautiful sun is out, tricking you into thinking it's springtime."

There's not too much more winter left. Soon the blossoms will be out and the playgrounds will be full again. I'll be with a new family, helping new children to grow and bloom. In the meantime, I've endured much worse than a few months without a job. I've got options. I could get a bar job, a waitressing job, even a cleaning job in the mornings or something that would keep my afternoons free for interviews. Anything will help pay the bills and ensure my savings are kept safe for Eddie and Dylan.

But I also need a room to call my own and a family I can be useful to, a child to jump in puddles with. I have to believe a nanny job is bound to come along soon. But until it does, I have to cast my net wider. I'm going to sign up with other nanny agencies and look into temporary work. I've heard of temp jobs that turn into something more permanent. Who's to say it won't happen to me?

I've got this. It's the truth, sure, but it's also a promise to myself. *You have to have this*, I remind myself.

You don't have any other choice.

SIX

Eira

I turn backward and push open the heavy metal gate with its chipped green paint and pull the buggy in after me. Coram's Fields is my favorite playground. Nestled in the center of London, in between Georgian town houses, it's a playground you can't enter unless you have a child with you.

"Shall we start at the swings?" I say to Elliot, who's not quite one. It's only my second day with him, covering for another nanny who's off sick. Temporary work isn't ideal, since it's uncertain and doesn't allow me time to get to know the children. But as my nanny Gabby would have said, needs must.

I unclip Elliot from the buggy and place him in the baby swing. "Hold on," I say. He grins at me, his chubby cheeks a little reddened from the frosty air. He tips his head back, enjoying the motion, then lets out a squawk that sounds like a tropical bird.

There's a bench next to the swings where an older lady

in a smart black mac and sensible lace-up shoes, just like the ones we used to wear with our nanny uniform at school, sits with a pram. I glance around to see if she has an older child with her as well, or whether she's just with the baby, but there aren't any other children nearby. There's a kid in the sandpit about ten meters away and another one on the zipwire at the back of the playground. It's otherwise empty because it's winter, not to mention the middle of a school day.

"Elliot," I call as he swings toward me. "There you are!" I catch the swing with one hand and tap him on the nose with the other before letting him swing back, giggling.

"Excuse me, young lady?" the woman on the bench says, her hand lifted in the air to get my attention. "You don't happen to have some paracetamol, do you?"

I walk around the swing so I'm swinging Elliot from the back, but I'm nearer the bench. "I'm sorry, I never carry them." In my experience, little fingers always find the one thing you don't want them to, so I try not to have things in my bag that I wouldn't be happy for them to play with.

She winces and swallows, but tries to smile. "That's okay. Thank you."

"Are you okay?" I ask. "Can I call someone for you?"

She shifts so she's sitting forward on the bench and bends her head. Her grip is white-knuckled around the buggy handle.

"I do think we need to find Daddy." She nods toward the football field, where teams practice on the all-weather court at the back of the playground.

"He's playing football?" I ask.

"Yes." Her voice is a wheeze and she's gripping her chest.

Never mind Daddy. I think we need an ambulance.

"Do you need to lie down?" I ask as I pull out my phone from my pocket.

She doesn't respond, but she leans back on the bench, her breathing labored. I dial for an ambulance.

Glancing around, I try to see if there's anyone official I can wave over who might have a first-aid kit. Obviously, I have some training, but this lady looks like she's having a seizure or a stroke or something.

I pull Elliot out of the swing, place him back in the buggy and bring the buggy around to the back of the bench so I can keep an eye on him. I take the pram from the woman's fingers and maneuver it next to Elliot so they're both safe. The baby in there is nicely wrapped up and sleeping peacefully.

I give details to the emergency services. UCH is just around the corner. I wonder if it's better to take her in a taxi? But it's impossible with two babies.

"Why don't you lie down," I say. The bench is wide enough and she looks like she's about to fall down if I don't help her. I help her lie on her side and glance back to the football pitch. We need the baby's father *now*. He can take his mum to hospital.

I hear a siren and wonder if that's for us. I hope it is.

"What's your son's name?" I ask.

"Who?" she asks. She's confused.

"Stay here," I say. "I'm going to find your son."

I can't leave the children, so I scoop up the baby, huddled in its blanket, and with my free hand, push Elliot toward the football pitch. The child in the sandpit seems to have disappeared. Where is everyone? I pick up speed and get to the wire fencing.

"Help!" I call. No one hears me. "I need help. Your

mum is sick." I don't know who I'm talking to, or whose mum I'm screaming about.

"Help!"

A couple of players nearer me stop and they hold up their hands to stop the game and come closer to the fencing.

"Who's mum is looking after the baby?" I ask. "She's sick." I glance back at the bench, and I see the ambulance pulled up to the other side of the iron railings. Thank god they got here fast.

Other players head in my direction to see what the commotion is about.

"Eira?" someone asks.

I search the faces to find the person who seems to know me and lock eyes with Dax, the hot single dad Eddie would have been delighted for me to work for.

"Dax Cove?" I glance down at the bundle of pink blankets in my arms. Am I holding Guinevere? When I look back up, Dax is sprinting to the gate. I look back at the bench. "I think your mum is sick."

Elliot squeals from the buggy but thankfully isn't upset.

"My mum?" he asks, glancing down at the baby in my arms. "How do you know my mum?" He doesn't reach for the baby. Maybe this isn't Guinevere.

"The lady on the bench?"

He looks toward the bench and starts to sprint again.

Some of the other players come out and follow him. "Can we do anything?"

I don't answer as I see the paramedics coming through the gate of the playground. I need to tell them what I know. I start to make my way back to the bench, pushing Elliot and carrying a still-sleeping baby in my arms. Dax is already there, kneeling at the woman's head as the paramedics arrive.

I can't tell them much, and she doesn't seem to be talking at all, although her eyes are open. She looks gray. I'm so pleased the ambulance is here.

"Fuck," Dax says as he stands and lets the paramedics take over.

They do some checks, load the woman onto a stretcher, and wheel her into the ambulance.

"I'll meet you at the hospital," he says to them. He glances at me. "I don't know who to call." He pulls out his phone. "I don't know—"

"Maybe your brothers. And your dad?"

He gives me a look that tells me my suggestions weren't helpful. "She's not my mum. She's Guinevere's nanny."

Oh. The older candidate he went with. The shoes make sense now. She must have trained at Portland.

Dax pushes his hand through his hair, and I try to ignore the way my stomach flips. I should definitely not be focusing on his hands or his hair or anything else about how attractive he is. We're in an emergency situation. "I don't have any emergency numbers for her."

"Call the agency. They'll have numbers for her." My phone is in my hand. "Let me do it."

I dial the agency and speak to Felicity. I hold the phone with my shoulder and put Guinevere back in her pram. She's still sleeping—gotta love a newborn. As long as they have milk regularly, they're rarely any bother.

I ask Felicity to call the nanny's emergency contacts. I discover the woman's name is Doreen.

"Can she give out your number?" I ask Dax, who nods. To Felicity, I say, "Give them Dax's number. He's going to the hospital now. He can keep them—ahh, right. Yes, UCH."

"Her sister is going to go," I say as I hang up.

"I've known the woman three days," Dax says. "I don't know what—" He looks around as if he doesn't know which way the hospital is. And then he glances at the pram.

"What do I do if she wakes up?" he asks.

"Just stay at the hospital until her sister turns up. It won't be long. And I'm sure Doreen has plenty of food and nappies in the bag."

He looks at me as if I'm speaking Chinese.

"For Guinevere. I'm sure you have enough to tide you over until you get home."

"Fuck," he says.

"Do you want me to check?"

Elliot is busy pointing at nothing in particular and shrieking, so I rummage about the bottom part of the pram and pull out the baby bag. I flip open the top. "Yes, two bottles. Ready-made milk. Nappies. You're good."

"So if she cries I offer her milk? Doreen was putting her in some kind of routine."

"Forget the routine. If Guinevere's hungry, feed her. If she needs her nappy changed, change it."

"Right," he says. "Feed her. Change her. Can't be that hard, right?" He's staring off in the direction of the ambulance like he's hoping time will rewind and suddenly he'll be playing football instead of worrying about how to feed his kid.

"Maybe while you're waiting, you can call the agency and get an emergency nanny. That's how Elliot and I met, isn't it, Elliot?" I screw up my eyes and then open them wide at him. He howls like he's a wolf and I'm the moon.

"Maybe I'll hire you," he says.

I laugh. "You passed, remember?"

He nods. "I do. I was an idiot." Clumsily, he takes the brake off the pram and starts toward the exit. "Thank you."

I shrug, uncomfortable with his gratitude. I hardly did anything. "Good luck." He walks away, a tall hulk of a man in knee-high socks, with hair that could do with a cut, pushing a pram that looks two sizes too small for him.

It's adorable. And a little bit sexy.

Thank God he didn't hire me. If I can feel attracted to a man in the middle of a crisis, working for him on a daily basis would have been a complete disaster.

SEVEN

Eira

Callie is in the bathroom and I'm just about to set the dishwasher when my phone rings. It's the agency.

"Hi," I say. "Felicity?"

"Darling, I have fabulous news."

"You're up late."

"Working my heart out. And I have the perfect job for you. Even better, you don't need to interview. I have an offer. You'll never guess who from."

"The Lebedevs?" I ask. The Russian family are due back to London about now. They are legendary at Portland. People who manage to get hired by them are able to put a deposit down on a house. They pay eye-wateringly well. They sweep into town, hire two nannies for six months or a year to work around the clock and travel the world. Then they disappear. To a yacht? A tax haven? In hiding from Putin? No one knows.

"Better," Felicity says. "Dax Cove."

My stomach leaps. "Guinevere's dad?"

I know exactly who she's talking about. I'm just trying to buy myself time to figure out how to react. Because I should be thrilled. It's a permanent position, with one child, in the center of London. It's the job every nanny wants.

Except I'm not sure I do.

Felicity click-click-clicks on her keyboard. "Yes, Guinevere. She's just over a week old. How sweet."

"What happened to Doreen?"

"Doreen?" she asks, as if I've just asked her how her window cleaner is. "Oh yes, Doreen. She's in hospital. Turns out she has a heart condition. Collapsed with the baby apparently." Her tone is matter-of-fact, like she's telling me about a tube strike.

"I know, Felicity. I was there. I called *you*, remember?" Poor Doreen.

"Oh yes, that's right. Anyway, what do you think about Dax Cove? He called me, adamant he wanted to hire you."

"What salary is he offering?" I ask. Okay, so I don't have a job and can't afford to be picky, but I should make sure there are no reasons *not* to take this job. A low salary would rule it out for me. I absolutely can't take a job unless the money is right. There's too much riding on it.

"Oh, it's good," she says and I pull in a breath, waiting. I've turned down plenty of jobs in the past because of the salary. I have a lot of outgoings, and maximizing my salary is my number-one priority. "Hang on a minute, I've got it here." I imagine Felicity in her office, surrounded by scribbled notes, knee-deep in paper. I'm not sure whether I'm waiting for her to tell me the salary is high or low. Why am I wishing for a way out of this job?

"Annual of sixty-five gross."

"This is a live-in role, right?" Sixty-five is high for an English family. You always get paid more by the Russians or the Arabs. English families always pay less, which is one of the reasons I almost didn't apply for the position.

"Yup, live-in. I told him your previous salary and said you could expect six figures in some circumstances."

I try and do the calculation in my head. Sixty-five would be slightly more than I was on before. I might be able to clear five thousand a month. With a salary like that, I might even be able to save a little, get ahead of myself. I could pay off Eddie's credit card bill. And if she wanted to do that masters she's been talking about, I might be able to make it happen.

There must be a catch. "You think he's good for it? He's young. I don't want to be out of a job in three months because he realizes he can't keep up with the payments."

"He didn't blink at the salary. You might want to do an internet search of his name. The family is semi-famous. Big in the medical world apparently."

That doesn't necessarily mean they have money. It's not like NHS doctors earn a fortune.

"You don't need to worry," Felicity says. "I've been doing this job a long time and I can tell the ones who can't really afford it. He's interviewed every candidate even remotely qualified on the books without even mentioning salary. His finances aren't an issue."

I'm out of excuses.

I've always been excited about starting a new assignment. Although Guinevere is a doll and there aren't any family dynamics to put me off, I'm still not one hundred percent sure. I didn't want to have a crush on my boss.

And Dax is more than just a little bit handsome. It's not just the brooding, befuddled dad thing going on. More that I can tell he wants the best for his daughter. I feel a pull towards him that I've never experienced before, like he's a song in the distance I recognize but can't place. For some reason, I know he means trouble.

"Let me think about it," I say.

Felicity shrieks down the phone. "Think about what? This is a dream job. Have you got something else lined up? What's the problem?"

"Nothing, it's just a surprise, and I obviously wasn't his first choice because he turned me down after the interview. I—"

"He's a new father. Never hired a nanny before. He's going to make mistakes. He realizes Doreen wasn't the right person for the job. He knows you are."

"Just give me an hour to think about it."

"You'd be a fool to pass this up." Felicity is a salesperson who works on commission. The only problem is, the product she's selling *to* me is me. She won't give up without a fight.

"An hour," I say. "If you make me give you an answer now, it will be no." I'm bluffing, but we're playing a game of chicken and I bet she gives in first.

"An hour. No more. I have to move on to other candidates if you don't want it."

I pull in a breath, pleased I have a bit of space to think. "Speak then."

"Who was that?" Callie asks as she comes in.

"Felicity. She's got a job for me. Permanent. Pay's good. In Marylebone."

"What's not to like?" she asks as she slumps on the sofa, a glass of Diet Coke in her hand. She's never going to sleep tonight.

"Right."

"So what's the problem? You don't sound like you want it."

"It's just a weird setup. It's a single father. And...he's..." How do I describe Dax Cove other than gorgeous? "A little taciturn. And...well, he's attractive. I don't really want to see my boss that way."

Callie laughs like I'm a stand-up comedian who's just delivered a punch line.

"I'm serious." Nannying is the most rewarding job in many ways, but every now and then it can be a struggle. It's impossible not to form real attachments to the children in my care. I grow to love them. Every now and then I get reminded that the attachment I have to them is...limited. The children in my care are only mine to love until the end of my shift. They're borrowed, even if the love stays behind forever.

Having a crush on the father of the child would only underline that feeling of looking through a window at other people's lives. It would emphasize the fact that I'm helping people live their lives and not living my own.

"Oh, gosh, I've had a crush on most of my charges' fathers."

I sit down next to her. "You have not."

She nods. "I absolutely have. I haven't tried to pounce on them or anything, but I'm a sucker for a good suit and handmade shoes. Together with a little salt-and-pepper hair, I'm one hundred percent heart eyes."

I smile like I can't quite believe what she's telling me. "Are you serious? It doesn't make you feel a bit De Mornay-esque?"

Rebecca De Mornay starred in *The Hand That Rocks the Cradle*, a film from the last century that every nanny at Portland watches at least once during their training. It's about a nanny who covets the life of the family she's working for and ends up impaled on a picket fence. It's shown to new nannies by graduating nannies as a warning about what you could become if you don't keep a boundary between your professional and personal life.

"Nah," Callie says. "I don't have the same deep-seated psychological issues. And it's not like I declare my undying love for these men. Or even flirt with them. I find them attractive. That's all."

"So you don't think I should be worried?" I ask. I need reassurance because I know I should take this job. There's so much good about it.

"You should keep a diary. A salaciously erotic diary about all the things you want to do to him. Maybe you'll get a book deal, become the next EL James." She sweeps her hand across the air, like she's reading a headline. *"The Diaries of an Insatiable Nanny."*

I pull out my phone and dial Felicity. "You've got a screw loose," I tell Callie.

"Several. Just don't tell my boss because I'm in charge of her children."

"I hope you're calling with good news," Felicity bellows through the phone.

"Let's do this," I say. "When do I start?"

"Not sure how you'll like this, but he'd quite like you to start tomorrow."

"Tomorrow's going to be busy," I reply. Callie squeezes my hand, her eyes full of excitement for me.

"This is going to be a great position for you," Felicity says. "I have a really good feeling about it."

Yeah, I think to myself. I'm not Rebecca De Mornay. And so what if I have a crush? I'll just talk myself out of it. I'll make a note of all his annoying habits and focus on them whenever I find myself looking at him the wrong way. It will be fine.

"Oh and I didn't find out, but is the mother involved at all?" I ask.

"Nope," Felicity says. "He's a single dad. Mother is in America or something."

So I'm going to be working for a rich, handsome, single dad. Eddie will love it, and I know Callie does. I just need to keep out of his way, focus on his daughter and make note of his bad points. What could go wrong?

EIGHT

Eira

I've borrowed Callie's car to help me transport my things into my new home. I'm surprised we haven't been pulled over by the police, because the car is so stuffed, there are things poking out of the windows. It's a good job it's an automatic, because there's a shoebox balanced on top of the gear stick.

"You have a lot of stuff," Dax says to me as he takes a box from the back of the car.

"I'm nearly thirty years old. Things accumulate." He doesn't need to know about my storage unit crammed to the brim with everything from our parents' house I could get out before my uncle noticed.

"You're cute. Anyone ever tell you that?" Callie asks Dax as she joins us with my jumbo-sized suitcase—a loyal friend that's accompanied me everywhere I've been in the last ten years. The suitcase. Not Callie, although she's been a good friend to me. She can just carry less.

"Excuse her. She has no filter." I try to fix her with a

stare, but I can tell she's deliberately not looking at me. I lower my voice and hiss, "How would you feel if I said that to your boss?"

"I would take you for a medical examination if you told my boss he was cute. He's a hundred and five and...not cute."

I give a little shake of my head. There's no point in telling her she missed what I was trying to say. Her brain is three miles ahead now and I'd just be wasting oxygen.

I'm doing everything I can *not* to focus on Dax's cuteness. Or the way his forearm muscles flex when he picks up a box and his t-shirt pulls tight across his back. Yup, I didn't notice any of it. Or how the scruff on his jaw suits him a little too well, or the way he keeps his house so bloody tidy is adorable. Everything is just so organized.

And not sustainable, given he just had a kid. But I'm not about to tell him that.

"How much more is there?" he asks as he glances over his shoulder.

"A few more boxes," I say. Or twenty. I'm pretty proud we managed to get everything into one carload. Probably because I took a carload to the storage unit when I finished at my old job.

I have a lot of stuff. But most people my age have their things stored at their parents' place. I don't. Besides, it's all useful.

"You saw the room, right?" he asks.

"I did. Don't you worry about me. I'll be able to fit everything in."

"You might want to keep the door closed," he says.

I don't make a quip about waiting until his child hits three and seeing if he can close the door on mess. This father is in for a rude awakening. I add it to my mental list of Dax Cove imperfections.

"The temp nanny who took over from Doreen left this morning. I had the room cleaned so it's ready for you."

"Thanks," I say, as we head into the lift. I pause. I've known some really clueless dads in the past. Not that they're stupid—because of the nature of my business, most people who hire me are smart and successful. But that doesn't mean they have any common sense. I swear, medical science should fund research into some kind of vitamin or supplement to create common sense. It would be worth a fortune. "Where's Guinevere?" I ask, trying to sound blasé.

"Sleeping."

We're standing like Tetris bricks in the lift—Dax at right angles to me, Callie behind me. It's awkward. I'm staring at his jaw, trying to distract myself from his response by memorizing the curve of his Adam's apple, the way his eyelashes look almost like they've been drawn on.

I nod, trying not to give in to the growing panic swirling through my veins. Has he left her alone to come and help me empty my car? "Sleeping, huh?"

"Yeah, my mum is keeping an eye on her."

I exhale. Thank god.

"Great. Guinevere can help me get my room straight this afternoon if you like."

"You don't start until tomorrow," he replies. Felicity managed to get me a day to move in before I start.

"Right, but if you need me to help out today, just let me know."

"I think you're going to need the time to move all your stuff in. I might need to get the floors reinforced or inform my insurer or something."

I assume he's joking, but he doesn't say it with a smile.

His expression says having a nanny with possessions is irritating AF.

Another item for the list: *unrealistic expectations of people's possessions.*

I shrug. "It will take me a few days. I have to figure out the space."

The front door to Dax's flat is propped open.

"You're going to have to move, Dax," a woman's voice shouts as we enter the flat.

Dax inhales wearily, like he's heard the comment before and he's going to ignore it. Again. I like the fact that he doesn't respond.

"I'm serious. The two of you can't live here. Your life is changed now. You need to change where you live as a result."

A woman appears in the corridor, her hands on her hips, an apron on and a partially peeled potato in her hand.

"Oh my, hello. You must be Eira," she says. I'm not quite sure how she knows I'm the new nanny rather than Callie, who's trailing behind me. "I'm Carole—Grandma." She beams as she tells me her title. "Is Eira a Welsh name?"

Most people guess Irish first. "Yes, my father was Welsh."

"It's beautiful, and so fitting, given you're a Welsh queen's nanny."

I laugh. "Absolutely. A perfect fit."

Dax has dumped the box in my bedroom and looks positively furious about our conversation.

"How is she?" I ask. "Still sleeping?"

"Yes. She's here in the kitchen with me in the DockA-Tot. So useful."

"I swear by them," I say. "Good for traveling too, because they provide consistency for the baby and flexibility for you." I duck inside my room and slide the box onto the floor, before going back out into the hallway to continue my conversation with Dax's mum.

"You're Portland trained?" she asks.

"Yes." I nod to where Callie is depositing her box. "Callie and I met at Portland."

"Oh?" she asks. "And you two are...a couple?" Her voice lifts at the end of the sentence, like she's unsuccessfully trying to be cool with the concept.

"In the sense that we're best friends, yes. But not lovers, no."

"Do you have a boyfriend?" she asks.

I deal with this kind of inappropriate question all the time. I don't know what it is, but parents always want to know about the private lives of the nannies looking after their grandchildren. I don't know why.

"Mum," Dax shouts. "Leave it. I only just hired her. I don't want her handing her notice in for at least twenty-four hours. Apart from anything else, my back won't take her moving out straight away." Is Dax being intentionally hilarious? I start to smile and then remember my negative list. No, not intentionally funny and charming. Just rude and unwelcoming.

Carole rolls her eyes. "I'll leave you to it. You probably want to get all your things in. Even though—" She stops and raises her voice. "You've got to move, Dax. I'm telling you."

I've seen babies raised in smaller places. And bigger places. Central London is expensive. And this place in Marylebone won't be cheap, even though it's not large.

We've finally emptied the car and I've convinced Callie to go home, despite my room being utter chaos. All I need is a bed to sleep in tonight. The rest will sort itself out over the coming days.

There's a knock at my bedroom door and Carole pops her head around. "I've put Guinevere down and I'm about to serve up roast chicken. Come and eat."

It's very sweet of her, but I don't expect to eat with the families I work with. In fact, I prefer not to. It's difficult because I live in, but I like to try and keep a professional distance. Otherwise boundaries can start to blur on both sides. "That's so kind, but—"

"I won't hear no," she calls from halfway back to the kitchen. "Come quickly or it will get cold."

I don't want to upset her, so I set down the box I was just carrying and follow her.

Before I get to the kitchen, I can hear Dax whispering. "She might not want to eat with us, Mum. Can't you just leave it?"

Dax hasn't come across as particularly empathetic, but maybe I'm wrong. I have a feeling there's a lot more to Dax beneath the surface.

"Nonsense," Carole replies.

I open the kitchen door before their conversation escalates to an argument.

"This is so kind," I say.

Carole hands me a plate. "Not at all. You're going to be looking after my granddaughter. It's the least I can do."

I'm struck with the realization that I've not actually seen Dax with his daughter other than at the park after Doreen collapsed. "Is she a good sleeper?" I ask.

"Yes, in her room. The temporary nanny seems to have her in a routine," Carole answers, even though I was looking at Dax when I asked the question. "Help yourself. We've carved up the chicken so you can take whatever you want."

I take a leg and some broccoli and sit down at the

reclaimed table at the end of the kitchen, feeling every kind of awkward. "Guinevere's a week old? Is that right?"

"Eight days," Dax answers.

"Nine days ago, nobody knew anything about her." Carole shakes her head, exasperated, and Dax sighs.

Had he been keeping Guinevere a secret from people? Is she a surprise adoption? Was she left on the doorstep? I can barely contain my curiosity so I keep my eyes on the chicken and try not to blurt out eleven questions at once.

"But she looks just like her father. There was no need for that DNA test."

"Mum. Please. Eira has barely moved in. She doesn't want to know all my dirty secrets."

"Don't you dare call my granddaughter a dirty secret."

Dax puts his knife and fork down and pushes his chair back from the table, then stands and heads to the sink. "I didn't call *Guinevere* a dirty secret."

"Can you believe it?" Carole looks at me. "Had the law been different in America, we might never have known we had another member of the Cove family."

"But we do," Dax says.

"You seem completely indifferent, Dax. Do you know how close you came to never knowing you had a daughter? That woman had no intention of telling you."

Dax comes back to the table with a glass of water for himself and one for me. It's thoughtful and kind and...unexpected.

"Thank you," I say as he sets it down in front of me.

"You're welcome," he replies as his mother continues to seethe opposite him.

The tension builds and I try desperately to think of a way to make things right. "But Guinevere's so beautiful. Hopefully that makes up for any difficulty."

Carole grabs my arm. "Yes, we should focus on the good. And not worry that her mother was going to give her up for adoption without even telling Dax."

I try not to physically recoil when I hear her words, but it's difficult.

"I'm so sorry," I say. "That must be...traumatic."

"More for my mother than for me, apparently," Dax says.

Carole rolls her eyes. "Nothing upsets my youngest son, Eira."

"There's no point in being upset about something that didn't happen. It makes no sense."

I want the ground to swallow me up. It's so awkward. I do a mental calculation on how quickly I can get out of here without being rude. I feel like I've taken an awkward pill and I've landed in Awkwardland.

"Anyway," Carole says, "Tell us about you. Have you started unpacking your room yet?"

Dax snorts like he thinks it will take three years to unpack my room given all the boxes he helped carry in. But he's wrong. Three days max until all the boxes are unpacked and then a couple of weeks to refine where everything needs to be.

I don't know if it's just my boxes that have gotten under his skin, but Dax is prickly when it comes to me moving in. I'm not sure if it's personal or if it's just who he is. Maybe it's better if he's just naturally a bit rude—another perfect item for my list. His attitude is like a safeguard for professional distance.

"Not yet. I'll get there."

"Do you have family close by?" she asks.

"My sister's at university in Exeter," I reply, half answering the question.

"Oh, that's a lovely part of the world. What about your parents?"

The scrape of Dax's chair on the kitchen floor means I don't get the chance to answer the question.

"Please excuse me. I have work to do." Dax seems to have eaten his food as quickly as a stray dog offered a juicy steak for the first time in a week.

Carole and I sit in silence while Dax stands and puts his plate in the dishwasher.

As he closes the kitchen door, Carole sits back in her chair. "I'm sorry about Dax. He's a good man, believe me. But having a daughter...a child...it's an adjustment for him. For all of us really." Carole's clearly worried about her son. It reminds me of the way I worry about Eddie and Dylan. I want life to be perfect for them.

"If there's anything I can do, don't hesitate to ask. Just know that Guinevere will be safe in my care."

She clutches my shoulder. "Thank you. Dax said you were very impressive dealing with Doreen in the park."

My head lifts a little, like a flower basking in the sunlight. "I'm glad I was there and able to help."

"Someone needs to help Dax. And Guinevere." She sighs, and I can hear the worry in her breath. "I'm going back to Norfolk after we've eaten. I'll give you my number before I leave. If you're ever worried about anything, do let me know, will you?" She looks at me like she wants to say more. I don't respond, because I want to hear it.

She lowers her voice. "He never wanted children. Was set against it from very little. I'm concerned he won't...bond."

To have fatherhood thrust on you without notice would be a huge adjustment for anyone, but to have it thrust on you when you never had any intention of becoming a parent?

"I'll encourage what I can," I say.

It's information I shouldn't know, but at the same time, I'm glad I do. It means I can do something. Dax is going through a lot and I can't help but think I need to help him. Help Guinevere.

———————

MY BED IS MADE, my alarm set for six tomorrow and I've unpacked my clothes, toiletries and at least half of my boxes. I pull out my hair tie and then retie it immediately, catching the ends that worked free over the last couple of hours. It's nearly ten and I need to get to bed. But first, tea. I press my head against the door but don't hear anything in the hallway.

Perfect.

I'm going to have to work hard to avoid Dax in this flat, but I'll figure it out.

Clutching my beloved box of chamomile, I tiptoe out into the corridor and head to the kitchen.

I gasp when I see Dax at the kitchen table, reading some papers and eating what looks like the roast chicken his mother made him.

"I was just going to make a chamomile tea, if you want one?" I ask, trying not to sound like I'm a little freaked out that I'm disturbing him.

He shakes his head. "I'm fine."

"Are you reading anything interesting?" I ask, and then immediately wish I hadn't. Dax doesn't strike me as a man who enjoys small talk.

"Work stuff," he says. "I had to work from home today

because..." He trails off, but I know what he's not saying. He's had to move me in, look after his daughter. "I'm catching up."

I nod, not wanting to ask him any more questions.

The kettle boils and I pour the water straight onto my teabag. "You're not a doctor who sees patients then?" As soon as the question leaves my lips, I mentally chastise myself. Why am I trying to talk to him? I'm clearly interrupting him, and he obviously doesn't want to talk to me.

"No, I'm a research doctor. My work is...it's important. There's a lot riding on it—millions of lives." His gaze stays on his papers as he speaks.

I can tell by his tone that he's not saying it to show off, but I don't know why he's giving me this information. Part of me feels he wants me to dig, like he's giving me the scent and asking me to follow the trail.

Except he's not exactly encouraging conversation.

I pull out a drawer to find a teaspoon, but it's filled with papers. I pull out another one. That's full of papers too. I glance around, trying to spot the place where spoons might be kept if it isn't this unit. Dax doesn't say anything. He's too engrossed in what he's reading.

I cross the kitchen and pull out another drawer. Finally, I find the spoons, no thanks to Dax.

Another negative point for my list: *not good at giving instructions about where the spoons are.*

"So I'll see you tomorrow morning at seven," I say, picking up my mug. He doesn't respond. "Anything in particular you want me to do with Guinevere?" I ask.

He turns his head. "Like what?"

"I don't know, do you like her to get some fresh air? Does she have an appointment with the health visitor? Do you have any little routines I should know about?"

He shrugs. "Whatever you think. You know better than me."

I've seen this in new mothers before—the few days or weeks before they bond with their new baby. It will come. It will just take a little time. And maybe a little encouragement.

"Great. We have a free day. Who knows what mischief we'll get up to?" I smile, but Dax isn't listening. He's focused on his work.

Looks like Guinevere and I have some work to do. But babies are magic, so we have that going for us.

NINE

Dax

My head hurts. It's the lack of sleep. I'm also probably dehydrated, but I don't want to leave the nursery because for some reason, Guinevere likes my hand on her tummy. Every time I remove it, she wakes up, her face scrunches up and she starts crying.

It's been like this since four. I glance up at the clock. It's just before six. Another hour before Eira starts and I can get on with my day. Another hour until I can readjust my brain and start thinking about important things: the research I'm doing and how we're going to fund the next stage. I haven't even started work and I feel groggy.

The door creaks open and Eira puts her head around. She's dressed in jeans and a t-shirt, her hair still piled on her head. Does she sleep like that? Does it ever get brushed?

"Good morning," she whispers. "Have you been up long?" She has two mugs in her hand and she hands one to me. "Black coffee, right?"

How did she know that?

"I'm just having a little honey and ginger." She says it in a singsong voice as she peers at Guinevere. Her face splits into a smile and her bright smile is...disarming. It sends a jolt through my gut. "She likes to feel Daddy."

She says it like it's totally normal. "Every time I try to move away, she cries."

"Aww, she wants to know her human is nearby. She wants to feel safe. That's all."

I sigh. Of course that's why.

"Have you done much skin to skin?" she says, placing her cup onto a bookshelf beside her and moving toward the cot.

She doesn't wait for an answer, just slides her hand under Guinevere and lifts her up. Every muscle in my body tenses as I wait for the expression of pain Guinevere wears every time my hand leaves her tummy, but surprisingly, she stays fast asleep.

"Sit back," she says. "Unbutton your shirt."

For a second, I wonder if things are taking an unexpected turn. Then I realize she's unsnapping Guinevere's sleepsuit. Skin on skin. Obviously I've heard of it. I've read all the books. It just feels so...unnatural. Once I'm dressed, I'm dressed. Why would I want to get undressed?

Eira maneuvers Guinevere around and places her on my chest, her head nestled under my chin. The baby hasn't made a sound.

"There. She'll be able to hear your heartbeat like that." She glances around for something. "It's chilly in here. We should get a room thermometer." She takes a blanket and places it over us both.

"What do I do now?" I say. *How long do I stay here?* I don't say, but I really hope she'll offer up the information.

I'm just sitting here, not doing anything at all. I should be in the office by now.

"Just be with your daughter," she says.

My daughter.

The daughter I never thought I'd have.

I'm not a monster. I don't want Guinevere growing up knowing I didn't want her, but I'm not what anyone would call a natural father.

"Should I read her a book?"

Eira shrugs. "Maybe later. She just wants to feel your heat. Breathe in your scent. She needs to learn that you won't abandon her. She's lost one parent and a nanny. She uses her sweet voice to make sure she doesn't lose anyone else."

Her words hit me in the chest like a rock to the rib cage. Fuck. This poor, helpless baby has already been abandoned by a parent. Just a week old and I already need to be saving for therapy. I take a breath and let my body relax, smoothing my hand over Guinevere's back.

"Guinevere's a beautiful name. Are you an Arthurian enthusiast?"

I let out a half-laugh. "Back in the day."

Silence stretches between us, and I shift in my seat. I don't normally mind silences, but I feel an expectation—from myself—to fill the gap. Eira doesn't seem to notice the lack of conversation. She's looking around the room, taking everything in.

"I suppose if you weren't expecting her, you didn't have time to prepare," she says.

"I'm not the sort of guy who would have painted Winnie-the-Pooh murals on the walls even if I had known she was coming."

Eira laughs almost silently, and I feel it travel down my spine.

"No, you don't strike me as that type of guy."

What does that mean?

What type of guy do I strike her as? And why am I even wondering that?

"We could do with some things. Like the room thermometer. And clothes. And muslins. Bottles. A baby bath seat. Some first-aid stuff."

"I can give you my credit card. You can order what you want."

She doesn't react. "And why don't you have the crib in your room?"

"Because the cot is in this room. This is the nursery."

"She should sleep with you. For the first six months at least. It's recommended, but given the circumstances, it will be good for both of you. When we go shopping, we can pick up a crib for your room as well. Do you have time today?" she asks, turning and unscrewing bottles and premade milk and decanting one to the other. Guinevere isn't awake. I hope Eira isn't one of those nannies who wakes sleeping babies to feed them. Can't we just let her sleep?

"Like I said, I'll give you my credit card. You can get everything we need. You can even paint a Winnie-the-Pooh mural in here if you like."

She gives me a tight smile, like I'm not amusing or charming at all. "We shall go shopping together," she says, resolutely. "When are you free? What about lunchtime today?"

Her tone is firm, which is quite at odds with my first impression of her as someone who thinks children should be boundaryless and run riot all over the place. I wonder if she'll be as firm with Guinevere.

"Where did you have in mind?"

"We'll have to be quick because you're on lunch. John Lewis will have everything we need in one place. Unless you have a better suggestion? Harrods and Selfridges are farther away and you pay a premium."

"John Lewis is fine." I don't know if it's my voice or maybe the smell of the bottle that Eira just prepared, but Guinevere stirs.

"Someone wants some food and a clean nappy," Eira says.

I expect her to lift Guinevere from my arms and take over. Instead, she moves my daughter from my chest into my arms, snapping closed her babygrow. She hands me the milk.

"How much do I feed her?" I ask.

"As much as she wants," she replies. "She'll know when she's had enough. She might enjoy a story."

Guinevere takes the bottle without opening her eyes. "You should put baby books on your list. I don't have anything to read to her."

Eira smiles, her eyes sparkling from the dim light of the hall. "Read your favorite book to her. Or even your research results. She just wants to hear the sound of your voice." She pulls out her phone and snaps a picture. "You'll want pictures of these times when she's older. Make sure there are far too many pictures of the two of you. She'll treasure them." She sighs like she's thinking about something important to her. "I'll be back."

She moves silently out of the room, leaving me and...my daughter. I think I might have just been given my first lesson in childcare by our new nanny.

And I didn't mind it.

TEN

Eira

Guinevere's asleep in her new crib, right next to her daddy's bed. She's snuggled up in new Grobag, much safer than the old bedding, clean from her bath in her new bath seat.

And now I'm in the bath.

I'm exhausted. Today's been fun. I've never had a newborn charge who wasn't all set up with every gismo, gadget and item of baby clothing ever produced. But then again, I've never been a nanny for a single dad who didn't know he had a daughter until the day she was born. It's like I'm starting from a blank slate.

Even though there's no doubt Dax is attractive, I'm having to actively keep that thought boxed up in the back of my brain, and really focus on my list of things I don't like about him. I've really enjoyed the last couple of days. As a nanny, you're always helping the family you work for, but with Dax and Guinevere, I'm not sure what they'd do without me. The feeling's like a warm blanket on a frosty evening. It's nice to be making such a difference.

My phone buzzes.

My brother's name flashes up on my phone screen. Immediately my heart starts to bang against my chest. He's the best little brother ever. Sensible. Kind. Hardworking. But he's twenty-four. There's a lot of trouble he could get into. What if he got a girl pregnant and she didn't tell him until after the baby was born?

I grab my phone, see his message and relax. He wants to borrow money for a rent deposit on his new flat. He has a good job in a technology company, but he's on an entry-level salary and living in London's expensive. When he was first out of university, he took out a small loan to cover his annual tube pass. When I found out, I was devastated that he chose to shoulder that burden. I made him promise he'd always come to me if he needed money. I have a savings fund ring-fenced just for him.

He calls as I'm reading the message.

"I'm sorry to ask you again." He's always so apologetic, but he needn't be. Looking after him is my job. I'm his big sister.

"It's fine," I say.

"Have you spoken to the lawyers?"

I sigh, suddenly feeling weighted down by a blanket of lead.

"Not since the last time," I say. Dylan always holds out hope that the lawyers will fix things—that one day, justice will be served. Unfortunately, over the last few years, my hope has ebbed away. What's done is done.

If I never speak to another lawyer again, it will be too soon. All they've ever managed to do is drain my bank account. I haven't told Dylan and Eddie, but I've given up hope that we'll ever get resolution. Our uncle is in the

Cayman Islands enjoying our inheritance and there's nothing we can do about it.

"You shouldn't have to pay for my deposit," Dylan says. "I'm really hoping to get a pay rise soon. I don't want to ask yet because they just made a round of layoffs. When the dust settles."

"It's fine," I say. Because it is. Because we're all healthy and happy and we have each other. "Tell me about the flat." Dylan graduated over three years ago now, just as Eddie started university. He's been working in tech ever since. Eddie wants to do the same thing although she wants to work for herself. Both of them following in the footsteps of our mother—not that we ever heard her talk about work. We've all read about who our parents were, what they did, the companies they founded, the empire they built.

"I can get really good broadband," he says. I can't help but laugh, heartily, just like I used to when he learned to play peekaboo. I was so proud of him then, just as I am now. "It's important. I've got a couple of ideas I'm playing with for apps. If one of them comes off, I might be able to quit my job completely. I can't tell you too much, but I need bandwidth."

I know the feeling of needing more time. Space to breathe. Maybe now I have a job and I'm not sleeping on someone else's sofa, I've started to feel I have a bit more time to myself. "Okay, well I'll transfer the money tonight. Send me your new address."

"Speaking of new addresses, did you start your new job yet?"

"I did. I'm enjoying it."

"I don't get how you want to live in someone else's house. Don't you want a place of your own?"

Yes. The answer is *yes*, I would prefer to live in my own

flat, rather than have my nose pressed against the window of someone else's life. But as a live-in nanny, I can maximize my earnings. A little brother who still needs help with his rent deposit plus a little sister who has university fees landing every term, not to mention the rent and food and books and all the rest of her living expenses—it all adds up. Their needs come before my preference for my own place.

"It's much easier this way," I say. "No commute to work. I don't have to worry if the boiler breaks down or my flat mate moves out. No responsibilities beyond buying my own shampoo."

"No one believes you have no responsibilities. For a start, you're a nanny, and you've practically raised me and Eddie since..." He trails off. I don't like the way this conversation is turning.

"I'm in the bath and the water's getting cold. I'll call you later in the week."

"I love you," he says, his voice a bit louder than before.

"I love you too. Never forget it."

We hang up and despite my bathwater being just the right temperature, I get out of the bath and wrap myself in my favorite towel. It's worn and fraying at one edge, but my first nanny used to wrap me in this towel as a child, and I can almost feel her arms around me when I use it.

I have a shower in the bathroom attached to my bedroom, but I've used the bath across the hall for a soak. I press my ear against the bathroom door, to make sure I'm not going to open the door and walk straight into Dax. It sounds like the coast is clear, so I twist the doorknob, poke my head out to check and then scurry across to my bedroom. I close my door and exhale.

Phew. I avoided my boss while I was half-naked. I feel like I deserve a cup of warm milk for that.

Dax's mother was right. This flat is the smallest place I've ever lived. Usually, I'd be on a different floor to the family I'm working for. In my first job, I was in the basement flat and had my own kitchen. In my third job, the family had an entertaining kitchen and then a separate kitchen that actually got used by the chef and the housekeeper and me. There was never any danger I'd cross paths with my employer getting hot milk. Here, it's different. We're on top of each other. I can't exactly hear him breathe in the next room, but it's close.

I literally let my hair down and get changed into my pajamas—white with embroidered dots all over—then pop my head out of the door to see if the coast is clear. It must be an adjustment for Dax too, going from living on his own to having two women in his space.

The kitchen looks dark, so I dart out of my bedroom and along the corridor to fix my hot milk and leave a little gift for Dax. His mother was right about that, too—he needs to bond with his daughter. I don't mind helping that along in any way I can.

I head straight to the cupboard with the saucepans. It takes me about three seconds to discover that I'm not the only one in the kitchen.

A bare-chested Dax is leaning at the kitchen counter right in front of me, and I jump so high, I nearly hit Mars.

"Oh hi," I say.

He looks at me, looks away, then does a double-take. I probably should buy a dressing gown. He shifts and lifts his plate up as if to offer explanation. I try to focus on what he's eating and not on the way his jogging trousers hang low on his hips, or the way a trail of hair disappears under the waistband. Looks like he's eating peanut butter on toast.

"You're in the dark," I say.

He shrugs but doesn't offer further explanation.

"I'm just going to make myself some hot milk. Do you want some?" This shouldn't become a routine. Dax eats late, I make myself a hot drink. We bump into each other, neither of us wearing much.

Maybe I should get a kettle for my room.

He turns to face me and I have to look away. The way the muscles in his arms tense and relax—it's too much. "No thanks."

If I'd known he was going to be in here, I would have sacrificed hot milk. It's definitely not worth being in such close proximity to my ridiculously hot, taciturn boss. I need to focus on the negative.

The negative.

The negative.

He didn't hire me right away. He's a little rude. Unwelcoming. Doesn't like small talk. Complained about the carful of personal items I brought on move-in day, and implied I might be a bit of a clutterbug.

That's better.

"Guinevere sleeping?" I ask as I pour milk into a pan.

"No, we're playing backgammon. It's her turn so I'm taking the opportunity to have a snack."

On instinct, I turn to see his expression. He's not laughing. But he doesn't look like he's irritated either.

"I didn't know she played," I reply. "I'll be sure to have a couple of games with her tomorrow."

"You play?" he asks, surprised.

"Since I was five years old."

He doesn't respond straight away. Instead he takes a bite of his toast and chews for the longest time.

"I have a set," he says finally.

I focus on the pan of milk on the hob. Stirring it with

the wooden spoon will help it boil more quickly. Or not at all.

"Let me know if you ever want a game." I want to slap my palm on my face. I don't know what made me say it. I don't need a reason to be in close proximity to him. In fact, it's the exact opposite. I need to find excuses *not* to be near him.

More silence. Then, "Sure. I'll play you."

He stands upright, and I squeeze my eyes shut, facing my milk. I don't need any more images of his bare chest scorched into my brain for eternity. I feel him head toward me and even though I know he's just going to pass by, I try to hold still like any sharp movements could lead to an animal attack.

The air moves with him and I get a waft of his scent. Grassy and earthy, like a summer afternoon paddling in streams, poking at stones and picking wildflowers. It feels fresh and free with undertones of the wild.

I take a deep breath after he leaves the room and try to refocus on the milk, which is starting to bubble. I stand on tiptoes and reach for a cup from the top shelf.

"You want me to get that for you?" he asks, appearing out of nowhere.

Before I can respond, the heat of Dax's body is behind me and our fingers catch as we both reach for the same mug.

I pull my hand away, but as I set my heels on the floor, my back presses lightly against his chest.

"Sorry," he mutters, even though he hasn't done anything. He moves away slightly and sets the mug on the counter.

"Thanks," I say, sending up a little prayer that he can't see the flush on my burning-hot face. I focus on pouring out my milk.

He lifts the leather case he's carrying. "I found it." As he passes by, he sweeps his hand over the light switches and the overhead light turns off, replaced by low lighting under the kitchen cabinets.

I slide my hand around the cup and take a seat opposite him at the kitchen table, the backgammon set between us. Why am I here? I should make an excuse to leave. I'll play one quick game then say I have to call Eddie or something.

"I have something for you." I reach into my pajama pocket and pull out the two white circular disks, threaded with ribbon and wrapped in tissue paper.

He frowns as I hand him the gift. "What is it?"

I don't answer, just sip my milk, waiting for him to open it.

When he does, he doesn't look like he has any more of a clue what I've given him. "It's a handprint on one and a footprint on the other," I say.

"Of Guinevere?" he asks, turning them over to see what's on the back. I wrote today's date on them.

"No, those are my hand and feet prints, Dax. I thought you might like to put them in your study."

He ignores me and still looks confused. "But what for?"

I sigh. "A Christmas decoration. You can put them on the tree. I know it's a bit early, but who doesn't like a sentimental Christmas ornament?" Looking at Dax's expression, I'm pretty sure I've found the one person on earth who wouldn't be moved by his daughter's hand-and-footprint on the Christmas tree.

"Right," he says, and puts them to the side. He opens the backgammon set and I move forward, taking in the red and cream worn leather. It's a beautiful set. It reminds me of the one I learned on as a child—my grandfather's, who left it to my father. I couldn't find it in my parents' possessions when I left the house. I wonder if my uncle ever uses it.

I pick up one of the cream counters and turn it round in my hand. It has a lovely weight to it. "Is it stone?" I ask.

He shrugs.

I watch, turning the counter over and over, pretending I don't notice how quickly his fingers move, setting out the counters. Then he retraces his steps, lining up the counters so they're straight and even, exactly central on the points.

He looks at me. "Ready?"

I take the cream dice from the leather-lined pocket and throw one. He throws one of the red dice he's holding.

He throws a five. Mine comes up as a six. It's my favorite move to start a game. I take my counter farthest from home and move it across the board.

Dax glances up at me and gives me a small nod. It's an acknowledgement that he knows I can play, since it's likely the same move he would have made. Warmth gathers in my chest. I get the feeling Dax's good impression is hard won.

I pick up my die at the same time he does and our fingers brush together.

I drop my dice to the table like they're on fire and pretend I didn't shiver when he touched me.

He rolls a five and a two. He makes the safe, standard move, and as he removes his dice, he glances up at me like he's waiting for me to acknowledge that he knows what he's doing too.

"Safe," I say.

He shrugs.

I would have played the same exact move.

We continue the game in silence. Dax has long abandoned his toast and sits back in his chair, his arms folded against the naked chest I'm definitely not looking at. I use my milk as a shield between us and take consistent, small sips to punctuate his turns.

A few moves later, he leaves a counter open and when I throw my dice, our eyes lock and he smirks. He knows I can take him if I want to.

I do, and when I scoop up my dice, I glance at him to see if he's a sore loser. His face only shows concentration.

He throws again, and manages to get his counter back into play.

In the end, I beat him.

"You play well," he says.

"Thanks. I've had a lot of practice, although it's been a couple of years."

He doesn't say anything. It's my cue to leave. "I should call my sister."

"Oh, it's like that is it? One game and if you're winning, you're out?"

A small smile curls around my lip. "We both have to be up early."

He nods and doesn't try to convince me to stay. Am I being rude? Should I play him again? "You don't have to work?"

He sighs. "I'm too tired to concentrate."

I laugh. "Oh, that must be the reason you didn't win." I'm smiling as I speak, but I'm also giving him salve for his ego.

"Not at all. You play well." It's the response of a confident man. It's just a game of backgammon, but there are plenty of men whose egos would have been bruised about losing. I gave him a plausible excuse but he didn't take it. I like him better for it.

"Let's do the best of three," I say. "That gives you a chance to win back your dignity."

He lets out a half-laugh. "Wow. I didn't realize my dignity was at stake."

I shrug and wonder if I've been unprofessional. I don't know if it's because he's not married, or he's a similar age to me, or maybe because this flat is so small, but the line I usually see so clearly between me and my boss is blurry. I forget myself around him.

This time, I set up the board. I look up when I'm finished and he's looking at me. Not at the counters. Not at his toast. He's looking at me, and he doesn't look away.

I throw my die and the game begins. Dax's fingers move decisively around the board. He's quick to make awkward moves, not lingering too long when it's his turn. Does he want this situation to be over as soon as possible? It was his idea to play.

This game is more interesting. He takes me. I take him. He gets all his counters home and when he blocks me from getting back on the board, he gives me a look that says, *I've won.* It takes everything I have not to slide onto his lap and kiss him.

I don't know if he's a closet mind-reader on the side, but without looking away, he sits back in his seat, sliding his legs out, grazing mine.

My heart boom, boom, booms in my chest, but I don't move away. *Can't* move away.

His lips curl into a smile and finally he throws his dice.

I lose. I lose *monumentally.*

"I guess you got your dignity back," I say.

His gaze flickers from where he's setting out the counters again to meet mine and then back again. "That's a relief."

The deciding game is quick and close. I beat him by a tiny margin.

I grin. "That decides it then, I'm backgammon champion of the world."

He shoots me a full, unreserved grin and my breath catches at how warm it is, how beautiful he is, how good it makes me feel.

I move my legs so we're no longer touching and as I stop feeling his heat against me, it hits me that we've crossed a line. It was just legs touching, but it's more than that. That doesn't happen if you're not attracted to someone.

I stand, a little confused and unsure whether I just messed everything up. I don't want to lose this job.

"I look forward to a rematch," he says. "Tomorrow night. I'll take your crown." He holds my gaze a little too long. I can't tell if it's gamesmanship or something else.

Whatever it is, I look away and stand, ready to retreat to the safety of my bedroom.

ELEVEN

Dax

I wake up, open my eyes and Guinevere is staring back at me through the see-through sides of her crib.

Is that normal? For a baby just to be lying there, awake but not crying? I sit up. Is she alive? She blinks, and I let out a breath.

"Are you okay?" I ask. What am I asking her for? I'm losing my mind. "Shall we change you?" Again with the questions. I pull my fingers through my hair and swing my legs over the bed. "I'm tired," I say. I didn't go to bed late last night, and I didn't have a beer like I normally would on a Friday night. There's no real reason to be tired, but I am.

I check the clock. It's just before eight. Has she slept all the way since midnight when I went to bed? Maybe she's just been awake staring at me all night.

The sound of the front door closing gets my attention. "Mum?" I call out. She's the only one who would let herself in without knocking. Then I realize. It was probably Eira.

She said she'd be out early. Something about going to see her brother.

"Do you like your new nanny?" I ask, reaching into the crib. Eira said I should talk to Guinevere so she can get used to my voice. I'm not a big talker, but Eira suggested narrating whatever I'm doing. Maybe it will mean that Guinevere is less fussy.

It's my first weekend alone with Guinevere and I'm regretting not hiring a weekend nanny. I really should look into it. I just can't bear the thought of even more people in my space. My brothers are coming round—there's no way I'm leaving the house. I need to get Eira to write me a list of things to take if I'm going out with the baby. But being here where I know where everything is seems more manageable than spending the day out.

I check the time on my phone. I have two hours and sixteen minutes to get us both washed, fed and dressed, while not causing any permanent damage to this kid.

I lift Guinevere and place her down on the floor, where Eira set out a changing mat, along with nappies and wipes and creams in a basket. I suggested that we change her on top of the chest of drawers. She told me that there was too much of a risk of Guinevere falling. But Guinevere doesn't move. Not really at all. But Eira's the expert. She spent two years training to be an elite nanny and she's already helped me so much. I need to listen to her.

And maybe I should have agreed to the changing table she suggested. There's just not enough room in this flat for more furniture.

On the tub of wipes, there's a pink Post-it.

Talk to your daughter. Tell her what you're doing. Tell her your secrets. You got this.

Eira's here, even when she's not.

I whip off Guinevere's nappy. "I'm taking your nappy off," I say. "Then I'm going to wipe your bottom." I've changed her nappy before and I've started to get faster. "No poos," I say, checking the nappy. I guess she knows that already.

After I've changed her and refastened her sleepsuit, I lift her up, careful to support her head. There are some things I remember from medical school. "So, Guinevere, I'm going to be honest with you, I never wanted to be a father. But there's no way I was going to let someone else fulfil my responsibilities. So here we are. We're just going to have to make the best of it. I'm sure we'll get used to each other."

I head out to the kitchen to make myself some coffee. When I get there, I realize there's nowhere to put Guinevere down so I can actually make myself the coffee. Then I remember the camp bed thing my mum brought. Park-a-Kid or something. "Do you know where they put that little bed?" I ask. I look around and spot it under the table.

And with it, another pink note.

Don't be tempted to put it on the table or the counter. It's not worth it. You got this.

Eira's reading my mind.

"She wants you on the floor," I say.

Guinevere moves her head to stare behind me as if she's looking at someone. She's so convincing that I actually turn my head to check there isn't anyone there.

"I need coffee. And you need milk, so...you're on the floor. I'm not going to overrule Eira. She knows best." Despite my first impressions, Eira's incredibly competent. Impressively so. She's also beautiful. I think back to playing backgammon a couple of nights ago. I was so close to pulling her onto my lap and kissing her. The only thing that stopped me was knowing it could scare her off. Guinevere needs her and so do I.

I put Guinevere into her bed under the kitchen table so the surface acts as a shield from any falling objects and put the coffee machine on.

There's another Post-it on the mug cupboard.

Get milk ready while the coffee machine works its magic. Clean bottles are in the sterilizer. You got this.

There's a heart on the end of this note and I stare at it, trying to figure out whether it's significant. She didn't move away when I slid my leg against hers the other night.

I pull out the bottles from the sterilizer and fill one with premade milk. "And you can have some breakfast."

I glance down just in time to see Guinevere scrunch up her face. It's the thunder rumbling a couple of beats before the lightning, because a couple of seconds later, Guinevere starts to cry.

Shit. What happened?

I scoop her off the floor and she stops. "Didn't you like it down there?" I tuck her into the crook of my elbow and move her bottle to the kitchen table, then pick up my coffee. "Let's get our breakfast and the paper, and let's chill." I'm about to sit down when I feel my arm warm where she's lying. I lift her up to inspect her and see an unmistakable brown sludge mark on her babygrow.

"Oh. I see. It's like that, is it?" I abandon my coffee and head back to my bedroom. I open her babygrow on the changing mat on the floor to find she's covered in shit. And now her changing mat is covered in shit. And so am I.

So much for a little rest and relaxation with the paper.

"We're going to need some house rules," I say. "The first one is 'no shitting on me'. If you want to shit on any of your uncles, that's absolutely fine. But not me. Do you hear me?"

I maneuver us into the bathroom, trying to make sure nothing drips. There aren't enough wipes in London to deal with this. She needs to be hosed down like a dog. And so do I.

I set her in her new bath seat and get to work. There were no Post-its for this scenario. "Mary Poppins missed something," I say to Guinevere. "You didn't foresee this, did you, Eira?" She's got me talking to her as well as Guinevere. Madness has set in.

"Second rule," I say. "No staring at me when I wake up like you're the ghost of girlfriends past. It freaks me the fuck out."

We make eye contact. I want her to understand the gravity of these rules. They're going to be lifelong requirements to ensure our peaceful cohabitation. "You hear me?" She moves her arm haphazardly, almost like she's drunk and lost control of her limbs.

"And then there's bacon," I say. "You've gotta love bacon if you're going to be my kid. Bacon sandwiches on a Sunday morning are the best things about Sundays. Oh, and you've got to be a good student. Grades don't matter as long as you're learning. Well, they do matter, but they don't matter as much. Do you think you'll become a doctor? It runs in the family, you know. But there's room for other things as well. Your uncle Zach writes books for a living, and uncle Vincent makes a lot of money doing god only knows. But really, science is where it's at. You get the chance to change lives, Guinevere."

My heart sinks a little. I've tried to put it to the back of my head how Guinevere is going to impact my career. Mum always says you have to play the hand you're dealt, but at the same time, I've always been clear about what I want out of my life.

"I'm not sure I'm going to be the best...father," I confess. Father.

I never thought I'd refer to myself that way. It was never a title I aspired to.

I wrap Guinevere in a pink towel with elephants on it. It's one of the three thousand things we bought on our shopping trip earlier in the week with Eira. I place her on the bathmat, step over her and into the shower. "I think we might need a weekend nanny." I'm pretty sure Eira would be appalled if she saw Guinevere on the floor of the bathroom and me covered in shit. "I'm going to work a lot and you don't have a mum. There are challenges ahead. But you've got an awesome grumpy grandfather and a grandma who already adores you. And one or two of your uncles aren't bad either. Then there are your aunts, who I'm rather fond of—although don't tell them that. It's a secret that stays between you and me. And you're going to have your cousins."

I stop. No mum. What will that be like? I can't even imagine. I might be Guinevere's father, but I'll never be a *dad*. It's just not who I am.

I'm not about to beg Kelly to come back into our lives. She made her decision about how to play the hand she was dealt, and I've made mine. Guinevere, planned or not, will grow up surrounded by people who love her. The Coves wouldn't have it any other way, even if I can't be the kind of father my brothers seem to want to be. Guinevere will be one of us—and for now, that has to be enough.

This baby may have changed a lot around here since her arrival, but I won't sacrifice my work for anything or anyone. The world is just waiting to be changed—improved—and I'm committed to leaving behind a legacy of innovation. My parents had five kids—six, if you count Vincent—and while

I wouldn't trade my family for anything, my parents traded career advancement in exchange for us. Guinevere will be my only child. I'll have an army of nannies to make sure I still give my all to my work, if that's what it takes.

"I'm not going to win any Father of the Year prizes," I tell her. "But I'll be reliable. And you'll always have a roof over your head and food in your tummy. And probably Chinese burns on your arms if your cousins are anything like their fathers. Don't take it personally."

I step out of the shower and Guinevere is gazing up at me. I should do an internet search on what she can actually see. She probably wonders if I'm about to attack her. It's likely traumatic seeing the world from down there.

Quickly, I wrap a towel around my waist and scoop her up. "I'll try not to be a complete fuck-up as a father, so long as you tell me you're going to love bacon and don't shit on me again. Deal?"

TWELVE

Eira

I step into the kitchen, half wondering whether Dax and Guinevere have moved out. It's so peaceful.

But there they are. Guinevere in her DockATot under the kitchen table and Dax sitting next to her, eating his cereal.

"Good morning, both of you," I say. "How was your day yesterday?"

I had to force myself out of the house yesterday. I knew Dax was perfectly capable of coping, but I also knew he'd doubt himself. Most of all, I knew he needed the time with Guinevere on his own to bond.

By the time I got home, they were both fast asleep. I crept into my room so I wouldn't wake anyone.

Dax swallows and gives me a thumbs up. Chatty as usual then. At least he's wearing a t-shirt.

I step closer and peer at Guinevere, just to make sure she's still breathing. "Good morning, my Welsh princess."

I turn back to the counter and set about making a cup of

coffee. "Do you want one?" I ask. I start emptying the dishwasher while I wait for the coffee to brew.

"That would be great. Thanks."

It's a cup of coffee, so it's not a big deal, but I'm pleased I can do something for him. He's likely had his hands full since Guinevere woke up and a cup of coffee is probably exactly what he needs.

"Do you always do two things at once?" he asks.

I turn to make sure he's talking to me.

"The dishwasher and the coffee. But you do it all the time. Folding the muslins and playing peekaboo. Doing laundry when you change her clothes. Putting out the bin when she has a dirty nappy."

He's been watching me. Observing. It sends a shiver down my spine.

"Just efficient, I guess." I smile at him.

"Efficient. Huh."

"Any plans for today?" I ask, wanting to get off the subject of me.

He takes a big breath in and then sighs. "Shit. I've got to cancel football this week." He shakes his head. "Or I guess, forever."

"Why?" I ask. Last time I saw him play—the day Doreen collapsed—it had been a Tuesday lunchtime. Does he play twice a week?

"Our team plays on Tuesday and Sunday," he says, answering the question before I have a chance to ask it. "Unless I get a weekend nanny, which I've been thinking about."

It must be difficult for him to adjust to being a father out of nowhere. But a weekend nanny wasn't going to facilitate the bonding he needs so desperately with Guinevere. "I don't have any plans today. In fact, I was going to go for a walk. Why don't I bring Guinevere to the park while you play football?"

"It's your day off. You don't need to do that," he says.

"Like I said, I don't have any plans and I'm offering. It's efficient—I get the walk and you get to play football. Then you're not letting anyone down at the last minute and you have some time to figure out if you can make something work for Sundays."

He fixes me with a stare that I feel between my thighs. "Are you sure you don't mind?"

———

HE PUSHES the pram to the park while I walk alongside the father-and-daughter duo. They're beyond cute—Dax is so tall anyway, and next to the pram, he seems even more elongated.

"I've noticed a lot of people have their babies in a buggy-thing where they sit up. But Guinevere is in the cot wheely thing," he says.

I don't respond. I've learned over the years not to offer my opinion on the raising of children unless it's immediately life threatening or explicitly solicited.

"Is that better?" he asks.

"Not in my opinion," I say.

There's a beat of silence. "You're not going to elaborate?" he asks.

It's a weird response. The usual response to invite elaboration might be something like, "Oh really? Why don't you think so?" or some other such question. I get the impression Dax doesn't comply with a lot of social norms.

I can't help but smile. His lack of instinct to make things

comfortable, his refusal to dance the usual steps in this situation, is disarming.

"Two reasons. Babies as young as Guinevere should be flat most of the time, which is why the *pram* is good. It helps the development of the spine. When she's a little older, she can go in a buggy or a pushchair—two words for the same thing. And the second reason is, studies suggest the higher up prams and pushchairs are, the more they protect children from pollution." I glance up at him to find his eyes narrowed. There's a ridge between his eyes that suggests he's listening. "Studies show that all prams should be a meter from the ground. Below that level is where most of the pollution is found. So, given Guinevere is in a pram in central London, I think it's good to keep her as high as possible. The pram is higher than the pushchair."

"Sounds reasonable," he replies.

"As opposed to?"

He shrugs, "You know, some kind of kumbaya, eating-your-placenta type shit."

"I read it in *New Scientist*, so that's really not their vibe."

"*New Scientist*?" he asks. "Is that your usual bedtime reading?"

"It's my job to understand how I can best help the children I work for. Childrearing is all about science. And love."

He grunts from beside me. "I'm interested in the science bit."

The love bit is coming, I don't say.

"I can send you some age-appropriate studies," I say. It might be a way to nurture the bond between Dax and his daughter—give him the science, let him apply it, let it foster interest in his daughter. Let it help him love her.

He doesn't say anything and we keep walking, past the

black wrought iron railings of Coram's Fields Park. He opens the heavy green gate as if it's made of paper and backs the pram in, exactly as I would have done.

"I bet you know a lot you never tell anyone," he says out of nowhere. "You don't want to tell parents how to raise their kids. You don't want to be overbearing." He's not asking me questions—he's making statements. And he's nailing my approach to nannying. "But you have all this knowledge inside."

He stops abruptly and turns to me. "I don't want you to hold back. Guinevere shouldn't be at a disadvantage because I'm not...a typical caregiver of a child. I want her basic needs catered to. So if you see me doing something you would advise against, or if you see something she needs, I want you to tell me."

My heart squeezes in my chest like a child's fist around the string of a balloon. Okay, so he can't bring himself to say father or daddy yet, but the bond between Dax and Guinevere is starting to grow like a crocus poking its head out of the ground after winter. He worries she's not going to have what she needs, that he's not going to be enough. It's every parent's concern.

"You're doing just great," I say. "Remember, I had two years of school to help me deal with kids. But new parents never have that training. You don't need to be perfect. You just need to love her and put her first."

"Love her, huh? Did you read that in *New Scientist*?" He shakes his head and starts to walk again, pushing the buggy.

I let the little barb roll off my back. Maybe he doesn't think he loves her now, but he will. He's starting to.

Dax strikes me as a person who's previously been used to dealing in logic. And now? As a father? The first whispers of love are beginning to infiltrate his heart. He just doesn't realize it yet.

"It looks like we're early," he says.

There are a couple of players on the pitch, and I'm surprised he hasn't released the pram and headed over there already. Or maybe I'm not. Maybe he's having second thoughts about leaving his daughter. Does he have new mum syndrome, where he wants the freedom to do things for himself, but at the same time, doesn't want to leave his daughter?

"Why don't we take Guinevere on the swings for the first time?" I suggest.

"The swings?" he says. "Is she old enough? Doesn't her neck need more support?"

"Not for the saucer swing," I say, heading over to the round swing with the roped, dish-shaped seat, big enough for five kids to pile onto.

"Is that clean?" he says, grimacing. He's already worrying about her. How can he think he's only interested in the science of development?

"She's in her pramsuit. No part of her will be touching the swing. We can pop a muslin down if it makes you feel better." I can't help but smile at his concern.

Dax stops the pram by the swing and I pop on the brake. "It's good to get into the habit. Even on flat ground." I'd never say it normally to parents, but Dax has asked me not to hold back. If that's what he needs, that's what I'm going to give him. "You want to take her out?" I ask.

"You do it," he says.

First I pull out a spare muslin from under the pram and place it across the ropes, then I pull back the hood of the pram and scoop Guinevere up. "Are you ready for your first go on the swings?" I ask. "Daddy's going to push you." I lay her down so she's staring at the sky. "Just a little push," I say.

Dax nudges the swing, his eyes pinned on Guinevere like he's waiting for her to drop through the ropes at any moment.

"Movement like this helps her develop her balance and her place in world. It stimulates the development of her senses. It might seem like a simple swing, but it's all science."

He doesn't take his eyes off his daughter. "I get it. It's just...like a dog could come along and bite her at any point. Or someone might have dropped some glass on this thing or—"

"That's why you're here. And I'm here. Kids have parents—and nannies—to protect them. And while you're playing football, I have my dog-fighting gloves and my glass-finding lamp. We're all good. For now."

"Does there come a point when you don't think they're moments away from death?" he asks.

I let out a laugh that's been building in me. "It's hard when they're little like this. But wait six months, maybe a little more. You're going to wish she would just lie here like this." I gaze at Guinevere. She's not smiling, but she looks so content, gently swinging, watching the bare branches of the trees above her cut out against the blue of the sky. "And then for fifteen years, she won't sit still. Then it will come full circle and hopefully, if everyone does their job properly, she'll be gazing at the sky in wonder, thinking about how amazing this world is."

I feel his gaze on me and on instinct I turn my head. Our eyes lock. Some kind of understanding passes between us. He respects me. He understands what I'm saying.

There's a connection. Again.

"Being responsible for another human being makes you feel everything a thousand times more," I say. "Life's more vulnerable and scary and tiring and draining, and also a thousand times more colorful and fun and miraculous and wonderful."

"I'm not sure about that," he says.

Not yet, I don't say.

Voices from behind us catch our attention. It's more people arriving for the football practice.

Dax turns back to Guinevere.

"Do you have to go?" I ask.

"I have a few more minutes." It's like he can't bear to leave her. It's adorable.

"We'll walk you." I take Guinevere from the swing and put her back into the pram. This time I push, because otherwise, Dax might have us heading to the slide and forget about the football altogether.

We get to the gate of the pitch. "Enjoy your football. We're going to enjoy watching." As soon as I say it, heat rushes up my cheeks. I didn't mean to imply we'll enjoy ogling his perfect male form running about the pitch, but...if the shoe fits, lace that shit up.

He nods and glances between me and Guinevere. He starts to say something and stops himself. Finally, he turns and heads through the gate. When he gets onto the pitch, he stops and turns. "Thank you," he mouths.

It feels intimate somehow, like we're the only two people in the park.

I smile at him and he grins back. It's boyish and sweet and sexy, and I try to ignore the way butterflies flutter in my stomach.

Because this is about Guinevere. And the money. Nothing else.

THIRTEEN

Dax

Jacob is the most irritating of all my brothers. And that says a lot, because they're all pretty annoying. I don't even think it's because he's the oldest. Even if he was the youngest, he'd still think he was in charge of everything. He's in my kitchen. *Again.* He never used to drop by. Why does he think that me having another human being to look after means he gets to visit more often? It's not like Guinevere can be pleased to see him. Can she?

"I'm just saying we're always all together. This is the one time in the year where everyone changes schedules and takes time to be together as a family." He sips the cup of coffee he made for himself without asking me.

"You don't need to school me in Mum and Dad's anniversary weekend. I'm in this family too. I know how it goes. But none of you are new single parents from what I can make out. Guinevere is not even three weeks old. She doesn't need to be pushed from pillar to post and taken to a new place with loads of new voices. It will be overwhelming for her." I'm not sure if what I'm saying is accurate, but it sounds about right, and honestly, I can't face a trip to Norfolk on my own with a baby. "And it will be overwhelming for *me*. I'm barely holding it together here, where I know I can get a delivery of nappies in fifteen minutes if I run out. Norfolk is the middle of nowhere. It takes forty-five minutes to get to the nearest supermarket."

"It does not. You're exaggerating."

"Only slightly." Everywhere outside of London was less convenient. That was a fact.

"And you're going to have tons of help with her. It's not like no one will pitch in. Plus it's a chance for all the family to see her."

There's no doubt my family will all want to coo and ahh over Guinevere. It's just too much hassle.

"It's alright for you. If you need to stop for petrol on the way, you just drive into a garage, put petrol in and pay for it while Sutton waits in the car. If I need to, I have to get Guinevere out of her seat, into a coat. I have to get the buggy out of the boot, then strap her into the buggy, go and pay for the petrol and then take her out of the buggy, out of her coat, into her car seat, the buggy goes back in the boot, and then she's probably shit herself so I have to deal with that."

"Or you could just unclip her car seat and save yourself a lot of bother." Jacob rolls his eyes.

I hadn't thought of that.

"If you want to find an excuse, you'll be able to," he says, and he looks kind of disappointed. He fails to see his own lack of logic.

"This isn't about excuses." The. Most. Irritating. Brother. Alive. "This is about practicality. I'm not coming."

"You need to switch into a problem-solving mindset,

rather than be a problem magnet. Bring a nanny. Bring Eira. That way, you have two pairs of hands for everything."

"You're fucking irritating," I say. "You do understand that Eira's a human being, don't you? She's not a personal robot that will do everything I program her to do. She doesn't work weekends. She needs time off."

Why can't Jacob drop this and let me be? I've done three weekends now. Okay, Eira helped with football practice, but other than that, I'd coped pretty much on my own. And honestly, I feel fucking proud of myself. But to go on the road with this show? It's too much.

"Have you asked her if she'd be willing to come to Norfolk, given how important this weekend is to our family?"

I haven't asked her. Partly because I know she'll say yes. She always says yes if I need her help. I don't want to take advantage. Beyond that, it would feel a little too much like we're parents taking our daughter to visit Grandpa and Grandma. Eira is so competent with Guinevere, so loving and kind, that I'm sure people mistake her for the baby's mother. And honestly, if I squint, it isn't hard for me to see it in Eira too.

I know that's a dangerous game.

And then there's the living together. The late-night cup of warm milk and game of backgammon that has never been repeated.

Thank god.

The memories of that night are all too vivid. Her white pajamas, slightly see-through in the low lights of the kitchen. More than once I'd caught myself staring at the outline of her breast or the dusky pink of her nipple and had to make myself look away. It took everything in me not to stare between her legs.

Things could easily get complicated with Eira.

Inviting her away for the weekend with me and Guinevere isn't going to simplify anything.

Eira comes into the kitchen with Guinevere, providing a timely interruption to this conversation and my thoughts. They look so at ease with each other. Our end-of-day routine is about to commence: Eira feeds Guinevere at six then hands her over to me in the kitchen at seven.

"Hey, Guinevere. Your uncle is here." She grins up at us both. I know by the way her smile stays in place that she's picking up on the tension between us, though she doesn't say anything. "You want to hold her?" she asks Jacob. "She's in a milky coma."

I don't look at Jacob. As much as I want to drop-kick him out of my flat right now, I don't want to deny Guinevere time with her uncle. She deserves a big family, even if they're as annoying as hell.

Jacob's chest lowers and he turns and washes his hands. The thick tension between us is punctuated by Eira's soft chattering to Guinevere. "You're such a lucky girl with all these men wanting baby cuddles. This is what it's like being a Welsh princess."

Jacob dries his hands and scoops up Guinevere in a confident way that sticks in my gut. He makes it look easy. But it's not. I'm still not as confident as he is just holding her. Taking her to Norfolk is a hard no. I don't want to be surrounded by people with far more experience with infants than me, watching me fuck it up.

I'd rather just stay here. Take her to the park. Hang out.

"You two are fighting," Eira says after she's handed Guinevere to Jacob.

"We're not," I snap. "Jacob's being unreasonable and I'm not giving in to him."

"Oh, I see," she replies. Her steady look calms me, like her gaze is the sun, soporific and sedative. "I'm going to make a coffee. Does anyone want one?"

"I'd love one," Jacob says.

"Jacob, she's not your servant."

"It's fine, Dax. Honestly. I'm making myself a cup. It's no bother. Unless you'd prefer me to leave the two of you to argue in private?" She smiles and it trips me up. I smile back, and for a second it's just the two of us in this kitchen. Then I remember I'm annoyed at Jacob.

"We're happy to argue in front of whoever's around," Jacob says.

Eira looks away. Guinevere is totally out of it in Jacob's arms. Milk coma central.

"Well, I'll be out of your hair in a couple of minutes."

"You're fine," I say. I don't want her to feel uncomfortable.

"Oh, that reminds me," Jacob says. "Mum told me to give you some stuff. It's in my bag." He nods at his rucksack in the corner.

I'm not sure I want to look, but I flip open the bag in any event and pull out a bunch of papers.

"Yeah, that's it," Jacob says.

I turn them over. Details of houses for sale. "From mum?" I ask. "Funny how they're all in Hampstead."

"It's very family-friendly," Jacob says. "Lots of good schools—"

"She's four weeks old."

"But you're not nomads," he says. "You don't want to be moving every five minutes."

"I don't want to be moving at all." He's really pressing my buttons today. Why is he invested in me moving house?

In how I organize childcare? Next he'll be checking on the contents of my fridge.

"You got anything to eat?" he asks.

I knew it.

"No," I say.

"I'm going to make myself scrambled egg and avocado if you'd like some?" Eira says, sliding a coffee onto the counter behind him.

"Thank you, but I should go home. It's my turn to cook tonight. I said I'd leave something for Sutton."

"That's a good idea," I say. "Go home. To your pregnant wife."

He acts like he hasn't heard me, presses a kiss to Guinevere's head, then whispers something into her ear. I don't want to hear what it is. I'm pretty sure he'll be complaining about me.

"Eira," Jacob says in a forced bright tone.

"Don't you dare," I say. I know he's going to ask her about coming to Norfolk and he absolutely must not.

"What?" he says, acting all innocent.

"Just respect my decision," I reply.

"Dax, we really want Guinevere there. And you. She's the newest member of the family and it would mean a lot to all of us. Especially Mum and Dad."

I clench my jaw. I hate it when he's winning an argument. "It's not like I don't want to be there. It's just early days and—"

"Why don't Sutton and I drive you up?"

"Because your car will be full to the brim."

"Okay, well, Sutton can drive up on her own and I'll come with you."

I sigh. I do really want to be there, but I can't let Sutton drive up there on her own when she's over five months pregnant. It's a long way, and I know she's nervous after the miscarriage. There's no way I'm putting her or Jacob in that position. I could call the agency to hire a short-term nanny for the weekend, but everyone would be more comfortable with Eira. Including Guinevere. Maybe I could just keep my distance. It would be easier to avoid her there, with lots of people around.

I sigh, breathing in the inevitable.

"Eira, my parents' wedding anniversary is next weekend and we usually make a family affair of it all. If you have plans or would rather not, that's completely understandable, but it would be really helpful if you could work the weekend and come up to Norfolk to help with Guinevere. To be honest, I'm not at the point where I feel confident bringing Guinevere to a new place by myself, settling her in a new room and..." I could list a thousand other things. "But I don't want you to feel obligated."

Eira seems to like to step in and save the day. To help people and look after people. She does it every damn day for me and it feels uncomfortable to ask her for more. "You already do so much for Guinevere." *And me*, I don't add.

"What days would it be?" she asks.

"Saturday," Jacob interrupts before I can say anything. "Until Wednesday."

"Sure," she says, barely missing a beat. "I can do that."

Jacob's eyes light up. "If you go up by helicopter, you don't even have to leave until mid-morning on Saturday."

Eira snaps her head around. "I'm not going by helicopter." Her voice is filled with such finality, it's like a physical blow. I daren't even ask why.

"We can travel by car," I say. "I prefer driving anyway."

"Where would we stay?" she asks, her tone back to normal, any talk of helicopters forgotten.

"You know they've rented a place for the weekend," Jacob says.

"For me?" I ask.

"No, you narcissist. For all of us. Because of the building works. It means we can all be together."

"Are there enough bedrooms?" I say, my eyes sliding to Eira.

"Eight. More than enough as long as the kids all sleep with the adults."

"There's room for you, Eira, or I could pay for a hotel if that would make you more comfortable."

"I don't mind," she says. "You decide."

"It's easier if you stay," Jacob says. "That way no one needs to worry about driving you somewhere. Everyone can relax."

"Ignore him," I say, turning to Eira. "If you want to stay in a hotel, I can drive you. You decide."

"I'm fine with whatever. It's only four nights. I'd prefer not to spend them under canvas, and no traveling by helicopter, but apart from that, I'm good with anything." She blushes slightly and focuses on her coffee. If we were on our own, I might be tempted to ask her what's got her embarrassed. So it's a good job we're not.

I know I'm asking too much of Eira, but Jacob's right—Mum and Dad will want Guinevere in Norfolk next weekend. Eira being there is the only way it will happen.

"I really appreciate this. I'll make sure you're compensated."

"And I'll match whatever he's paying you," Jacob says.

I roll my eyes. Of course he has to have the last word. At least Guinevere will never have a brother she'll have to put up with.

FOURTEEN

Eira

The flat is starting to feel smaller. It's as if I can feel Dax everywhere, even when I'm tucked up in my room. He features in my dreams most nights, and I find myself thinking about him during the day. It can't just be because he's attractive and understatedly kind and focused and and and. We're just living in such close quarters. I feel like I'm surrounded by him.

I need to distract myself.

Eddie's name flashes up on my phone. *Thank goodness.*

I answer with, "I was just about to call you."

"I'm so stressed out," she replies.

I tuck a pillow behind me and lean against the headboard. "What's going on?"

"I've got a lot of deadlines coming up. They've all sort of crescendoed at the same time. And the economics is... I'm just finding it really difficult."

Sometimes I wish I'd gone to university. I loved Portland, but I didn't find any of it *really difficult*. I wasn't stretched intellectually. And it wasn't the university experience—there were few nights out, and only one guy in our year. I can't compare my further education to Eddie's. I could have gone to university, but I was set on being a nanny. Portland always felt like the right decision, especially after the accident. But when Eddie talks about university, I'm aware that I missed out.

"Do you think you need an external economics tutor?" I ask. "Maybe just for a few months to get your confidence back." With this job, I can definitely afford it.

"I don't know. I just don't feel like I'm in the right frame of mind."

"Hmmm, like you're self-sabotaging or something?"

"Yeah. Maybe. I've got to the point where I'm almost scared to sit down and open the textbook. The lectures are so intimidating."

"Are other people in the lecture feeling the same way?" I ask.

"Not Milton," she says about her best friend. "He's loving it."

"Would he tutor you?"

She sighs. "Maybe. I haven't thought about that actually."

"Sometimes you're too hard on yourself. You probably understand more than you think."

"Not in this case. I just didn't expect it to be so...mathematical."

"But you can do mathematical. I bet you're avoiding it because you *think* it's difficult, but if you spent as much time on the economics as you did the lectures you enjoyed, you'd find it a lot easier."

"That's probably true. I'm making it worse for myself."

"It's a natural response. We want to do what we're good at already, and avoid the things that take more work to unpack. Don't beat yourself up. You got this."

"Maybe if I just did fifteen minutes a day..." she says, almost to herself.

To my mind, that doesn't seem like enough time, but fifteen minutes might lead to half an hour, which might lead to more understanding, which might improve her confidence. "That sounds like a great plan. De-chunk it."

She chuckles. We're both thinking about the same thing —the summer we went to Wales when I was thirteen. Even though Eddie had only been four at the time, the three of us had talked about it so much ever since, I think it kept the memories fresh for her. It was one of the few family holidays we had where we actually spent time with our parents. We'd been like a proper family, playing with our dad on the beach. I remember looking around, seeing if anyone was looking at us with the same feeling of jealousy that I used to feel, looking at kids playing with their parents in the pool or on the beach. I remember feeling...proud. Proud that I had a dad who wanted to play in the sand.

"That sandcastle was awesome."

Dylan had found a picture of an oversized, intricate sandcastle and announced at breakfast that he wanted to make it. Gabby, our longtime nanny, said she'd try to help. Dad looked up from his paper and examined the picture. Dylan didn't ask Dad to help. There's no way he would have considered that Mum or Dad would come down to the beach, let alone play with us. None of us would have expected it. We spent our days with Gabby, while Mum and Dad did...who knows what. Looking back, Dad probably worked. Mum probably went to the spa or worked. It was what happened in London, but we just transported to Wales for a couple of weeks.

And we had fun, the three of us and Gabby.

But that one day in Wales, Mum and Dad came to the beach and Dad helped us build the most awesome sandcastle ever seen in Europe. I'm sure it's the memory the three of us think about most when our parents come to mind. Dad kept reassuring us that the key to replicating the sandcastle in Dylan's picture was to "de-chunk it."

And he was right. We stopped looking at the sandcastle as one structure and focused on distinct parts. The base. The middle. The turrets. The decoration. The flag at the top. What we ended up with was awesome.

Whenever I have a problem, I always give myself the same advice. *Just break it down. De-chunk it.*

"Thanks, Eira. You've always got the right answer."

I laugh. "You came up with that all by yourself."

"But only because I'm talking to you. Your wisdom slithered down the phone." She gives me too much credit. I didn't do anything at all. "Tell me about you," Eddie says. "How's the new job?"

I stop staring at my bedroom door, knowing Dax is there on the other side of it, and focus on the screen of my phone. "Different. You know, I've never worked with a single dad before." As soon as the words are out of my mouth, I regret them.

"Single dad? You didn't tell me you were working for a single dad!" I can hear the excitement in her voice. "What's he like?" she asks. "Is he hot? Rich? Arabian? I bet you end up married into royalty."

"No, no, and no," I say. "None of that is going to happen." A series of images flash through my brain: Dax bare-chested at the dining table, playing backgammon, a look in his eye that says he's holding something back. The sparks of electricity passing between us every time we touch. The blush that takes over my cheeks whenever he's in the room, since just looking at him sometimes makes me feel embarrassed. The way he looks at me like he knows me better than anyone else in the world.

We never did play another game of backgammon. I had an excuse all figured out if he ever asked, but he never did. Maybe he realized, just like I did, that the line between the professional and the personal had encircled us that evening. Even though we didn't cross it, we'd had our faces pressed against it.

I didn't want that to happen again. I guess, neither did he.

"But it's nice looking after a newborn again," I say.

"Do you worry you'll become too attached when there isn't a mum there all the time?"

"I always become attached. It's an occupational hazard." Not all our nannies had gotten attached to us. Some did more than others. Gabby was with us the longest and all of us still hear from her from time to time. Then there was Tina and Flavia. Others I've all but forgotten, their names lost to memory.

"What's the kid's name again. Merlin?"

I roll my eyes but appreciate that she asks. She relies on me more than I rely on her, but she makes an effort to understand and be interested in my life. Dylan does the same, to a lesser extent. "Guinevere. What father is going to name his daughter Merlin?"

"Merlin's a pretty name. But I like the idea of my children having Welsh names, just like the three of us. It's a... connection. It's nice." Even though none of us were born in

Wales, our father's insistence that we all had Welsh names makes me feel like he...wanted to live on through us somehow. Eddie's idea of us passing that down to the next generation is lovely.

"I like that idea. You can have Glynnis."

"Seren is my first pick," she says.

"You're not thinking about this seriously, though, are you? You're not..."

She bursts out laughing. "You don't need to worry, I'm not preggers. And have no plans to be. Gotta figure out how I'm going to rule the world first."

"Sounds like a good first step."

"How's the flat?" she asks.

"It's fine," I reply. *It's small*, I think. Dax's mum isn't wrong—moving house would be no bad thing. For a single man, this place is more than big enough. But if he can afford it, a little more space would help me breathe again. "My room is nice. Looks out onto the garden."

"And he's not handsome at all?" she asks, her tone a little disappointed.

I laugh. "Stop with the romance novels. Or maybe just give up fifteen minutes a day of them and dedicate the time to de-chunking your economics." I make a mental note to ensure Eddie and Dax never meet. I'll never hear the end of it if she sees him. She'd have me married off before they'd shaken hands.

I don't mention the fact I'm going to Norfolk, where I'll be surrounded by what seems like a loving family. I don't tell her how it will make me ache inside, how I don't want to go but agreed because Dax needs me. Guinevere needs me. So I'll be there, my face pressed up against the glass Saturday to Wednesday, before coming back to this too-small flat to look after a beautiful baby girl without a mother.

I don't mention the way I wonder what my life would have been like if any one of a million things had been different. There's no point in dreaming about a life that can never be mine.

FIFTEEN

Eira

I step out the building, pushing the pram with a sleeping Guinevere inside. Dax is already coming toward me.

"Is that everything?" he asks.

"I don't think there's anything left in your flat to bring, even if we had room in the car."

He nods earnestly. "Yes, you're probably right. And I can go out and get anything we forgot once we get there."

I'm a conservative packer when it comes to taking a newborn away, but there's nothing of Guinevere's left in the flat. We have literally brought everything with us. I'm not sure how it's all fitted into the car. Then I look up and see the car, which is more like a bus.

"That's a big car," I remark.

"Yeah, I bought it yesterday," he replies. "I had a Golf that looked like this guy's lunch. I didn't see how we were going to fit everything in."

"So you...bought a bigger car," I say slowly. I never thought Dax was poor—employing me, the flat in one of the nicest parts of town, the way he's always dressed in casual but undoubtedly expensive clothes—but dropping six figures on a car as an impulse buy?

"Bigger and safer. I figure most cars that drive into us are going to come off worse for wear."

I nod. There's no denying that. This vehicle is the size of a small house.

"Plus I got to drive it away. So...that's the story with the car." He sounds like he's uncomfortable offering so much information. It's kind of adorable, and I feel oddly pleased that he feels comfortable enough to share stuff with me. Dax isn't an over-sharer by any stretch. Even if it's about his new car. He also usually speaks less. Maybe he's stressed about the journey.

"Wanna lift her in?"

He nods vigorously and unfastens Guinevere from the pram. Before lifting her, he unzips her pramsuit, just before I was going to suggest it. "I saw some awful videos online about kids in coats—how dangerous it is to keep them on and then put them in the car seat."

"Absolutely," I say, slightly proud that the science is Dax's gateway drug into loving and caring for his daughter. "They need to be strapped tightly and securely."

"I also went out and bought this new car seat. It means she can be flat lying down, which is better on long car journeys. And it's adjustable."

"That's great," I say as Dax lifts the sleeping Guinevere from the pram into her new car seat, in the brand-new car-slash-bus.

Dax's love for his daughter is growing by the day. Warmth gathers in my chest.

He clips her in and turns to take the blanket I'm already

holding out to him. "Right," he says, laying it over her. "She didn't wake up."

"Milk coma," I say. "If we get going now, we'll get a couple of hours driving in, I reckon."

He flips off the carrycot and slides it into the boot, the wheelbase going in next to it. I can't believe there's room.

I have my bag, along with a big bag of supplies for Guinevere that I didn't want disappearing in the boot.

"Okay," he says. "I think we're ready." He opens the passenger door for me, which is...a surprise. I don't think any man has ever done that.

"Actually, I'm going to sit next to Guinevere," I say, and shrug. "It's not that I think she's in any danger," I reassure him. "But being right next to her, if anything *were* to happen, I can get to her in a second. If nothing else, I can stroke her gorgeous rosy cheek and hold her tiny hand and make sure she knows she's not alone."

Not to mention the secondary advantage of putting a little space between me and Dax. The backseat gives me room to breathe, despite being in close quarters with Dax for so long.

"Oh," he says, straightening. "Yes. Of course."

Once we're inside, he waits for me to have my seat belt fastened and then pulls away. It's still early, and there's less traffic on the Euston Road than I've ever seen before.

"Do you go up to see your parents a lot?" I ask.

"Define 'a lot'," he says.

"I don't have a definition in mind," I reply. "It's not a trick question. You don't get scored at the end of it."

He clears his throat. "No, right. I suppose so." He seems a little stressed and it's ten out of ten adorable. "Usually one of my brothers is with them at the weekend."

"How many brothers do you have?"

"Five," he answers. "Four and my cousin Vincent."

"Wow," I say. Three sometimes felt like we were an army. I can't imagine what six must have felt like.

"But you come from a big family too, right?"

"It's me and my brother and sister. Not that big." My family always felt like the three of us, rather than the five of us. We were a team. A gang. A unit. I can't help but wonder if my parents were still alive, whether we would ever visit them. I can't imagine it. Even as we grew, they weren't particularly interested in us. We were an adjunct to their lives—a compartmentalized section of their existence they'd dip in and out of. They didn't know us particularly when we were children, so it's hard to envision a world in which we would have been close to them as adults.

"Do you use it as a base to see all your brothers?" I ask. "Or do you go to spend time with your parents?"

We catch each other's eyes in the rearview mirror. "Both," he says with a hint of uncertainty that tells me it's an unusual question. "But don't tell my brothers that."

I smile and see the corners of his eyes crinkle, so I know he's smiling too. I look away. I've got to keep some kind of wall between us but it's becoming more and more difficult. The more I know Dax, the more I like him and the more I want to know.

After a couple of beats of silence, he asks, "Do you see your parents a lot?"

"They died," I say. "Six years ago."

"Fuck, I'm sorry. I had no idea."

"You don't need to apologize." People always say they're sorry when they find out my parents have died, and it never makes much sense to me. Maybe because I'm not sure what they're sorry for—obviously no one is apologizing for murdering them in cold blood. I suppose they're apologizing for my loss. Except I'm not sure it *was* much of a loss. They were alive and then they weren't. And honestly, it hasn't made a whole lot of difference to me. Okay, so we don't join them at Claridge's for Christmas dinner. We don't write them birthday cards. But our family is intact.

It's still me, Eddie and Dylan.

As it always has been.

I felt like a fraud at the funeral. So many people crying and saying we were too young to lose our parents. I suppose on the outside it looked that way, but what they didn't understand was we never had them to begin with. Not much changed for us. Dylan was at university, I was about to graduate Portland. It was only Eddie who was still living in the Mayfair town house. She was fifteen and every spare moment of her day she was studying. That year, my first job was a live-out position, so I could move back into the town house to live with Eddie. The plan was that once I turned twenty-five and inherited, things would change.

"My brother and sister and I are close. Like you and Jacob, except we hate each other less."

He laughs and I get a flutter of butterflies in my stomach. "We don't hate each other." He pauses. "No, we really don't. He's just irritating. He's the oldest, and he tries to over-manage situations. Over-manage me. He just needs to stay in his lane."

Now it's my turn to laugh. "I'm sure Eddie and Dylan think the same about me."

"But you're so capable," he says. "They must need you." The sentence lingers in the air as if he wants to add something to it but knows he shouldn't.

I take it as a compliment. It's good to be needed.

I stare out the window, watching the oncoming traffic trying to get to the place we just left. Did my parents *need* each other? Or anyone? Would they have grieved if Eddie, Dylan or I had died suddenly?

"My parents were pretty busy when we were growing up. They had really demanding jobs, working long hours," Dax says. "And then I was the youngest. It's easy to get...*forgotten* isn't the right word, because I never felt that, but I was able to get on with things in my own way because of the chaos and the sheer numbers of us."

Something snags inside me—a sense of understanding. "I know that feeling," I say. I've never thought about it like that, but as I grew up and the nannies were more focused on Eddie and Dylan, I was able to do pretty much do as I wanted, how I wanted.

"Really? But you were the oldest."

"I flew under the radar in the way you're describing."

"Yeah, that's a good way of saying it. Under the radar."

"I didn't do anything bad," I say.

He lets out a half-laugh. "Right."

"I just did what I wanted."

"And you always wanted to be a nanny?" he asks.

"Yeah. Nannies were kind and helpful and made a real difference. I liked that."

"Does the role live up to what you thought it would be?"

I pause before I answer. "It absolutely does."

"But that's not the end of your answer," he says.

Our eyes catch in the rearview mirror again and I look away. How could he tell that? "Sometimes I think I'd like to do...I'm not sure *more* is the right word. Different, maybe."

He doesn't respond, but the silence isn't awkward. It's like he's left room to breathe. To think. He's not asking questions, one after another, or trying to fix anything. As a result,

I'm thinking about what *more* could be for the first time in a long time.

I'm always so busy, my head so full of Dylan and Eddie and whichever children I'm looking after, I rarely think about what an alternative life might look like. There's no point, is there? I'm not even sure if I'd be able to come up with something else. There's an old niggling gap where I wish I'd gone to university, but to study what? Archeology? Sociology? Biochemistry? I don't know what would interest me. Maybe it all would.

If our inheritance hadn't been stolen—or if our parents hadn't died—I might have become a perpetual student. But it was and they did, so I can't think about what *more* might have been.

SIXTEEN

Eira

We arrive in Norfolk nearly five hours after we set off. We've stopped twice. Once to feed Guinevere and once just to take her from the car seat when she seemed a little out of sorts. Or maybe it was me who was out of sorts. Going away with a new employer always has its challenges. Even when they're not Dax Cove.

"So this isn't your parents' house?" I ask, looking around at the buildings surrounding us.

"No," he replies. "They're having some building work done on their place, so..."

It's a beautiful red-bricked barn conversion, with buildings at the end of the driveway and either side. I just hope I don't have to share a bathroom with anyone but Guinevere. I don't want to bump into anyone in my PJs. Especially not Dax.

As a child, we never holidayed anywhere in the UK but Wales. Norfolk's just like I imagined it: wide skies and flat, flat roads. Windmills and the gray sea.

"Hey Guinevere, we're at Grandma and Grandpa's house," I say. "There's going to be a lot of people who want cuddles with you. If you don't like it, you just let us know, and Daddy will come and get you." I'm trying to signal to Dax that he might need to manage his family when it comes to Guinevere. I can't tell if he's heard me.

I slip out of my side of the car as Dax opens Guinevere's door. "Let's get her in first and then I'll come back for all the stuff."

The temperature is chillier than it was in London.

"Should I put her pram-suit on?" he asks.

I glance at the door. It's three steps away. "I would wrap her in that blanket and get her inside as soon as possible." I pull out some bags and follow Dax. He reaches out to open the front door when it swings open.

"Daddy," a tall guy in a suit says, beaming at Dax. I've not met him before, but there's no doubt he shares Cove genes. He's gorgeous.

"Don't make that word sound dirty," Dax snips. "Eira, this is Nathan," he calls over his shoulder. "Second brother down." He pushes past Nathan to get inside.

Nathan takes the bags I'm carrying and leads me inside. "Delighted to meet you. Thank you so much for coming with Dax. He's the last person any of us expected to be a father. Two years ago he was still playing with Star Wars figurines."

I hear Dax groan, but he doesn't bother to respond, and I like him better for it. Eddie used to have a talent for pushing Dylan's buttons and he'd bite—Every. Single. Time. I never understood why he didn't just ignore her.

"Turn left under the staircase," Nathan says. "Every-one's in the kitchen."

The four of us caterpillar through the house and as we

round the corner, I hear the shrieks before I see who they're coming from.

"My baby!" Carole says, her arms in the air. "My grandbaby!" She scoops Guinevere out of Dax's arms and I half brace myself for her to start screaming, but she doesn't.

"And darling Eira," she says, putting her free arm around me to give me a half-hug. It's a lovely and slightly unexpected welcome.

"I'm John." A ruddy-faced, scowling man approaches me, offering his hand. I take it and he pats our handshake with his free hand. "Can't believe you're having to live with this one." He nods at Dax. "I hope you're not sharing bathrooms. Since he was a baby he's clogged the loo eleven times. Eleven. Can you believe it?"

"John," Carole reprimands her husband. "Don't be saying stuff like that. No one wants to know that about our son."

"But it's true," he says defensively.

"Well it might be, but it doesn't need to be said. Eira doesn't need to understand Dax's loo-busting habits. She can find out in her own time."

Dax looks at me, his eyebrows slightly raised in silent apology, and I offer a small smile. I don't think my dad would have been able to tell people how many fingers and toes I had, let alone how many times I'd blocked the loo.

"Ignore my father." I turn toward the familiar voice and see Jacob. "We all do. Thanks for coming. Do you want a cup of tea?"

"Oh, if you tell me where everything is, I'll make everyone a cup," I say.

"Good grief," Carole says. "You've just got here. I'll make the—no, I've got Guinevere. Jacob, you make the tea. I could do with a fresh cup, although I don't like the water here."

"Yes, I just offered to make the tea, but thank you for reassigning me the job," Jacob says. "Eira, this is my wife, Sutton. She'll introduce you to everyone else while I make the tea. We can't leave it to Dax. He probably doesn't know everyone's names."

Sutton laughs and swats her husband on the arm. I feel a surge of protectiveness toward Dax. It's obvious they're joking, but it's unnecessary.

"We're still waiting on Vincent, Kate, Zach and Ellie. They should be here within the hour. They're coming by helicopter."

A shiver runs down my spine at the thought of four of Dax's family members in a helicopter.

"Oh, just in time—this is Madison, Nathan's wife," Sutton says. "And his daughter."

Madison has a child who looks about one on her hip, and she grins at me. "Hey, Eira. First time at the Coves' can be a bit daunting." She comes closer. "They tease each other relentlessly and it can be exhausting. But deep down, they all love each other."

"Deep, deep, *deep* down," Sutton says, laughing.

"You know the thing that I love—they're not like this when they're apart," Madison says. "It's like this switch they flip when they see each other. You'd never think it, but they're fiercely loyal and they don't just love each other, they *like* each other a whole lot."

"I hope you girls are behaving yourselves," John says as he passes me a cup of tea. "Don't be telling Eira anything that will put her off us." He pats me on the shoulder and there's something about the way he's protective of me that has the bridge of my nose fizzing. This man had five kids and a distinguished career by all accounts. He's not cold and standoffish. He's warm and welcoming and...clearly a beloved father.

"Don't worry, Dad, we'll leave that to you," Jacob says. He turns to me. "You'll get used to this."

Don't they get it? I'm just the nanny. I don't need to get used to anything. They don't need to worry if I'm put off. It's not like I'm a part of all this. They're talking to me like I'm...one of them.

"Oh, I don't know how I forgot," Jacob says. "I got you something, Dad."

Jacob holds something in the air and I can't quite make out what it is. Everyone busts out laughing. "There was no point putting any of our faces on there when we all know, Dog is your favorite." He loops something over his father's head, and I realize that Jacob's gift to his father is an apron. With pictures of a dog's head all over it.

"Where is Dog, anyway?" Jacob asks.

"Asleep in the front room," John says.

"Getting away from all of us, no doubt."

The alarm of my phone vibrates in my pocket. I take it out and silence it. Guinevere will be hungry soon. I need to prepare her bottle.

I don't want to interrupt anyone and ask where I'll be sleeping, so I quickly wash my hands and set about preparing a bottle. As I'm screwing the lid on, Guinevere starts to become unsettled. She's a good baby and loves her routine, so she rarely gets to full-on meltdown mode.

Carole starts to jiggle her around, but it doesn't help. Because she doesn't need reassurance. She's hungry.

I catch Dax's attention and hold up the bottle. I don't want to be the one who takes a granddaughter from her grandmother if I don't have to be. Much better for Dax to do it. I also get the feeling that Dax needs his family to see how competent he is. He's not a gushy father. Not yet anyway. He's intensely practical. Scientific.

"Mum, can I just take her for a minute?" Dax asks, reaching for his daughter.

Apart from a walk to and from football practice, there haven't been many times when Dax and I are both around Guinevere for an extended period of time. I make sure I disappear into my room when my day ends so he can have time with his daughter. In the mornings, he leaves before Guinevere has breakfast. But now? How much does he want me to do? I want to encourage their bonding. But at the same time, I want to make sure he has time with his family.

"Would you like me to feed her or would you like to?" I ask as I stand as close as I can without touching him. I don't want to embarrass him.

His eyes fix on mine and back down to his daughter, then across at his family. He's obviously torn and I'm not sure why. Does he think I'm trying to shirk my responsibilities?

"I'm happy to, but I know some parents who really enjoy feeding time with their newborns," I whisper.

He nods. "I'll take her somewhere quiet." He takes the bottle from me, and I hand him the Peter Rabbit muslin I'm holding, too. He heads out. I follow a few steps behind.

"Eira," someone calls. I'm torn. I want to be on hand for Dax if he needs anything, but at the same time, someone else wants my attention.

I fix my smile in place and turn.

"Here's your tea," Sutton says, handing me the mug I'd placed down. "Is everything okay?"

"Absolutely." I grin as if to underline my point. "Guinevere just needs to eat."

"Is she on a schedule?" she asks.

"She is. Some babies just are happy to slot into a timetable."

"It's no wonder, given her father," she says.

I make no comment and try to keep my facial expression neutral.

"How's he taking to it?" Her expression shifts from amused to concerned, her eyebrows pinching together.

"Amazingly," I say, that defensive feeling rising up in my chest again. "Takes all humans a while to learn to live together at first."

She laughs. "I guess you're right. Some humans are easier than others. But it helps that Jacob likes a schedule. Me too, I suppose."

"We're all different," I say. That's what I would tell Eddie and Dylan as they got older and asked questions about our family. Why our parents were gone such a lot. Why we didn't have dinner all together like they saw on television. *Every family is different,* I would tell them.

The Coves couldn't be more different from the Cadogans.

"But Dax is so caring," I say.

"He is?" says Jacob.

"Yes," I say at the same time as Carole.

"Just because he's not as verbal as the rest of you doesn't mean he doesn't have feelings. It doesn't mean he doesn't care," Carole says. I want to applaud, but I don't. "I'm glad things are going well," she says to me. She holds my gaze as if she's waiting for me to contradict her.

"Yes, very well," I reassure her.

"Well, we're all delighted you're here," she says. "I knew the first time we met that you'd fit right in."

That's my job. Fit in, become part of the background. Useful scenery, unnoticed until needed. Hopefully that's how things will go this weekend. Dax won't notice me and I won't notice him.

Something tells me that's wishful thinking.

SEVENTEEN

Eira

I stand at the door to Dax's room, looking between the monitor and the travel cot. Guinevere doesn't seem to be concerned about being in a different place at all. Maybe because she knows she's surrounded by her entire family who clearly adore her already, despite her barely opening her eyes this afternoon.

"How is she?" John asks in hushed tones from behind me.

"Sleeping like a princess," I whisper in reply.

"Are you ready to eat?" he asks.

I wave him away. "I can fix something later. I'll keep an eye on Guinevere."

He takes a breath. "You have a monitor." He pauses. "And better than a monitor, you've probably got a good instinct and excellent hearing. Guinevere will be fine while you eat. While we all eat. Together as a family."

Gravel collects at the back of my throat at the word *family*, but I'm out of excuses.

"I don't want to impose and—"

"I insist," he says. "If you're looking after my grand-daughter, we want you well-fed. And my apple pie is the best in the world. Mark my words, you won't want to miss it."

He practically herds me back to the kitchen, where there seems to be people everywhere.

"And now Eira's here," Carole says. "We've got a full house."

I glance at Dax down by the dining table, chatting to his brother. Will he mind his employee joining him at dinner? It's not like we *never* see each other in the evening—and then there was Backgammon Night—but it's not normal to socialize with the family like this. Not in my experience.

The helicopter arrived safely and now, at the end of the kitchen, a huge dining table is full of Coves. Some have been born into the family. Some have married into the family. But they're all family.

I don't belong here.

"Eira," Carole calls, "come and sit next to me."

"Mrs. Cove, I'm very happy to fix myself a plate and—"

"Absolutely not," John interrupts, and Carole fixes him with a look.

"If you would prefer to eat on your own, that's fine. We would love you to stay. Wouldn't we, Dax? Jacob? Everyone?"

The table falls silent. I'm sure I'm beetroot red as everyone turns to face me.

"Of course," Madison says.

"Absolutely, you have to eat. We don't bite," Jacob says.

Everyone else chimes in with similar words of encouragement. I'm entirely mortified that I've made such a spectacle and am now the center of everyone's attention.

My gaze catches on Dax's. He's opposite me, the expression on his face incomprehensible. Then he gives me a small nod and I just make out the word *stay* under the hubbub of everyone's chatter.

I sit and the spotlight slides off me. Everyone focuses on the food.

I'll eat quickly and quietly and then creep back upstairs. No one will notice I'm gone.

"She's such a pretty baby, Dax," Kate says. That's the absolute truth. Of course all babies are lovely in their own way, but many aren't pretty.

"Are you sure you don't need a second DNA test?" Vincent says.

I check on Dax's reaction but it's as if he's an enormous iceberg in the middle of the ocean, his brothers and cousin the little waves lapping at his sides. He doesn't even notice them. I can't help but wonder if he's only stoic with his family or if he has the ability to not sweat the small stuff in general. It's a skill I would love to have.

I like to dodge the small stuff. I'd love not to sweat it when it invariably lands.

I can't help but be more and more intrigued by what's going on beneath Dax's surface. They say only a third of an iceberg is visible above the surface. The rest is kept hidden.

What's Dax hiding?

"She looks exactly like Dax when he was a baby," Carole says. "He was always being mistaken for a girl." She pauses. "But that could have been the pink cardigan I dressed him in." She hoots with laughter. "And the rest of his clothes were white or yellow, no blue at all. After Beau, I vowed not to have any more and donated all the boys' clothes."

Dax takes a deep intake of breath as if he's bracing

himself. Clearly, he's heard this story before. Looking around, it seems like most everyone else has, too. Which means Carole is telling this tale for my benefit. But...why?

"When I got pregnant with Dax, I was convinced I was having a girl. I picked up the pink cardigan at the hospital charity shop and then realized I was tempting fate, so bought yellow and white for the rest of his clothes."

"Dax, what's it like being a disappointment to your parents from birth?" Jacob asks.

Dax continues chewing his mouthful of food, and I definitely *don't* watch the way his jaw tenses with the movement.

"He doesn't know," John says. "Maybe *you* could explain?"

There are a few *ooohs* and *arrrs* around the table, acknowledging the sting of John's remarks. But everyone's smiling and it all feels genuine. Warm.

John starts chuckling and stands. "Vincent, come and help me with some wine, will you? The Malbec's still in boxes in the entryway."

Jacob doesn't look chastised. No one's taking anything personally.

"She's very beautiful," Carole says. "And she's very relaxed for a first baby. Don't you think, Eira?"

"I think she's very beautiful, and I find most babies are relaxed as long as their caregivers are relaxed."

Carole chuckles. "That's so true. It's the same with patients. A relaxed doctor makes a relaxed patient. Isn't that right, John?" she asks as her husband returns, carrying a box of wine bottles, followed by Vincent with two boxes.

Carole rolls her eyes. "How much Malbec are you lot going to drink?"

"All of it!" booms John.

John and Vincent uncork the wine and pass out fresh glasses, while me and a few others clear plates and Carole and Dax plate the main course. There's so much activity, it's chaos, except it's not. It's like a crowd scene in a movie: everyone is doing their own thing, but everyone knows their lines and exactly what they're meant to be doing.

I've never seen anything like it.

The noise. The banter. The warmth. The love.

It's so different to anything I've seen or experienced before.

"Tell us about you," Carole says when we're all seated again. "We really should have a short questionnaire for newbies to fill out to get us up to speed."

"Mum," Dax groans. "You're starting to sound like Dad."

She chuckles. "I do, don't I? I thought you of all people would like that idea. It would be efficient. You could create some kind of spreadsheet." Carole isn't distracted and turns her attention back to me. "Do you come from a big family?"

"I have a younger brother and a younger sister."

"Lovely," she replies. "How old are they?"

"My brother Dylan is twenty-four. Eddie, my sister, is in her final year of university. She's twenty."

"Babies," Madison says.

"Eddie?" John asks. "Is that short for something?"

"Her real name is Efa." Anytime I ever use Eddie's real name, it feels like a betrayal. She hates it so much. She renamed herself at three years old.

"Efa, Dylan and Eira. Names of a proud Welsh family," John says. "What do your parents do?"

As a nanny, I'm not used to people being interested in my background beyond my experience with children. The

Coves seem lovely, but I can't help but wonder why they keep asking me questions.

"My father was a businessman," I reply. "My mother worked in the city. They died a few years ago."

A hush settles on the table and I keep my gaze on my plate. Death makes people feel uncomfortable, but not as uncomfortable as someone who doesn't seem that bothered by the death of her parents. I don't want to look anyone in the eye in case they see it.

"I'm so sorry." Carole clasps her hand over mine.

"How did they die?" John asks.

"Dad," Dax reprimands.

"John," Carole says and squeezes my hand. "I'm sorry, Eira. John...well, it's easy to be very matter-of-fact about death as a doctor."

"It's fine. They died in a helicopter crash."

The expected gasps and condolences flood the table. My gaze snags on Dax's as soon as I look up, and I see understanding on his face. I'd take a five-hour road trip over a helicopter ride any day of the week.

"That's heartbreaking to lose both parents so young," Madison says. "Your brother and sister were even younger."

I don't think any of us misses them. Of course, I can't say that out loud because everyone would look at me differently. The people around this table would diagnose me with a personality disorder or worse, sociopathy. But it's difficult to miss what you didn't have.

"Helicopters...they scare me," Madison says. "I remember when the Cadogans died in that horrific helicopter crash. It was all over the news. Awful."

Yes, it made the news at the time because my parents were high profile. They'd been coming into London when the accident happened. But why on earth does Madison remember their name?

"The guy who was named Dealmaker of the Decade by the *Financial Times*?" Nathan asks.

"Yes," Madison says. "Aled Cadogan and his wife. She was—I can't quite remember what she did, but she was successful too. They both died in their prime. It was awful. Left three kids apparently."

Dax and I look at each other again—and realization spreads across his face just before I say, "Yeah, they were my parents."

Cutlery falls onto china. Immediately, I wonder if I should have said anything.

"You're one of the daughters of the Cadogans?" Madison asks.

I nod. How does she know so much?

"Didn't your uncle run off with your inheritance?" Madison asks. "Sorry, my mind is like a steel trap. Occupational hazard of being a journalist for years. I was fascinated by this story."

I try and push down the ball of betrayal and hate and frustration that lives permanently in my stomach. "Yes, he did," I say. How far will this interrogation go?

I glance at Dax again, and I see a glimmer of panic in his eyes. Has he heard of our family?

"Everyone needs to stop pestering Eira with questions," Dax says. "I know it's difficult for most of you to comprehend, but some people don't like answering deeply personal questions from complete strangers. Give it a rest. Everyone."

Silence tumbles through the room.

"Darling girl," Carole says. "You have to forgive us. We

can be a little overfamiliar and overbearing. I'm terribly sorry."

"It's fine," I say. I don't want to make anyone uncomfortable. It's understandable that people are curious.

"It's not fine," Dax replies, his gaze on mine. "Let's move on to other topics. I have a baby, for Christ's sake. And I'm a terrible father. Never wanted children. Haven't a clue what I'm doing. Let's talk about that."

It's like he's jumped into the ring in a clown costume to distract the bull.

That's usually my job.

Time stands still for a few moments as I try to figure out what's going on. It feels like tangled spaghetti in my head. I was uncomfortable being questioned, but I understand the interest in my parents. I was ready to endure whatever questions they wanted to ask.

Dax put a stop to all of it.

No one's ever done anything so kind. No one has ever made my journey easier, just because they can see my struggle. It's such a shock, such an unfamiliar feeling, that I don't know what to think. But I'm intensely grateful.

EIGHTEEN

Dax

I'm boiling with rage. I love my family, but boundaries are not something any of them comprehend. Or certainly they couldn't this evening with Eira.

I head to my bedroom, where Eira went to give Guinevere her ten o'clock feed.

The door creaks as it opens and the light from the landing spotlights Eira sitting in the chair by the window, cradling Guinevere as she feeds her.

"Hey," she says, smiling up at me. "She's totally fine. Go and enjoy your evening with your family."

I sigh and close the door behind me. "I've had just about as much as I can deal with tonight. I'm really sorry for how they were at dinner. Give them a glass of wine and a dining room table and nothing's off limits. They forget themselves."

"Oh, don't be sorry. It was a little awkward, but not for the reasons you think. Being around that dining room table was an experience I don't think I'll ever forget."

I groan. She doesn't sound pissed off, but I'm pretty sure

there's a ninety-five percent chance she'll resign as soon as we're back in London. "I'm sorry."

"In a good way," she says.

She's humoring me. She doesn't need to.

"Seriously, I never had a meal like that with my family. Sometimes Dylan and Eddie and I will have lunch or dinner together, but..."

She trails off as if she's trying to pinpoint the difference. I can help her out—her family aren't rude arseholes.

"I would have loved to have grown up like this. There's so much warmth and love and...it was a lot of questions, and some of them weren't so sensitive, but none of them came from a bad place. It was thoughtlessness, not nastiness."

I nod and take a seat on the bed opposite her. "That's true. They didn't mean to make you feel uncomfortable. They're just a little too comfortable themselves."

She smiles at me, and I don't know if it's the light coming through the window or because she's holding Guinevere, but she's luminous.

This is why I shouldn't be in here.

This is why I should have insisted on staying in London this weekend.

This is why I should have never hired Eira as Guinevere's nanny.

"I'm sorry about your parents," I say, leaning forward, my elbows on my knees.

"Can I tell you something?"

My heart starts to canter. "Of course." I want to know far too many of Eira's secrets.

"I grieved my parents a long time ago. Before they died. I was raised by nannies and teachers. Not by my parents." She fixes me with a look. "They didn't want children. Not really. I think they had us because that's what people did.

But they weren't interested in us. They were always traveling or working or out who-knows-where." She pauses. "I don't know why I'm telling you this. I'm sorry."

I sit upright and place my ankle over my thigh. Eira watches my movements. "I want to hear. Tell me."

"That's it really. They were parents in name. But they didn't love us. We didn't love them. We lived in the same house and we shared the same surname. That was it."

She says it in a matter-of-fact way, but my heart gently clenches at her words. I don't know what it would be like to not have known my parents loved me.

"I was uncomfortable answering your family's questions because I feel like a fraud whenever the accident comes up. People expect me to be a grieving orphan. Problem is, I was never particularly sad that my parents died." She glances up. "I do wonder whether or not I'll get struck down for even thinking like that."

"Of course you won't," I say, trying to be reassuring. "But you and your brother and sister are close?"

She nods. "Always. We had each other, no matter what. That's what I'd always say when they were little. We have each other."

"I feel the same with my brothers. I know they bait me, but like you say, it's done out of love."

"You're lucky," she says, and our eyes lock.

Eira looks away first. "You know, becoming a parent is an adjustment for anyone. But just spending time with your daughter will create a bond between you. I'm sure it would have created a bond between my parents and me and my siblings, had they made the effort."

I suck in a breath. "When I made the decision not to sign the adoption papers, I didn't think much past the point of fulfilling my responsibilities," I say. "Doing my duty."

"Most people don't think through the implications of having children," she says. "To be honest, most of the time, it's impossible to imagine." I know she's trying to be comforting, but she's giving me too much credit.

"I thought it would be like you describe it with your parents. I would share a house and a last name with Guinevere. I'd be her father in name only. Because I love my work. I was put on this planet to carry out the research I'm involved with. It's going to transform people's lives. Guinevere would have a loving extended family. She'd have the best of everything materially. Go to good schools but...she'd be raised by nannies—just like how you described it."

There. I've said it. She's seen the worst of me.

Her lips twitch, and I know she's got something to say, but she's holding back.

"Say it," I urge her.

She shakes her head. "It's really none of my business."

"You're right. But I want to hear it anyway."

"She'd have the best of everything, but not you? You're the only thing she wants or needs. A human being in her corner, entirely on her side. Someone who will shield her from the worst of life's twists and turns, teach her how to navigate them and comfort her when she's lost. That's all any of us want, isn't it? That's what I've tried to be for Eddie and Dylan, because none of us had it from our parents."

"I bet you're a great big sister," I say.

"Dylan and Eddie would disagree, I'm sure. They'd probably say that I was pushy and overbearing and that I need to be..." She shrugs. "I don't know, different. Sometimes I feel more like a parent than a sister. It's just, I don't want them to feel they have no one they can rely on but themselves. Because I know that feeling."

"But you have them," I say.

"I do. But it's different. For a start, I don't rely on them financially. And I'm the oldest."

"You give them money?" As soon as I've asked the question, I regret it. It's none of my business.

"Not an allowance or anything, but obviously I pay Eddie's university fees and expenses. And Dylan still needs me from time to time."

"Jeez, Eira. You're..." She's so kind. And generous. "That's a lot of burden."

"It's not a burden. I *want* to do it. My uncle didn't do a lot, but my Portland fees were paid for through my trust."

"And he didn't help Dylan and Eddie?"

I shake my head. "He ran off to the Cayman Islands just before I turned twenty-five, which was when the trust was meant to be dissolved and I was supposed to come into my inheritance. I suppose I feel a little guilty that I got my education paid for but Eddie and Dylan didn't."

"Except they did. Because you paid."

She shrugs. "I guess. But Guinevere isn't going to have to worry about that. You just need to keep out of helicopters. And her uncles are a lot more trustworthy than mine." She smiles like she's made a joke, but I can't help but think how awfully life has treated her.

She nudges me. "Whatever you do, you're not my parents. You're not my uncle. But maybe you might grow into wanting to give her more of you."

I push my hands through my hair. It's difficult hearing about her situation and relationship with her parents, especially when she thinks I'm going to make the same mistakes. But it's different for me. "My work is—I know it sounds like I'm an arsehole, but I'm not talking about working to make money. I don't need or want any more than I already have. I'm not doing this for selfish reasons—quite the opposite."

"I get it," she replies. "My father and mother wanted to be remembered. But mainly what drove them was wealth and status. I understand that's not what you're aiming for. You have much more altruistic goals." Her lips press together and I can see her brain working. I want to know what she's thinking—what she's not saying. But I won't press her. Not again. She's had enough of that tonight.

"I think you have two loving parents who are incredible role models."

Of course that's what she sees. That's what everyone sees. All I see is lost potential.

"But think what they could have done for medicine—for the human race—if they'd not had kids."

She smiles at me, like she knows a secret that I don't. "Oh, Dax." My name from her lips scatters goose bumps over my body. "Did you stop to consider that they were only able to be as good as they are *because* they had children? Each other? A family?"

I shake my head and uncross my leg from my knee. "You're a romantic. Even though you're dealing with kids' shit and vomit and god knows what else. You're *still* a romantic. Or maybe it's not romanticism. More like... you're on the inside of a conspiracy. Everyone is too scared to tell the truth about kids and marriage. The fact is there are only so many hours in a day. I don't have time to be a great father and a great scientist. It's just impossible."

"Okay," Eira says. "If that's how you feel, that's how you feel."

What's she thinking? That I should have given Guinevere up for adoption? That I'm just as bad as her parents and Guinevere won't miss me when I die either?

Sacrifices have to be made.

"You think I'm a selfish idiot." It's not a question. I can see it in her eyes.

"I think you're a new parent, trying to figure stuff out. But no, I don't think you're going to end up like my parents, if that's what you think."

I pause, wanting her to say more. Because I don't see this going any other way.

Guinevere has finished her bottle and fallen asleep, if she was ever awake. Eira stands and places Guinevere back in the travel cot right next to my bed.

"I think you come from a loving family. I think you like to get on with things your way. Maybe you're the brightest among them. Maybe you're in a position to make more of a mark on this world than any of your brothers or your parents. You might be different than them, but your values, who you are inside, that was fixed a long time ago. And you're already more of a father to Guinevere than my father ever was to me."

I stand, and we're inches from each other.

"You can't know that about me. I sometimes wish her away. I think about getting a weekend nanny. An overnight nanny—"

She presses her finger to my lips and I'm silent. The heat of her buzzes against my skin.

Maybe she feels it too, because she drops her hand. "Sorry. I—"

"It's fine," I say. *Touch me again.*

"All parents feel like you do at one point or another. All I'm saying is, being a wonderful father and being great in your field, it's, well—the two aren't mutually exclusive. In fact, quite the opposite. What greater motivation to make the world better than having a child?"

She turns and looks at the cot. It creates a little distance between us, and I get the overwhelming urge to pull her toward me. To close the gap. To feel more of her heat.

Guinevere hasn't stirred.

"Give yourself a chance. Flirt with the possibility that the two of you will rub along quite nicely together. You do so far."

She looks back to me and I can't stop staring at her. How her pillowy-soft mouth curves, how her hair seems to glow in the moonlight, how her almond-shaped eyes are every shade of blue at the same time.

"You're amazing," I blurt out. She looks down at my collar, no longer meeting my gaze. "You're kind. And insightful. And patient. And...beautiful."

I stop. I know I've gone too far.

"I should go," she whispers.

I can't disagree with her. Everything that could come after this moment is too complicated if she stays.

NINETEEN

Eira

John sets down some eggs on the kitchen island. "The key with scrambled eggs is not to overdo it. Never whisk. Always use a fork."

When I woke this morning, I quickly got ready, not knowing when Guinevere would wake. It's a new environment and her schedule might get a little wonky.

"Good tip," I say, cracking eggs into a bowl. "How many shall I do?"

"Twenty, I think. Some will want fried."

I laugh at the idea of making twenty scrambled eggs. "I better get cracking," I say and give John a wink.

"Oh dear," he says, his expression crestfallen. "Your puns will have to get better than that if you're going to be influencing my granddaughter's sense of humor."

I laugh. "It was pretty bad," I say. "I'll try to do better next time."

Dax wanders into the kitchen, Guinevere in his arms. My entire body goes up in flames. I don't want to look at him in case he can read my mind, because then he'd know I was a second away from sliding my hand over his chest last night and asking him to kiss me. I force myself to smile.

"Is she ready for her breakfast? Does she want eggs?"

Dax frowns at me like I've pissed him off and a shiver skates down my spine. What have I done? I'm not really going to feed his daughter eggs.

"What are you wearing?" he asks, his tone terse.

I glance down at myself. "Jeans and a shirt. If you—"

"The apron. I can't have you wearing the apron with Jacob's face on it. I'll never hear the end of it." He strides toward me and starts to undo the tie at the back as if it's about to explode if he doesn't get it off me as soon as possible. I may or may not have imagined Dax peeling my clothes off, but it wasn't motivated by his brother's face.

Once untied, he lifts the apron at the front and I dip my head so he can slip it off.

"Okay," I say. "No apron."

"You boys are ridiculous," John says from where he's putting sausages into the oven. "There's no reason to be jealous, Dax. It's an apron, not an engagement ring."

Dax and I lock gazes, our eyes wide as if we've been caught keeping a secret.

"I don't believe in feeding the beast," he says, recovering quickly. "That's all. Don't want him with any more ammunition than he already has."

"Shall I take Guinevere and give her some milk?" I ask. "Dax, you could take over eggs?"

"Actually," he says. "I'll do the milk."

There's a boom in my chest, like a mallet on a kettle drum.

"No problem," I say, trying to sound like it's no big deal that Dax has chosen to be a father above any other choice he had this morning. Even if the other choice was eggs. Baby steps.

I start cracking eggs into the bowl and watch as Dax sets Guinevere in the DockATot and starts preparing her milk. His hair is still damp from the shower and his navy t-shirt clings to his chest a little too closely.

Not that I'm looking.

Not that I got up extra early so I could wash my hair.

Not that I'm wearing my most flattering jeans and I've actually put on some mascara and lip gloss.

"Hey Guinevere," I say, as Dax fixes her bottle. "Did you sleep super well? Did your brain grow? One day it will be as big as your daddy's."

I hear Dax's huff of a half laugh behind me. Maybe I'm imagining it, but he passes just a little too close to me, grazing my arm with his.

Our gazes snag again and all I'm aware of is heat. Everywhere. All over me.

Shit.

Dax settles himself into one of the kitchen chairs and gives Guinevere her bottle.

"Right, that's tomatoes and sausages in. Baked beans are heating. Eira's on the eggs. What else?" John looks around as if searching for clues about what he might have forgotten.

I smile and sneak a look at Dax. He's smiling too and then he rolls his eyes. "Mushrooms."

"Oh yes. A little fungus. And black pudding. How could I have forgotten black pudding?"

"And you're not doing bacon?" I ask.

Dax chuckles. "Don't mention the bacon."

"We don't do bacon," John says, a serious expression on his face.

I smile, but don't ask any questions.

"Is that some beautiful unsmoked back bacon I can smell?" I hear Zach before he appears at the kitchen door.

Ellie dips under his arm. "Don't start. Seriously. It's not even funny anymore."

"You're right," he says, following Ellie over to the kitchen table. "It's not funny. I don't see why we can't have bacon just because we can't agree which bacon is the best."

"Because it causes too many arguments."

Everyone gets to work setting the table and getting drinks. More and more people flood the kitchen.

I glance over at Guinevere. She's taking it all in her stride.

I transfer the cooked eggs into a warmed dish and put them on the table, just as Guinevere finishes her bottle.

"Why don't I put her down while you have breakfast," I say to Dax.

He shakes his head. "It will only take a second." He stands and heads out of the kitchen.

Is it wrong to feel kinda proud of him? I don't know if he regrets what he said last night, or whether he's had a change of heart. He doesn't strike me as the kind of man who puts on a show for his family or me. Maybe he's starting to feel that tug of love I'm convinced is already growing.

We take our seats at the dining table, but this morning, I'm sitting next to Vincent and not Carole. Everyone has changed seats. I don't try and slink off or suggest I take a plate somewhere else. My intention is always to make the minimal amount of fuss. I know now, sitting down with everyone is the fuss-free option.

Vincent hands me a dish of tomatoes and I'm just setting it down when Dax comes up beside me. My heart begins to race and I scan the table.

There's one free seat.

The one next to me.

Heat floods my chest and I try to catch my breath.

As he slides his chair in, his leg brushes mine, but I don't dare look at him. The last thing I want his family to see is some pathetic nanny with hearts in her eyes for her boss.

Because that's not who I am.

I'm just adjusting to having a hot, single dad as my boss.

Once I've gotten used to him—used to sharing a small space and accidental brushing hands, used to the dip and curve of his muscular arms and the intensity of his stare—this heated feeling suffusing my chest will ease. I know it will.

I'm just not quite there yet.

I lower my voice. "Is she okay? Do you want me to check on her?"

His hand touches my back, and I have to stop myself from pushing harder against him. "She's fine," he whispers. "Sleeping peacefully." I feel his breath on my cheek like a caress.

What is the matter with me? I need this phase to pass quickly or I'm going to say or do something inappropriate. I was so close last night. I thought it would have passed this morning, but I think it might have gotten worse.

"Is she a good sleeper?" Kate asks.

She looks at me, but I turn to Dax to let him answer the question. He's not shaved this morning and the stubble on his face dares me to run my finger along it. My body starts to throb as I imagine the drag of it between my thighs. I clench, trying to reset myself, but it just makes it worse.

What's happening to me? It's like I can't cope with him sitting this close. I mentally high-five the past version of myself that was smart enough to sit in the backseat with

Guinevere on the ride up. I'm not sure I would have survived five hours of close proximity.

I'm a grown woman, and I can't lose this job. I need to get myself together. I need to erase him from my mind somehow. Put some kind of shield between us.

I focus on my plate, tuning out everything other than the scrambled eggs, the tomato, the mushrooms, the toast. I count the number of pips on the tomato. I estimate the number of mouthfuls of egg left on my plate. I contemplate how I'd arrange the food if I were photographing it for a magazine.

Anything so long as I'm not thinking about Dax and how close he is to me.

Eventually, my heart rate drops and my body seems to relax. As long as he doesn't touch me again, I should be okay.

I chew each bite as many times as I can, trying to focus on the flavor, the texture, the way it would feel if it hadn't been cooked.

Then breakfast is over and finally, I can move. Finally, I can get some space.

After breakfast, I convince everyone I should stay back with Guinevere while they go for a walk along the coastline. Dax tries to convince me to come and that Guinevere would be fine in the fresh air, swaddled cozily in her buggy.

She would be. But I'm not sure *I* would be.

"You go," I say. "It will recharge you. It will be nice to have some time with your family."

He raises his eyebrows and I smile.

"Take some time," I say.

He stares at me for a second, then two, then three. I have to look away. Is he deciding whether or not to go? Does he want to say something? Want *me* to say something?

"Okay," he says. "We'll only be gone a couple of hours."

I nod vigorously.

"Then tonight," he adds, "we should talk. About last night."

The pulse in my ears pounds.

Talk about last night? What does that mean?

The time alone with Guinevere should be a relief, but instead the quiet that descends over the house just gives my brain the freedom to wonder what Dax wants to say. Is he going to fire me? Is he going to apologize or claim he had a little too much wine at dinner? Say he didn't mean it, and he doesn't think of me as anything more than the nanny?

I almost can't decide which outcome I dread the most.

Whichever way it goes, I want to be in London when it does. I don't want to be surrounded by his family, in the middle of nowhere, without being able to escape.

"Can we press pause and talk when we're back in London?" I suggest. "I would prefer that."

"Yeah. We can do that."

At least if he fires me, I'll be able to go over to Callie's in the evening. I'll be able to escape. Lick my wounds. And then work my notice.

TWENTY

Dax

Guinevere won't take her bottle. The sounds of her fussing down the hall are a distraction from the article I'm trying to read, but Eira is with her. I need to tune her out and focus, though I'm realizing that's easier said than done. I've been spoiled until now—she's never been fussy before. Maybe I shouldn't have taken her to Norfolk. She's gone from an environment of nonstop noise, being passed around like we're playing day-long games of pass the parcel, people cooing and ahhhing, to...still, quiet, peace. It's just the three of us, now we're back in London.

I'm bracing myself for a talk with Eira. Things between us have been... I've been so close to kissing her. More than once. But I'm her boss. She's my daughter's nanny. She lives in my home. She's more than off limits, but I could probably be thrown in prison for some of the dirty thoughts I've been having about her.

It has to stop. I have to explain that things should stay professional between us. I can't go through another nanny search again. I don't want Eira to resign when I fuck things up or can't give her what she needs. What she deserves. And she deserves *everything*. I'm just going to have to grit my teeth and do the impossible: tell her we have to keep things strictly professional.

Eira appears in the doorway.

"Are you ready to talk?" I ask. I squint as I notice her pallor, white as the shirt she's wearing.

"We need to take Guinevere to the hospital," she says, her words tight and firm. "I think it will be quicker than calling an ambulance."

My stomach drops to my knees as she turns and heads out of the kitchen. I scramble after her. "What's happened?"

I follow her into my bedroom, where she pulls out the baby bag we took to Norfolk.

"She has a fever of thirty-eight point four. That's up since the last time I checked. She's not eating. She's fussy. She just threw up. Not just some spit-up—actual vomit." She moves to the crib and pulls open Guinevere's sleepsuit. "There's mottling and a spot. In fact there are three. They're fading at the moment but—"

The room starts to spin and I have to remind myself to breathe.

Eira thinks Guinevere has meningitis.

"I'll get the pram out." She doesn't need to say anything more. Instantly, I feel a bloody useless fool not to have caught it first. I'm the doctor in the house, but the diagnosis didn't even occur to me. "Can you get some things together?"

I turn to find Eira already filling the bag full of nappies and milk and bottles.

Shit.

Shit.

Shit.

The nearest hospital is UCH and it has a specialist children's A&E. She'll be in the best possible hands.

Eira pulls bags onto her shoulder and then takes Guinevere in her arms.

"Keys?" she asks. "You need your phone and your coat." She's already wearing hers.

I nod and follow her as we head out.

Eira works quickly, strapping Guinevere into the car seat. "Do you want me to drive?" she asks. Her tone is calm and comforting but I can barely think straight.

"I think—"

"I'll drive," she says. "Get in the passenger seat."

I do as she asks, unable to do anything but leave Eira to put the pram in the boot and the bags next to Guinevere.

She gets in beside me and starts the car. She's not panicking or flustered, but I've never seen her move so quick.

"Call your brother," she says. I look at her blankly. "Jacob. Call him and ask him to meet us there. He'll probably know the doctors in pediatric A&E. He'll make sure she's taken care of."

I nod and pull out my phone. "I only have twenty percent battery." Shit. I'm not prepared for this at all.

"Plenty to call your brother, and I have my portable charger with me."

She turns out of my underground car park and speeds onto the street.

Jacob answers the phone on the second ring.

"Guinevere is sick," I say. "It might be meningitis." My voice collapses as I speak the words. "Can you meet us at UCH?"

"I'll be there in twenty minutes," he says without hesitation, and he hangs up.

I don't even need to tell Eira to park on a double yellow line. She just pulls up opposite the hospital entrance and gets out.

Within seconds we're at the children's accident and emergency check-in.

The receptionist is disinterested. She can barely look up from her phone.

"I'm a doctor here. I want my daughter tested for meningitis," I say.

"Name?" the receptionist asks.

I'm so angry at her apathy, I'm only vaguely aware of Eira giving the necessary information as I stalk around the corner, Guinevere in my arms, looking for someone who can help us.

"I need a doctor who can test my daughter for meningitis," I call out as I head to the nurses' station. I can't remember the care pathways for meningitis. It's been a minute since I did my A&E rotation. "Should we start her on steroids?" I ask. "A drip at least."

A nurse comes towards me and guides me out of the station and into one of the triage bays. "Let's take a look, shall we?"

"I'm a doctor," I say. "Here. Research. I do—I want a doctor to see her."

"The doctors are all seeing other patients at the moment," the nurse says. "But they'll want a temperature and a pulse check. Let me do that."

I know she's right. I note the time. I want to see a doctor within two minutes.

Once some basic stats are done, the nurse removes Guinevere's babygrow and starts to examine her, talking to her while she does. Guinevere is increasingly fussy. I step forward and stroke her head. "Hey, Guinevere. Daddy's here. Eira's here. You're safe."

I hope I'm right.

Have I kept her safe?

A heavy ball of regret lodges in my chest, threatening to pull down my entire body. It's my job to keep her safe.

Eira appears at the curtain. Our gazes meet and she gives me a reassuring nod.

The nurse finishes the examination.

"I'm going to find a doctor. I'll be back."

I want to go with her, but I don't want people focused on the father who can't keep it together. I want to have all the attention on my daughter.

"It's going to be okay," Eira says, placing a thin muslin over Guinevere's naked body. "It's okay, sweet girl," she says to her.

I bend and place a kiss on Guinevere's forehead. For a second or two she settles as we both look over her.

In a matter of seconds a doctor arrives, Jacob right behind him. Thank god Eira suggested I call him. As a consultant pediatrician in the same hospital trust, the junior doctors accept his authority when he starts ordering people around. Within minutes, Guinevere has blood taken, is put on a drip and is prepared for her lumbar test.

Eira and I stand at the edge of the bay, watching as the doctors and nurses work.

"Is she going to be okay?" I'm not sure if I'm asking Eira or god or the universe. But I need something from someone. I'll do anything, I think. I never wanted to be a father, but I don't want to lose her. She's mine. So tiny and vulnerable and completely dependent on me, her dad, to keep her alive.

I close my eyes and try to think. What can I trade for her?

If she survives this, I'll move out to Hampstead and buy a house with a garden, with room for a playroom and her friends to come and stay.

If the universe gives me another chance, I'll be the best dad. I'll take her to the park. Sing to her, even.

If the doctors can just make her well again, I will do everything I can to make sure she's safe.

Eira sucks in a shuddering breath. "Yes," she says. "I think so."

I fumble for her hand. I don't know if it's our version of a prayer, or maybe I'm just taking comfort where I can get it, but it makes me feel slightly better that I can feel her beside me.

GUINEVERE IS FINALLY ASLEEP, but I can't take my eyes off her. I'm holding her hand between my thumb and forefinger. I want her to know she's being cared for, that she's not alone.

That she's loved.

I don't know when I started to love her. It didn't happen right away. I just know that right now, I'd stand in front of a train for her.

The swish of the curtains gets my attention and I turn. It's Jacob. His expression is blank. I can't read him. What's he going to say?

"It's viral meningitis."

I deflate like a balloon without a knot. "Thank god. So she's going to be fine? No kidney damage or swelling?"

"There's unlikely to be any permanent damage. You caught it very quickly."

"Eira did," I say.

I'd been a fool. Asleep at the wheel. I make a mental note to book her in for some tests. I should have done it anyway. Check-ups. Maybe monthly. Just to make sure I'm not missing anything. I'll get Jacob to tell me who's the best pediatrician in the UK. Besides him. I don't want him missing something either because he's too close to her.

I'm vaguely aware of Jacob talking to Eira. "As you know, much better than bacterial meningitis. Just need to keep her hydrated."

"Does she need anti-viral meds?" I ask. I pull out my phone to check the protocol for infant viral meningitis.

Jacob puts his hand on my shoulder. "She's fine. Now she's hydrated, she's happy. But she'd be happier at home where she can sleep without the noise and the lights of a hospital."

I'm not sure I want her to leave the hospital yet. "Is it safe to take her back home?" I ask.

"Mate, she's safer at home than here. You know this."

"And you're sure it's viral?" I ask. "One hundred percent?"

"One hundred percent. The blood test and the lumbar test both confirmed it."

"I've looked after children with viral meningitis before," Eira says. "Rest and cuddles and a bit of Calpol. We can try her with water if she doesn't want her milk."

I glance back at Guinevere, her little arm covered in bandages holding the cannula in place. She's so vulnerable. "I don't know," I say. I'm clearly not able to look after Guinevere. I'm not focused on her enough. I don't notice things.

"I'll take the bags and the pram to the car and come back," Eira says.

"No," I call after her. "We'll all go together." Eira was the one who noticed Guinevere's symptoms. She shouldn't be away from her. I catch her eye. I want to know if she really thinks it's a good idea to leave.

"Okay," she says. She nods at me as if she knows the silent question I'm asking. "This is good, Dax. She's going to be fine."

"I'm going to take her cannula out," Jacob says. "And then you can go."

In a few minutes we're back at the car and Jacob is helping us put the pram in the boot.

"Did you strap her in?" I ask Eira as she shuts the back door.

A small smile curves around the edges of her lips that says no, the baby is hanging out the window. "Yes. She's all strapped in safely. I'm going to sit next to her. You're going to drive us home." She holds up my car keys. "You are fine. Your daughter is fine."

"Thanks to you," I say.

By the time we're home, my shoulders have relaxed a little and my breathing has returned to normal. I didn't realize how tense I was until I had some time to think in the car.

We bundle Guinevere inside. Eira manages to give her some Calpol and even gets her to have some milk. She's a fucking miracle. Thank god for her.

"You need to sleep," Eira says, coming into the kitchen. "You look exhausted."

"I'm a lot better than I would have been if you hadn't been here."

"But I was here. And if I hadn't been, you'd have caught

it, because you would have taken her temperature and checked her for spots and—"

"But what if I didn't?" I ask. "What else am I going to miss as she grows up? And not just the physical stuff. What if she's getting bullied at school and doesn't tell me or she gets depressed or—"

Eira comes towards me and places her hands on my upper arms. "All these thoughts are entirely normal," she says. "It's called *the mental burden of being a parent.* And it's intensified because you're a single parent. The only thing you can do is your best. And your best is pretty good from what I've seen."

"You're incredible," I blurt. "Absolutely amazing. Calm and capable and you care so much." I cup her cheek in my hand, all thoughts of boundaries shattering with every breath.

"I really do," she says. "I really care about Guinevere. About..."

"Thank you," I whisper, sweeping my thumb across her bottom lip. "Thank you so, so much."

I shift forward a little and her hands move to my chest. I close my eyes at the feel of her hands on me. I've thought about her touching me like this for so long, in so many ways.

"Dax," she whispers. Her voice is full of doubt. We both know this isn't a good idea. But it feels so fucking inevitable. If either of us walks away now, we'll just be delaying the unavoidable.

I silence her doubts by pressing my lips against hers. She gasps as our mouths meet. She tastes like honey and fresh flowers, and I want to drink her in and eat her up.

I take her face in both my hands and deepen this kiss. It's better than I thought it would be, and I expected it to be phenomenal.

Her hands travel up my chest, heating my skin and making me want to strip naked. I want to make this woman in my hands feel everything I feel for her.

She's beautiful inside and out. She deserves to be worshipped.

She moans into my mouth and the sound travels across my body and into my balls, making me vibrate with wanting her.

As if I've confessed how desperately and intensely I'm feeling, Eira steps back, panting, her lips reddened, her cheeks flushed. "I think we should..." She trails off.

My gaze travels from her eyes to her mouth, down her throat to her breasts, down, down between her legs. I close my eyes and try to imagine how sweet she'll taste.

"We should stop," she says. "We were going to talk and then—"

And then everything changed.

I step back, trying to ignore the pounding in my chest, the way my hands twitch with the need to touch her, the way I feel like I'm a magnet and she's every ounce of iron in the world. "We can stop," I say.

"It's been an emotional evening," she says.

I nod. She's right. It has been emotional, but that's not the reason I kissed her. It's not the reason I don't think I'll be able to *not* want to kiss her until the end of time. That's all about who she is and who she's shown me she is.

"We can stop," I repeat, "if that's what you want."

"What did you want to talk about?" she asks.

"I honestly don't remember. All I can think about is how beautiful you are, how you feel, how you taste."

She blushes. I don't know exactly what it is about her reddened cheeks, but I feel myself lengthen in my jeans.

"I thought you were going to say how this wasn't a good idea and how I'm—"

I tuck a loose strand of hair behind her ear and it silences her. "Hey, listen, if I've misread this," I say, "if you're not...feeling this, then—"

"It's not that."

Heat gathers in my chest. This is happening. I've not got this wrong.

"It's just the consequences," she says. "The stakes are so high for me."

I get it. Or I don't get it. I'm past the point of being able to sift through my emotions, to look at the logic of this situation. Is that what having a daughter does to a person? Does becoming a parent override sense? "Let's press pause on the stakes. On both sides. For tonight at least."

She looks at me as if she's asking if that's even possible. I don't have an answer for her. All I know is that she's looking at me like she needs me, and I *know* I need her.

I link my fingers into hers and she smooths her free hand over my chest. Inhaling, I try to commit this to memory. For some reason, this moment feels like it will stand out as an important juncture in my history.

"Eira," I whisper. She closes her eyes in a slow blink.

I drop my forehead to hers and it's as if our bodies are connecting and aligning, just as our breathing is.

I cup her face in my hands and kiss her.

I have an overwhelming sensation of regret that we haven't done this sooner, that we've wasted time. I deepen our kiss.

Her fingers skirt my sides and I can barely keep quiet. If we stay like this the entire evening, just kissing and feeling and pressing, that will be more than I could have ever hoped for.

But I want more. I want much more.

A screeching sound propels us apart.

What the fuck?

I look around and run to my bedroom to check on Guinevere. She's fine. Sleeping peacefully. She won't be due any more milk for a few hours at least.

When I come back into the kitchen, Eira waves her phone at me. "I set an alarm to check on Guinevere every forty minutes."

I chuckle. "Right. So I checked on her and she's fine."

"Good." She nods resolutely. "That's really good." Her reddened lips and mussed hair make her look wanton. It's sexy as hell.

"We really need to keep a close eye on Guinevere," she says. "It's been a long evening and the next few days might be disruptive. We should probably sleep."

"We probably should." I just don't want to not feel her right next to me for the next eight hours. "Come and sleep in my bed."

Her eyebrows shoot through the ceiling.

"We'll both keep all our clothes on," I caveat. "We're just going to sleep."

"Just sleep?" she asks.

"You have to promise to keep your hands to yourself," I tease.

"I'll do my best," she says.

I take her hand and lead her into my bedroom.

TWENTY-ONE

Eira

I pull away from our kiss, pressing my fingers to my lips to stop myself from saying something I shouldn't. All the words I should be saying are buried deep at the bottom of the back garden of my brain.

There should be boundaries between a boss and an employee.

I can't afford to lose this job.

We should keep this professional.

I can put my feelings to one side for the good of my career.

Unfortunately, logic has left the building.

"I'll see you after work," he says. "But call me if anything changes. And..." He smiles and it releases a thousand tiny butterflies in my stomach. "Call me anyway."

"I won't call you at work unless it's urgent." I put on my most professional voice.

"Then I'll call you," he says.

"Go to work," I remind him. He didn't want to go in

today. Last night with Guinevere was intense and it's understandable he's worried, but I know how important his career is to him. There's nothing he can do here to help. Guinevere is out of any danger and he's working at the very hospital where she was treated last night. If anything happens, I'm bringing his daughter right to him.

Guinevere just needs to sleep and eat and she'll be fine.

I know this.

Dax leaves. I lean back on the closed front door and look to the heavens.

What am I doing?

I'm Miss Sensible. I'm the girl who never crosses the line, the nanny who always knows how to sink into the background.

What am I doing?

Perhaps it was the heightened emotions of Guinevere's illness. Perhaps tonight, after we've both had some time apart, things will have fizzled between us.

It's unlikely. But it's possible.

If things haven't fizzled...then what?

I start sleeping with my boss? Until when?

Until he fires me.

I set about my day, unpacking from Norfolk, tidying, and doing three thousand loads of washing, in between checking on Guinevere and giving her milk, which she takes really well. All the while I try not to think about Dax, but it's impossible. He lives here. I'm surrounded by him. I'm looking after his daughter.

I put Guinevere down after her third feed of the day, and head to the kitchen to start preparing dinner for Dax. He'll be exhausted when he's home and he'll appreciate a proper home-cooked meal he doesn't have to prepare himself. My phone interrupts me as I pull vegetables out of the fridge.

Immediately I assume it's Dax, and I smile as I pull my phone from my pocket.

It's Eddie.

"Hey!" It comes out like I'm having the time of my life in an open-topped jeep on my way to a Mexican resort for a week. Maybe I'm overcorrecting because it's my sister and not Dax.

"What's the matter with you?" she asks. "You sound really happy."

"I always sound happy," I reply, toning down my exuberance. "What's the matter with *you*?" It's unusual for Eddie to call me when she knows I'm working. I glance at the clock. Dax will be home in less than an hour.

"You always sound happy? If you say so," she singsongs. "But if you thought you were happy before, you're going to be flying to the moon when I tell you my news." She sounds excited and I pause, waiting to hear what she's going to tell me.

"I won a scholarship." It bursts out of her. "They just called to tell me ten minutes ago."

"You did?" I ask. "I didn't know you applied for one. What's it for?"

"That's the thing—I didn't! Everyone in my year was automatically entered apparently. And I got it!"

"That sounds...weird."

"Who cares how it sounds. It covers all my tuition for this year and for last year."

I freeze. That can't be right. "It pays you back what we already paid for tuition?"

"What *you* already paid for tuition," she corrects me. "Yes. Can you believe it?"

Frankly, no, I can't believe it. "Where did this scholarship come from? Who's funding it?"

"The university, I guess," she says. "They said it was a brand-new scholarship and a letter would follow giving all the details. This is good, Eira. It means you can do something else with all that money."

It sounds way too good to be true. "Let's wait until the money's in your account, shall we?"

"What are you so suspicious of?" she asks.

"I don't know, this kind of thing doesn't happen to us, does it? If you had your inheritance and our uncle hadn't stolen it, you wouldn't need a scholarship."

"You're right, but we have to roll with the punches, not look a gift horse in the mouth. Look on the bright side!"

I laugh at her list of corny phrases. "Are you trying to do an impression of me?"

"Kinda. You're always good at seeing the positive, so it's weird that it's me trying to make you see that this is a good thing."

I'm not sure I always see the positive side of things. I've just tried to put a positive spin on things for the sake of Eddie and Dylan. If I fall apart, who would they rely on? I have to be the one to buoy their spirits, otherwise we'd all drown.

Deep down, I've always been able to see the truth of our situation. Partly because I'm older, but also because I've never had the option to ignore reality. If I dig for the truth, demand it and refuse to look away, I can fix whatever's wrong. Being in denial doesn't serve a purpose. All the same, I try not to consider what that means for me and Dax.

"It's a wonderful thing," I say, trying to fit the pieces together in my brain. I can't see a downside unless Eddie is lying to me about how she got the money. If she's really won a scholarship, worst-case scenario, it doesn't pay out and we're back where we started. "Really wonderful. Congratulations."

"Thanks." I can hear her smile through the telephone. "Before long I'll be completely financially independent from you and you can keep that hard-earned money for yourself. Maybe even get yourself a flat or something. You won't have to live in where you work."

Eddie and Dylan understand we are a team. Each of us knows what role we play to make the little machine of our family hum along. I'm older and able to earn money, so that's what I do. Dylan is working and will climb the corporate ladder. He won't have to rely on me financially forever. Eddie focuses on her studies. Each of us relies on the others to do their part.

"Living in isn't the worst thing in the world."

"You always say that, but I can't imagine you don't want your own place. You've always been so independent."

Having my own flat in London is a faraway dream I only allow myself to think about every now and then. Making it a reality will require years working with some really wealthy families, and I'm not prepared to work outside the UK when Eddie and Dylan might need me. They've had enough disruption in their lives. We all need stability.

All good reasons not to kiss the boss.

"So how's it going with your single dad?"

"He's not *my* single dad." I can't help bristling at her words, even though I'm sure her comment was innocent enough.

"The guy you work for. Is he...hot? I need you to be working for a hot, single guy who's going to realize how beautiful, caring and wonderful you are."

My insides clench at the memory of all the things Dax said he liked about me last night.

"Okay," I say. "I'm going to leave you to go back to your romance novels and change the ending so it reflects real life —the girl loses her job and is blacklisted from every nanny agency on the planet. She turns to prostitution to make ends meet, then dies alone in an alley before rats eat her toes."

Eddie tuts. "Don't you know? Romance novels always have a happy ending."

I roll my eyes. "Exactly! Not like real life."

"Good things can happen, Eira," she says softly. "Look at my scholarship. This is a turning point for us. You never know—the solicitors might find a way to get that money back from our uncle."

"Oh you've moved on to fantasy now, have you? Bored with romance?"

She laughs. "I'm hanging up so you can spend more time with your single dad. Don't forget to wax. I love you."

"Love you more."

Maybe Eddie is right. Perhaps the clouds are parting and we're in for a period of sunshine. Her scholarship buys me some breathing room. If I do get fired for kissing my boss, I won't be destitute—at least not right away.

For better or worse, the thought just makes me wonder how soon I can kiss him again.

TWENTY-TWO

Dax

I can't remember ever feeling so pleased to leave the hospital and get back home. Something smells absolutely delicious as I walk through the front door. What is that?

Last night changed everything. It's like the clouds have parted and I realize how much I love my daughter. She's no longer a duty and responsibility. The idea that I could have lost her was so horrifying that I now understand the most important job I'll ever have is being a dad.

Work's important. It always will be. But being with Guinevere, watching her grow, keeping her safe—it's the best thing ever.

I can't stop smiling. I pass the kitchen and laugh as I hear Eira singing along to the radio. Before I investigate further, I sneak into my bedroom and find Guinevere sleeping soundly.

The restlessness has gone and she looks so snuggly and sweet, I want to scoop her out of her cot and hold her close.

I settle for a kiss on her head and a stroke of her cheek. I don't want to risk waking her.

I head to the kitchen and stand, leaning on the door-jamb, watching as Eira stirs whatever's on the hob while she sings along to some rap I've never heard.

I imagined her to be all about the show tunes rather than Lil Wayne.

She turns and freezes at the sight of me, her eyes going wide.

"Rap?" I ask. "Really?"

She shrugs. "I'm selective in my love of rap. It has to be old school. Classic."

I nod, trying to bite back my grin. "Okay."

She shrugs. "I made you dinner. Chicken and mush-room pie. With broccoli and carrots."

"Wow," I reply. "I thought it smelled good, but pie?"

"You ready now or do you want to go see Guinevere?"

"Oh, I saw her already."

A smile uncurls on her face like I couldn't have given her a better answer. "She's been such a good girl. She's had all her milk."

"Thanks for keeping me updated," I reply. I'd messaged her on the way to work asking for regular updates and Eira dutifully messaged me every sixty to ninety minutes, telling me what was going on with a picture. The photo was usually of Guinevere sleeping and the messages were just as benign. It was all very appropriate.

Just as it was last night. I slept on top of the covers, while Eira slept underneath. Occasionally our fingers touched. But that was it. I don't know how I managed to sleep with her so close. Probably the relief after such a tumultuous evening, but also, it just felt that having Eira in my bed was as it should be. Like everything was right.

But now? Seeing her again? My entire body responds to her, the hairs on my arms standing to attention, my insides heating, my heart straining to break out of my chest. I'm done ignoring it. Last night woke up a part of my brain that had been dormant until then—a part of my brain that doesn't include my research or changing the world. It's the part that wants to be a dad. Wants to kiss Eira. The part that wants to want more than I've ever had before. I'm ready for it all.

She dishes up a plate and sets it on the table. When I don't move, she turns to look at me, her expression asking what's wrong.

I shake my head. "Not without you." I nod at the chair kitty corner to me. "Eat with me."

She narrows her eyes slightly and takes a breath as if trying to decide. "Okay."

She fixes another plate for herself and sits at the small kitchen table. I can't help but stare, mesmerized by her every movement. The way she places the plate down with elegant, purposeful fingers. The way she sits to the side then twirls herself around in the chair. The way her gaze flits across the table, making sure we both have everything we need.

"It's good to see you," I say. It's not quite *I miss you*, because that would be too...intense and not what I mean. I didn't miss her. I was just looking forward to coming home and seeing her all day. There's a difference.

Her cheeks flush. I chuckle at her visceral response to a simple sentence.

I know how that goes.

"How's the pie?" she asks.

Neutral territory. I get it. The situation is awkward. I'm her boss. She's living under my roof.

"The pie's...spectacular," I say. I haven't tasted it yet.

She nods and takes a mouthful.

I can't not stare at her as she chews.

She stares back, her eyes brightening, a smile threatening at the edges of her mouth. She swallows. "What?"

"I like watching you," I reply honestly.

Her gaze hits her plate. "Dax, I...I...this is..." She looks up, and I smile at her inability to form words.

"Just say it. Whatever it is, it's fine."

She pulls in a breath like she's bracing herself for what's next. "You're my boss."

I nod. She speaks the truth.

"And...my kinda landlord. I mean, I live under your roof."

More nodding from me.

"It's a lot to...lose."

My eyes narrow, trying to think about the negative points of kissing her. Of feeling her naked body wrapped around me. Of making her come. "Yeah."

"I'm serious. There's a lot at stake. For me."

She has a lot to lose. All I can see is everything we have to gain.

"And then it doesn't work out and...you bring dates home and...this is a small flat."

This is where my mother went wrong. If she'd have wanted me to move, she should have pointed out that in a bigger house, I could bang the nanny and not worry about things being awkward if it doesn't work out.

But I'm not thinking about whether or not it could work out. I'm thinking that if I don't get to touch Eira, I might actually lose my mind.

I reach out and hook my fingers under her chair, pulling it across the floor so she's sitting right next to me.

She squeals. "Dax."

"You want to say no?" I hold my palms up. "We stop. No questions asked." I suck in a breath. "You don't want this?" I shrug. "We stop. No questions asked. You're not attracted to me?" I shake my head. "We stop. No questions asked."

I fix her with a stare. "But don't say no because you're scared." I hold her gaze. "Or because of what might happen if it goes wrong."

She looks away.

"What?" I ask.

"Easy for you to say. You..."

"You're right. It is easy for me. I know what I want, and I have the power here. But I don't want to overanalyze this. I'm not asking you to marry me. Right now, at this moment, I want to kiss you. And I think you want to kiss me."

I drop my voice and cup her head in my hand. "Let's just deal with right here and right now." It's not ordered or logical. In fact, it's the kind of wishy-washy bullshit I've absolutely teased my brothers for in the past. But it's what feels right.

Things change.

People change.

Fatherhood is changing me.

Eira sighs. Her sweet breath hits the side of my face and it feels like velvet.

I reach for her and pull her onto my lap, reveling at the feel of her, so soft and warm in my fingers. I slide my hands up her thighs and brush my lips across hers. Once, twice, three times.

She relaxes against me and her eyelids flutter shut as I press a kiss against her collarbone.

"What am I doing?" she asks the heavens.

A knock at the door has her leaping from my lap.

I bet that's a fucking delivery guy.

We both head out of the kitchen at the same time and it's almost comical as we both try to squeeze through the door.

"I'll get the door," I say, gesturing her ahead of me.

"I'm going to check on Guinevere," she says.

I swing the door open and it's Jacob. He always had a habit of ruining things with women for me.

"What?" I ask.

"Good evening to you too," he says, barging past me. "I think you meant to say, *thank you, Jacob, for coming to check on my daughter after you've spent the entire day at the hospital. You're the best big brother ever.*"

I groan and close the door.

"She's in..." I call after him as he enters my bedroom.

I watch from the doorway as he and Eira work together to move Guinevere, remove her clothing, check her temperature and discuss fluid intake and medications.

"She's bouncing back nicely," he says. "Just got to ride it out."

"Thanks, Jacob," I say.

"You need to move," he says as he passes me. "Takes too long to get here. There's a house just gone on the market opposite me. I'll send you the details."

I don't have the energy to argue with him. "Okay." Maybe it wouldn't be a bad idea having a pediatrician I share a gene pool with living directly opposite me. "I'll take a look."

He shoots me a glare that says, *did I hear you right?*

Everything's changed.

"I really appreciate you coming over to check on her. Do you want some pie?" I ask.

"Pie?" he asks, incredulous. "What kind of pie."

"Chicken and mushroom," Eira says. "There's plenty."

And of course, Jacob stays for pie, because that's the kind of cockblocker he is.

TWENTY-THREE

Eira

I can't make out what they're saying, but Jacob seems in no mood to leave anytime soon. It's giving me breathing room. Anytime Dax is near me, I lose all sense of judgement. I know that kissing him is a bad idea. Him touching me is a bad idea. Letting him near me is a *very* bad idea.

But whenever he's around, I just can't help it.

I don't know what's the matter with me, but all my self-control abandons me as soon as I'm alone with Dax.

In fairness, I've never had a boss who's single and sexy as hell. I've never been tested to this extent as a result. But if every single one of my friends were asked to vote, none of them would say I'd risk my job for a roll in the hay.

So what's different about Dax?

Everything, my body sings.

It's not logical. It's chemical.

I've been pacing the length of my bedroom since I excused myself from dinner with Jacob and Dax. I step over the still-disorganized books and trinkets, hoping my thoughts will slot neatly into place if I just keep moving.

Maybe we need to get it over with. Sleep together once, and maybe that will be that. If it's just once, then maybe he won't fire me. Especially if I'm super professional and the next morning act like nothing happened.

That's the answer—scratch the itch.

Then be done.

Someone must have opened the kitchen door, because I can hear both of them now. I stop by my bedroom door. Waiting. Listening.

For what? I don't know.

Then silence. Did Jacob leave? My heart speeds up, like an overexcited puppy.

What now?

I hear them in the hallway again. They must have gone to check on Guinevere.

Are they going to go back into the kitchen, or will Jacob leave?

And then what? Do I leave things hanging, or do I put on my big-girl pants, open my bedroom door, and...

An image of my sister holding a sign saying "go get your man" flashes in my brain. I shake it off.

All I can hear now is muttering, then the click of the front door and the slide of the lock.

My heart is thud, thud, thudding in my chest. In my fingertips. Between my legs.

I reach for the door handle and pull back, as if it might bite me.

What do I want? I ask myself.

A job, I think. To be able to support my brother and sister.

A place to live. I haven't had a home since my parents died.

A period of quiet, where I'm not firefighting or untangling a catastrophe.

Dax.

Dax.

Dax.

I grab the door handle and yank.

And yelp as I come face-to-face with Dax.

"I was debating whether to knock. I get that the power dynamic is weird and this is your space."

I nod, a nugget of pride burrowing into my chest. His mum did a good job. I don't know why *I'm* feeling proud about it, but here we are.

"I want..."

His eyebrows lift as he waits for me to finish my sentence.

One night, I think. Just one night when I don't have to think about anything but right now.

"You," I finish.

A smile curls around his face. "I want you too."

He hooks his fingers around my waist and pulls me toward him. Every pound of responsibility I usually feel weighing down my shoulders drops to the ground.

I look up, his gaze so completely enveloping it's like he sees more than anyone else. Like he knows me better than I know myself.

He reaches behind my hair. "I want to see it down."

"My hair?" I ask, a little confused.

He nods once and I reach back, pulling out the two clips that keep it in place.

"You're so beautiful," he whispers, cupping my neck. "I

don't think I realized how beautiful until I saw you that first night with your hair down."

"Backgammon night?" I ask.

A grin spreads across his face. "Backgammon night."

That was the night things started to shift.

"You know I let you win that second game."

He chuckles. "Sure you did."

We stand there in my bedroom doorway for seconds, minutes, hours, staring at each other, on the precipice of something.

His thumb sweeps across my lips and then he bends to kiss me. My body sags in relief. It's been such a long time coming. In this moment, I feel I'm right where I'm meant to be. What's happening brings so many complications, so much ambiguity, but it doesn't stop me. It's like there's an external force keeping me where I am, preventing me from running, from letting my logical brain take over. It's as if the choice has been made for me by forces bigger and stronger than I could ever hope to be.

It feels like being here with Dax is my only option—and I'm not looking for an out.

TWENTY-FOUR

Dax

There are a thousand reasons why this is a bad idea, but I can't think of any of them right now. All I can do is feel Eira's soft skin under my fingers, smell the scent of honey and rose petals, and listen to the sounds of Eira's breathing falling into the same rhythm as mine. It's as if every minute we're together, we bind tighter, like the external world falls away and we exist on our own plane, free from consequence.

Her fingers trail under my t-shirt and I groan. I'm not sure I'm going to survive this.

She pulls at my waistband and we tumble back into her bedroom and onto her bed. I crawl on top of her and press up on my hands, looking down at her, her hair splayed out on the bed behind her.

She looks like a goddess.

All goodness and light and beauty.

A sudden pull inside me warns that I can't fuck this up, that this is important. It's the start of something.

My gaze snags on her mouth as she bites down on her bottom lip.

She's not just sweet. She's also sexy as fuck.

"You okay?" she asks.

I answer her with a kiss. She tastes so sweet, and instantly I regret waiting this long to kiss her again. There's been too much wasted time.

Her fingers thread into my hair and grasp my shoulder. My body tightens at her touch. She shifts her hips under me and my jaw slackens. Every move she makes is totally mesmerizing.

Her fingers move down, down, down to the edge of my t-shirt and she pushes it up. I take it off, then she reaches for her shirt. I watch as she peels the white cotton from her body, slowly revealing the skin I know is so soft. I dip and press kisses from her collarbone, down between her breasts, over her bra, to her stomach. I enjoy how she writhes and shifts, wanting more.

I snap off her bra and continue my exploration, kissing, pressing, licking—*feeling*.

"My underwear is...it's not exactly sexy."

I let out a grunt. "I'm not looking at your underwear." I shift down the bed and peel her jeans off as I go. She's wearing plain white cotton knickers that come off perfectly easily—my only criteria for Eira's underwear.

I press a kiss to her pussy and breathe her in. Her scent fills me up and I'm so hard, I could knock down a wall with my dick right about now.

But that's not what I want to be doing with it.

"Dax," Eira whispers.

I press my tongue against her clit and soak up her heat and wetness. God, this feels so good. *She* feels so good. It's like every sensation with Eira is magnified tenfold. I part her legs and then slide my hands behind her bottom. I want to make sure I'm in complete control of what happens now. Something tells me it's what Eira needs: me to give her pleasure. Me to lead the way. Me, period.

The realization is like the tremors of an earthquake in my chest.

She needs me. And I think I might need her.

She squeals and tries to move away as my tongue dips into her folds. I dig my fingers deeper into her bottom to keep her in place. She's not avoiding pleasure. Not anymore.

She's hot and luscious and I need her. More of her. All of her.

"Dax." Her voice is hoarse and sexy and desperate. Her fingers are in my hair, clawing at me. "Oh no. I—"

She comes on my face, her body shuddering around me. She's a goddess who makes me feel like a fucking god.

And I can't wait another second to be inside her.

I grab my jeans, pull out the condom from my wallet and rip it open. I can't get it on fast enough. I must look like a fumbling teenager.

"You okay?" I ask as I grip the root of my cock.

She's staring at my dick, nodding. "I'll try not to come so quickly."

I groan at her words and lean over her, guiding my cock into her, just a little. "Don't ever worry about coming too quickly."

Our gazes meet and we stare at each other as I push into her, slowly, deliberately, perfectly.

As I get to the end of her, I let out a guttural groan. She feels so good. This feels so right. It's like fastening the last button on a shirt or pressing save on your work for the day. It feels utterly important, integral to life.

Not that I'm done. I'm just exactly where I'm meant to be. *We're* exactly where we're meant to be.

I start to move and can't look away from her as she stares back at me. I see every feeling in her expression: when it's good, when it's *too* good, and when it feels to her exactly how it feels to me. We're entirely in sync. It's like nothing I've ever experienced before.

It's as if my insides are being tightened with every move and thrust. Everything's intensifying. Every one of my senses is growing more powerful.

She sweeps her fingers over my face, pressing her thumb over my lips. I have to have more. I dip and kiss her, craving more connection when I already have more than I've ever experienced.

Our kisses grow fractured and desperate, punctuated by groans and cries. I feel so raw, like Eira has cracked me open and seen to the very heart of me.

I'm not going to last much longer. "Eira," I groan. "Eira."

She doesn't answer. Can't answer. She vibrates underneath me. Maybe I'm shaking too. We're both so connected, I can't tell where I end and she begins.

A roll of thunder echoes in my ears and I'm so close, so desperately close—and then Eira breaks apart under me just as the thunder claps through our bodies, a low, guttural grumble that envelopes us both.

It feels like I've just finished a marathon.

It might be hours later, but Eira's fingers tracing circles on my skin bring me back to consciousness.

I roll to the side, bringing her with me.

"So," she says, pressing her palm against my chest.

"So," I say.

"That was...interesting."

I can't read her expression. She's looking at me like she's looking for explanations. But I'm out.

"*Interesting* isn't how I'd put it."

"Oh yeah?" she asks. "How exactly would you describe that?"

I laugh. "You're looking for me to describe the most incredible, connected, world-tilting sex of my life?"

She smiles a timid grin and wrinkles her nose. She's so fucking sexy, if I had any feeling in my legs, I'd have her again. "Wasn't just me who felt that then?"

I let out a breath. "Nope."

We lie there for a few more minutes in contented silence, thinking about everything and nothing, before she shifts beside me, sitting up. I open my eyes and the sway of her breasts has me hardening again. There's no way I'm going to be able to get enough of this woman.

"Can I try something?"

"Everything," I say.

She smiles. "I mean, I've always wanted to..." She glances down at my cock.

"You have my permission to do everything you want, as long as it doesn't hurt." I'm harder than steel now, despite my orgasm still echoing in my ears.

She straddles my legs, and my eyes widen. "We need a condom."

She shakes her head. "You said anything. I just want to...just quickly."

I'm not quite sure what's she's getting at, but if this goes how it looks like it's going, I'll flip her over to her back and get a condom on so fast, she won't have time to complain.

Slowly, she lowers herself onto me, so she's right up to the hilt. Her eyes flutter closed and she stills. I'm just about to flip her over when she slides off me and shifts so she's eye level with my dick.

She takes my crown in her mouth and it's all I can do not to explode when she meets my eyes.

She's so unexpected in every way.

"That's what you wanted to try?" I ask. "You wanted to taste yourself?"

Her mouth leaves my dick with a pop and she nods her head. "I wanted to taste me on you."

I groan and pound the mattress with my fist.

So.

Fucking.

Sexy.

I expect her to stop now that she's completed her experiment. But she doesn't. Instead, she takes me deep, deep, deep in her throat, and pulls back so slowly, I don't have breath in my body by the time she's done.

"Eira," I call out, as she continues to lick and suck and the sounds—I try not to breathe in case I miss any of them. I need to repaint every room in this house the color of her reddened lips, it's so fucking perfect. The way every now and then she shifts and her breasts jut forward as if they're asking for attention. In that moment, I realize, I won't ever have enough of her. I'm insatiable for her.

She meets my gaze and I can't help but thrust my hips off the bed, needing more of her, getting deeper into her mouth. Eira moans like that's just what she wanted me to do.

I'm gone.

I cry out, wanting to warn her that I'm coming, but she just takes me deeper. I'm lost, out of control, completely powerless.

My orgasm hits me like a baseball bat to the chest.

I don't know when I'm next conscious. An hour might have passed. It could be a week. All I know is that when I come round, Eira is tucked into my chest and our legs are wrapped around each other's. Her skin is so soft and warm and it feels like home. Like I've known her my entire life and have just been waiting for her to reappear.

I tighten my grip, slide my hand over her hip and she shifts, sleepily, pressing a kiss into my shoulder.

Fuck, I'm getting hard again.

She smiles against my skin. "I'm so tired," she says. "But I want you again."

She turns in my arms, so she's facing away from me and shifts, her bottom grazing my erection.

Thank fuck.

I grab a condom and position myself behind her, both of us on our sides. I wrap my arms around her and close my eyes, sliding home.

I could stay like this forever. Fucking, sleeping, kissing... being. With Eira.

TWENTY-FIVE

Eira

It's just before seven but I've been awake for the last hour and a half. I've showered, and even washed and blow-dried my hair. I've put on makeup. Not to impress Dax. Absolutely not. I was just awake and...I don't normally get the time.

Everyone who graduates from Portland gets a pin alongside their certificate. It's a sky-blue porcelain and gold metal 'P' lapel pin. I don't normally wear mine, but I treasure it. I keep it in a trinket box my first nanny gave me when she left when I was six years old, alongside a dried-up Play-Doh bee my first charge made for me for my birthday, a photograph of me holding Eddie when she was born, and another of me and Dylan when he graduated. My most treasured items in the world.

Today I've put the pin on. I don't know if it's armor. Maybe I need to remind myself it's just another workday. There's nothing to see. I'm just a nanny looking after a newborn. Please move along and get on with your day.

Guinevere needs me. She's recovering and I'm going to be entirely focused on her, the youngest Cove of the clan.

I'm a nanny. Not Dax's lover, despite what the last twenty-four hours have brought. I don't know how things will feel between us today. I'd planned to scratch the itch and move on, as if being with him for the night would be like defrosting the windscreen of my car and then being able to continue my journey.

But as he pressed a kiss to my forehead and headed back to his room and Guinevere, I knew it wasn't going to be that simple. Dax Cove is more than an itch that needs scratching.

I head out to the kitchen and start to make up a bottle. Just as I'm screwing on the cap, Dax appears in the doorway, Guinevere a bundle in his bare arms, held closely to that rock-hard chest of his.

"Hey," I say. Despite trying my best to sound breezy, my voice sounds forced and awkward to my own ears. I feel fifteen years old.

"Good morning." His voice is gravelly and it sends a shiver across my skin.

"How did she sleep?" I ask.

"What are you doing up?" he asks, closing one eye and pushing his hands through his hair. I look away from the expanse of skin he exposes.

I glance at the clock over the door. "It's seven. What do you mean?"

"I thought you'd want a lie in," he says. "We were up late and it's your day off."

I freeze. Dax Cove has scrambled my brain so much, I've lost track of the days of the week. It's Saturday.

He chuckles. "You've lost track of the days?" he asks.

"Committed to checking on Guinevere," I say, my eyes wide, my smile about to erupt. "I did her bottle."

"Thanks." He takes it from me. Our fingers brush and our gazes lock.

"How did you sleep?" he asks as he takes a seat at the kitchen table. He has a muslin over his shoulder already. He's come prepared. "It was late when we went to bed."

I exhale and turn to the coffee machine, trying to hide my blush. Some of the things he did to me last night—well, I'm not sure which bits were legal. "It was. You want coffee?"

"I really do," he says, then, with his leg, he pushes out the chair next to him. "Then come and sit. Unless you want to go back to bed."

My eyes widen, but I'm facing away so he doesn't see. Yes, I want to go back to bed. With him. But I know that's not what he means.

I take a deep breath and scan the kitchen, looking for something to put away or clean. A red flash catches my attention and I look more closely. It's the red ribbons of the Christmas decorations I made of Guinevere's hand-and-footprints. He's hung them up on the pin where he usually hangs his keys, and his keys are on the counter below. I can't help but think it's a real shift for Dax, and I smile.

"What are your plans for today?" he asks. "We're going to head to the park if you want to join us."

I do. But I shouldn't.

Last night was a one-off, right? I'm still trying to keep my job. If we draw a line now, there's a chance that can happen.

"I have some unpacking and organizing to do."

He chuckles. "I bet you do. You have a lot of stuff."

Not really, I think. I'm nearly thirty, just a couple of

years younger than Dax, and he has things to fill a three-bedroom flat. What do I have? Enough to fill one room.

"That's why it needs to be organized."

"You think it's okay to take Guinevere out? It's still cold."

"Fresh air is good for her. You don't need to isolate her now you've had the diagnosis of viral meningitis."

"Right," he says.

"Am I teaching my grandmother to suck eggs?" I ask.

He laughs. "I think I've forgotten everything from my medical training. It's like my brain has wiped entire sections of my hippocampus clean to make room for other stuff."

"For your research?" I ask, sliding his coffee onto the table.

"Thanks. For the coffee. And yeah. There are a lot of moving parts. I had my first breakthrough at the beginning of my career because I saw some results in my research that connected with some results from some things being investigated by another team and...I don't want to bore you—"

"You're not boring me," I say. "You don't talk about your work a lot."

"My family shut me down often enough that I've learned not to share."

"You don't think they're supportive."

"They are," he says. "But I don't practice clinical medicine, which sets me apart from Jacob and Beau and my parents. We don't...I guess we don't get excited by the same things."

"They love you," I say.

"I know." He's completely sure in his tone, entirely secure in his parents' love for him. I can't help but envy him that. "But we're different. Did you feel the same with your parents? Did they get you?"

"They didn't know me," I say. "We were...almost like cars in the drive. Just something in their lives. Our nannies raised us. The cook fed us. The housekeeper paid the schools fees and..." I shrug. "When I look back at my childhood, it's not my parents I remember."

"Wow." He glances at Guinevere and then back at me. He's piecing the puzzle together. "And now you're a nanny, putting your sister through university. And you can't sue your uncle who took your inheritance. How come?"

"We're trying to take him to court, but it takes a long time and a lot of money, and we don't have a lot."

"Shit, that...that's awful. People are awful."

"I have to look on the bright side. I earn relatively good money. I can put Eddie and Dylan through university. So... things could be worse."

He fixes me with a stare. "You're amazing."

It's like I can feel his body pressed up against mine. I look away.

"I'm anything but." I cross my arms, trying desperately to keep him out. "You seem to be managing with Guinevere." I nod at the pair of them. He looks like an expert, holding her, the bottle perfectly positioned. He looks like he's an enthusiastic father of three, not a reluctant father of one.

"You're bad at taking compliments. Doesn't mean they're not true." He grins at me like he knows how easily he gets under my skin. "And yeah, she's...does it sound weird to say I feel like I know her better now?"

I can't hold back my smile. "It doesn't sound weird at all. It sounds completely normal. She's a tiny human with her own personality. Her own likes and dislikes—even at this age. It takes a while to figure each other out."

"My brothers must have felt the same when I was born

—that they had to get to know me." He picks up his mug and takes a sip of coffee.

"Probably. I remember feeling such love when Dylan and Eddie were born. They were everything. I loved them, I worried about them, I wanted everything to be good for them."

"And your role model for a caring, nurturing person was your nanny. So that's who you became."

I've never thought about it, but of course that's what happened.

"I suppose," I say. "My parents never expected me to work. They saw Portland as a kind of finishing school for me. As long as it kept me busy and I didn't ask them for anything, they were happy. Like I say, they didn't take much of an interest."

"How did you feel when they died?"

I pause. I don't think anyone has ever asked me that question. People just assume you're upset when you lose a parent, and losing two? Well, how could I be anything but devastated? "Vaguely disappointed. I think there was a part of me that thought that one day things might be different between us." A heaviness sits on my chest. I still wish things could have been different, that I could have missed them more.

"I can't imagine what that must have been like. I was lucky, I suppose," Dax says. "My parents were always busy and they were always coming and going and life was crazy. We had help—someone who'd look after us after school. And there were times when Dad couldn't come to my school play and Mum never came to my football practice because she always had something on. But I never doubted my parents' love. I never thought of myself as an add-on or an accoutrement to their world."

"You're right," I say. "You were—you are—very lucky."

He glances down at Guinevere. "I've never felt responsible for anyone in my life. I don't know if it's because I'm the youngest or I never had a pet or something. Maybe my brothers felt responsible for me. Until Guinevere, I never felt this intense weight that I have a human to care for."

I nod, understanding that feeling far too well.

"Jacob came round to check on you and your daughter last night, without you asking him to," I say with a smile. "He loves you and I'm sure feels that sense of responsibility as the older sibling."

"Yeah, I suppose I've labeled Jacob as bossy and interfering. Maybe I've been a little harsh with him over the years."

My heart swells in my chest as Dax shifts the pieces of his history around to make a slightly different picture—one where his brother loves and cares about him, doesn't just bait him. One where he loves his daughter.

"Are you all done?" Dax asks Guinevere in a singsong voice I've not heard him use before. "Shall we have a little burp before we go out?" He lifts her and puts her over his shoulder. Her body is all sleepy and floppy, like it normally is after her morning milk. It melts me to see them together like this. So in-tune.

Dax is falling in love with his daughter.

"I had a great time with you last night," Dax says, his head tilted towards Guinevere.

"Yeah," I say, flustered and not quite sure what the correct response is.

He laughs so heartily, he has to hold Guinevere so she doesn't fall off his shoulder. "What does 'yeah' mean?"

"It means I haven't quite figured out how to feel."

He nods. "Fair enough. Just so you know, I *have* figured

out how to feel, and I had a great time and I want..." He hesitates and glances away before saying, "More."

What does that mean?

"No, that wasn't clear," he adds, as if he wants to press the delete key and start again. "I want to hang out more, talk to you more, listen to you talk about...everything. Kiss you more...and..." He shrugs. "I'm not expecting any of that, but I want you to know where I am. In terms of you, I want more. In every sense."

So much for one night to scratch an itch.

"Good to know," I reply, pressing my eyes closed and wrinkling my nose so a smile doesn't erupt on my face. I can't tell him that I want more too. Because if I do then... what? I play house with my employer? It doesn't make sense.

He laughs again and this time he wakes Guinevere.

"I think someone did a poo in her nappy. Shall Daddy change you?"

Dax stands and before he leaves, bends and presses a kiss to the top of my head.

TWENTY-SIX

Eira

I pull out a wedge of paperbacks from the final box and stack them on my windowsill. I've just finished unpacking my room, but with every item slotted into its place, my confidence that I'll be here—in this job, in this house—in a month has waned. I'm only a few weeks into the position and I've gotten myself into such a tangle, but at the moment, I can't regret it.

My phone rings and I smile. I bet that's Dax.

But it's not. It's Felicity from the agency.

She doesn't even say hello. "I have the most incredible opportunity," she blurts.

"Hi, Felicity."

She ignores my attempt at politeness. "It's the Lebedev family. They want you. Of course, if you're happy where you are, I wouldn't steal you. You know that's not me. But I wouldn't be looking out for the interests of one of our best nannies if I didn't bring you the opportunity."

"The Lebedevs?" My stomach clenches and I tense.

Everyone wants to work with them. The pay is phenomenal. It's a legendary position. When I first started at Portland and heard about the perks of the job and the salary, I never thought I'd ever have a chance to work for them. "How do they even know about me?"

"No one knows how they hear about nannies. They came to me with a few names, but you were top of their list. I told them I'd just placed you, but they begged me to put the offer forward to you."

I never would have considered the job previously, since the role requires months of international travel. When Eddie and Dylan were young, there was no way I was prepared to do that.

But now?

"The package is incredible," Felicity says.

"But I only just started working here." I know the current situation isn't sustainable. I've slept with my boss—it's not like I don't know things here are going to end badly. Either I'm going to end up fired or I'm going to quit. It's just a question of time.

"The Lebedevs are prepared to reimburse the family of the nanny they pick for all recruitment costs."

Money really is no object for them.

"Can I send you the job description?" Felicity asks. "And details of salary and benefits?"

I stare at the books I've just stacked on my windowsill. "Let me think about it."

"What's there to think about?" she asks. "You're not committing to anything by looking at a job description."

The problem is that if I find out exactly what's on offer, the decision might be made for me. I've always tried to strike a balance between salary offered and how much I'll enjoy the job, but because of Eddie and Dylan, salary normally outweighs everything else. If I see the salary for the Lebedevs, I'm pretty sure I'll take it. Old habits die hard, and even with Eddie's scholarship as a buffer, there are always rainy days ahead.

"Give me twenty-four hours," I say.

I can practically hear Felicity's eye roll. "Don't keep them waiting too long. This is a once-in-a-lifetime opportunity."

I thank her and hang up. Almost immediately I get a message. Felicity is nothing if not persistent.

But it's not Felicity. It's a picture of Dax and Guinevere. She's sleeping, so clearly having a great time. It's captioned, "We miss you. Come join us in the park!"

I glance around my room. Well, I *have* finished unpacking. And it is my day off. I can do anything I like, right? Especially when I know there's another job waiting for me.

In less than ten minutes, I'm at the gates of Coram's Fields. Just as I'm about to open the gate, I spot someone familiar sitting on the bench opposite the entrance.

It's Doreen. Guinevere's first nanny. The woman who collapsed in the park.

I let go of the gate and walk over to her. "Hi, I'm Eira. We met here a couple of weeks ago."

It takes a couple of seconds for her to recognize me. "Oh, yes dear. You were very kind to me. Thank you so much."

"I see you've got some color back," I say. "How are you feeling?"

I can see her attempt a smile, but it doesn't quite work. "I'm okay. Just watching all the children come in and out. This is my favorite park and I won't be able to come here any longer." She sighs and her entire body sinks lower into the bench.

I take a seat next to her, looking through the iron railings into the park.

"I'm officially retired," she says. "No more playgrounds for me." She pats me on the hand. "I wasn't as lucky as you. Couldn't have my own children. That's why I became a nanny."

"I'm so sorry." I don't correct her and tell her the little boy I was with at the park wasn't mine.

"I thought it would be enough. But it never is. Your charge is never yours, you see. You always have to give them back." She shakes her head. "In the end, we nannies end up alone."

My scarf seems to pull a little tighter around my neck. I pull at the length of fabric but the feeling doesn't lessen. "I know nannies who have children," I say. I've never thought about my life so far in the future to consider having my own children. I'm so focused on getting through the present, trying to make sure Dylan and Eddie are happy, that I don't think about the future.

But soon, they won't need me.

Then what?

She nods. "The lucky ones."

I spot Dax pushing Guinevere's pram over to the edge of the football pitch. There's a game going on. Oh gosh, is he meant to be playing?

I should go and offer to watch Guinevere.

I turn back to Doreen. "Can I do anything to help? Do you need anything?"

She pats me on the hand again. "You run along," she says. "Live your life, my dear. Live your life."

Her words stick like a thorn in my chest.

"Why don't you come with me?" I suggest. "We can go inside and if anyone questions us, we'll just say you're with me—with us." The last word feels stuck, as if it doesn't belong. Guinevere, Dax and I aren't an *us*. I'm a *me*. They're an *us*. Nothing's going to change that.

I'm always going to be on the outside looking in.

"You're very sweet. But I'm going to stay here," she says.

I stand but pause, wondering what I can do to make things better for her.

I type out a text to Felicity, asking her to send me the job description for the Lebedev family when it comes through.

TWENTY-SEVEN

Dax

I look up and see her straight away. Her hair streams behind her as she heads in our direction like some kind of goddess, her hands stuffed in her pockets, her smile lighting up the dreary sky. She looks even more gorgeous than usual. Maybe I'm playing with fire, but I can't wait for tonight, when Guinevere's in bed and it's just the two of us. Again.

"Here comes Eira," I say to Guinevere.

"Hey," she says as she approaches. "Are you having fun?" She seems lighter than before in the kitchen.

"Better now that you're here," I reply. I lean forward and place a kiss on her cheek. A blush spreads from where my lips were and I chuckle at how...demure she seems. Today. Not so much last night. "Shall we get a coffee?"

She nods, glancing at me from under her lashes as she burrows into her coat.

"Did you get your room unpacked?" I ask as we make our way down the steps to the coffee shop within the park.

"Pretty much. All the boxes are done."

We order our coffees and head to a table by the window. Given she's just finished unpacking, she's not going to like what I'm about to say. "Well, you might be repacking them in a couple of weeks."

Her face goes as white as snow and her mouth drops open.

"My mum and Jacob keep talking about me moving. And I've said I'll think about it."

Her chest rises as she takes a breath and the color returns to her cheeks. "Oh, I see. Moving house." She laughs. "They may be little, but babies take up a lot of room. You've been through quite the transition in the short time I've known you."

"I guess so." She's right of course. I started off thinking Guinevere would just be an additional obligation, but she's burrowed into my heart. Talking to Eira about her family and her relationship with her parents, I can't imagine what kind of man I would be to turn over the entirety of raising my kid to a nanny, like I'd planned to do when I first found out about Guinevere. That's not how I was raised, and that's not how I'm going to raise my daughter. Like Eira said, maybe having a child can add to what I bring to the world, rather than take away from it.

Our names are called and Eira goes to get our coffees while I prepare Guinevere's bottle.

"My brother sent me a listing for the house for sale on his street. It's in Hampstead. Would you be prepared to live there?"

"In the house? I've not seen it. I'm sure it's fine. Are you planning on doing renovations?"

"I meant Hampstead, but you could come to see the house with me, too. I'm trying to make an appointment for later today." Guinevere begins to stir. "You think she smelled the milk?" I ask.

"That, or you're preparing the milk right around the time she's due for a feed."

I roll my eyes, smiling. "You're so logical, Eira." It's an accusation I've had leveled at me more times than I can count. The thing is, being a father makes me see the benefits of the illogical—staring at someone sleeping, loving someone who's only existed a few weeks, making deals with God.

Taking Guinevere from her pram, I tuck her into my arm like I'm now used to doing when my phone rings. I can see my phone on the table. It's the estate agent.

"You want me to take her?" Eira asks, standing, ready to take her before I've even said yes. That's what Eira does—positions herself to fix a problem before it becomes a problem.

When Guinevere is safely in Eira's arms, I swipe the phone open. I arrange to see the property in thirty minutes.

"You think she'll be safe in the back of a cab?" I ask.

"I think plenty of people take their babies in prams in the back of a cab."

That wasn't the answer to the question I was asking. "We should drive and Guinevere can go in her car seat," I say.

Eira's grin is unmistakable.

"I'll call the agent back."

By the time we pull up outside Jacob's house, it's an hour and a half later.

"They're tiny little things, but they really do change the way you live," I say.

Eira nods. "It's a huge transition having another life in your hands. But you seem to be adjusting."

"Yeah," I say. "I am." I open the car door and stare at the

house opposite Jacob's. Unlike his, the one I'm going to view today is modern.

"You said Jacob lives on this street?" Eira asks.

I nod toward his place. "Yeah, over there. And we're going to see this place." I stare up at the red and cream building. "We really are directly opposite. I can't exactly see in his windows, but if I got a telescope…"

"Guinevere would grow up right across from her cousins. That would be nice. Is it far for you to commute?" she asks.

So practical. My commute was the first thing I figured out when Jacob sent the link to the house.

"It's a five-minute walk to the tube station and an eight-minute tube journey."

"So twenty minutes if you factor in waiting times. Maybe a bit more because you have to get to UCH."

"Right. Which is about what it takes now, except I walk the entire way." I hadn't quite figured out that my commute time wouldn't change, but Eira's beautiful brain got there almost immediately. "This would give Guinevere a garden. And like you say, we'd be closer to Jacob and Sutton."

"It's a garden flat?" she asks. "Nice. Shall I stay here with Guinevere?" she asks.

"Absolutely not. I need your opinion. I like the way you think. You're logical, but you have more understanding of what children need than I do." I set about getting Guinevere's car seat out and ferrying her up the steps.

"Happy to help."

I catch Eira's eye and smile. That should be her motto. "Happy to help." I wonder if anyone ever helps her.

The agent meets us at the door.

"I'm Muriel," she says as we introduce ourselves. "Let's start in the basement. We can see the pool and the screening room. There's also a downstairs bedroom. Perfect as an in-law or nanny suite."

I don't look at Eira, but I can feel her gaze on me. She's probably wondering if we're in the right place. This house is probably ten times the square footage of my place in Marylebone.

"The developer had planned to keep this property for himself and his family, so he's really thought of everything. No expense has been spared on materials and finishes."

"But no one's ever lived here?" Eira asks.

The pool is a good size, and I can imagine Guinevere making a lot of use out of it as she gets older. Maybe I could take her for a dip even now, so she'll grow up without any fear of the water.

"No, he's found a new project he wants to invest in and needs the cash," Muriel says.

I like the idea of being the first person in this place. The first family to create memories here.

"Screening room is in here," Muriel says. I don't know if she catches the disinterest in my expression, but she quickly adds, "Great for sleepovers as they get older. And here's the bedroom. I don't know if you have a live-in nanny or housekeeper?"

I don't respond as I give the room a cursory glance.

"This is lovely," Eira says, stepping farther into the room. "It's big and has a window. And because you have the butler's pantry, it's like a little flat down here."

She seems excited, which is...uncomfortable.

It's hard to think of Eira as staff. She's more than that. Without her, I wouldn't have a clue what I'm doing with Guinevere. But it's not just the practical stuff she's helped me with; I swear, if it hadn't been for Eira, I'm not sure Guinevere and I would have the bond we do. I'm not sure I would be quite as much in love with my daughter as I am. Eira's encouraged that, nurturing the two of us—me and Guinevere—as a unit. I'm not sure anyone else would have managed the feat in such a short time, or ever.

I reach out to her and slide my hand up her back. I want her to know she's more to me than staff. And it's not just about the sex. I care about her.

"Let's take the lift to the top floor and then work our way down," Muriel says.

There are six bedrooms with views across London, and the living areas are bright and spacious. It feels like a family house—the kind of place I always imagined my brothers living in. I never saw my life unfolding the same way, but lately I've been realizing a lot of what I envisioned for myself is part of a future that no longer exists.

I'm not mad about it.

I could set up a real office here. Maybe even work from home a day a week. The garden is beautiful, the pool is a bonus. Even the proximity to Jacob doesn't put me off.

It's perfect. I think. But I don't know what children need as they grow.

"Do you have anything to sell?" Muriel asks as we come to the end of our tour.

"No," I say. "You say the developer wants the cash to invest in something else. Does that mean he's looking for a quick sale?"

"He's definitely open to offers."

I nod and glance at Eira.

"I'll leave you for a few minutes to discuss things," Muriel says. When I look up, she's gone.

"What do you think?" I ask.

She lifts her shoulders. "It's a lot bigger than what you have now."

I laugh. "That's for sure."

"The garden and pool are wonderful. And the staff room is really nice—natural light, its own bathroom and a kitchen down there too. Not that this is about me, but it's really nice and I'd be happy to..." She trails off, making a vague gesture that encompasses the house, Hampstead, maybe all of the UK.

I didn't ask her opinion on the staff bedroom, but she's clearly picturing herself there. And right at this moment, I don't have an alternative proposal. I inwardly cringe at the awkwardness of loose ends and unanswered questions. All that—and room configurations—can wait. The need for a family home, a place Guinevere can grow up in, surrounded by people who love her, can't.

"Muriel?" I call. As she approaches, I say, "I can offer seven percent under asking price. Cash. I can sign as fast as the lawyers can make it happen."

Muriel's eyebrows hit the high ceilings. "I'll certainly present the offer to my client."

"It's open until close of business today," I say. "You've got my number."

With Guinevere safely strapped into the back of the car, Eira and I get in the front. The car doors close and Eira turns to me.

"You like the house then?"

I laugh. "It works."

"And you made a decision just like that," she says, snapping her fingers. Then she waves her hand in front of herself like it's a fan.

"Oh, you like that?" I chuckle and reach across the center console to slide my hand over her thigh. "When I want something, I want something."

"It's like your heart and your head came together and made the decision. It's...attractive."

"You're attractive," I counter.

She pushes her lips together as if she's afraid she'll say something she shouldn't.

She doesn't get it yet. I want to hear every last thought she has. *Today and every day,* whispers a voice in my head. I don't speak the words aloud—just put the car in drive and go.

TWENTY-EIGHT

Eira

Maybe I'm imagining it, but it feels like the air is vibrating between Dax and me. I've abandoned all hope of being able to have sex with him and then just get over whatever was brewing between us. Especially when he says he wants more, which opens me up to the possibility that we might be able to have...*something*.

He's an itch I want to keep scratching.

In the meantime, I'm putting together a cheeseboard to try to satiate our appetite for food.

He appears at the entryway to the kitchen, his hair tousled like he's on a modeling assignment, but I know it's because he's been snuggling with his daughter.

It's like a dam bursts inside me and the blood in my veins starts to race around my body, finally free.

"I had a great day with you today," he says. I pause to make sure I heard him right. When I realize I heard him perfectly, I want to melt right into him.

Instead I turn back to preparing the cheeseboard. "I'm

not sure I added much." I try not to meet his eye because if I do, I swear he'll be able to read every thought. I'm doing my best to live in the moment and not start panicking about the future. "Your mind was pretty set on that house. What convinced you?"

He approaches me and it feels like time slows, every movement protracted. My skin tightens with every centimeter he gains on me, and I have to work to keep my breathing steady. He slides his arms around my waist, his front pressed to my back, his head burrowed in my neck, breathing me in.

"It solves a lot of practical problems. The space, the garden, the pool, the proximity to Jacob, the commute. And..." He pauses and presses a kiss to the top of my shoulder. "I could imagine a life there," he says.

I lean my head to one side, giving him easier access. "Your head and your heart are in alignment," I say, then immediately wish I'd kept it as an inside thought. I don't want to start talking about hearts and feelings.

"Yeah," he says, pressing kisses up my neck, his hands dipping lower. "I think you're right. Normally I try and keep my heart out of life decisions but it doesn't feel right since...Guinevere."

I turn in his arms to face him. "She's softening you."

He smooths his lips across mine. "She is. You too."

My heart throbs in my chest.

He slides his hand down, down, down and presses his fingers on the denim between my thighs. I feel like I'm on fire, his fingers trailing heat wherever he touches me.

He groans, and I bite down on my lip to stop the sounds I want to make from ripping out of my body. The way he wants me...it's intoxicating.

"I've been waiting for you all day," he says. "I've been waiting to do all the things I want to do to you."

A small smile forms on my lips. "I think you may have done them all last night."

Slowly, he shakes his head. A ribbon of longing tugs deep inside of me.

He slides his fingers into the waistband of my jeans, unbuttoning and unzipping and unpeeling. He lifts my legs one at a time to remove my jeans. He's kneeling at my feet as he tugs at my underwear. "These are...cute."

I groan in embarrassment. I'm wearing the light pink knickers with hearts all over them that Eddie bought me for Christmas. Hot underwear isn't high on my shopping list. I go for comfy, or in this case, available. "I wasn't planning on you seeing them."

He slides his fingers under the elastic and my embarrassment disintegrates. All I can focus on are the sparks I feel whenever he touches me. "Hmm, what's this? Looks like you might have been having some very dirty thoughts," he says. "You're all wet down here."

"I don't think that's my fault," I say, gripping the edge of the kitchen counter.

"Oh yeah?" he asks. "Did I do that to you?"

He gets to his feet and holds my gaze as he slides his hand down the front of my knickers. "Did I do this?" His fingers find my folds and he laughs. "Fuck, Eira. You're so wet."

My breaths are short. If I wasn't holding myself up, my knees would have buckled by now.

He removes his fingers and brings them up, brushing them over my lips, painting my mouth. I'm sure I'm completely crimson. Then he slides his hand back between my thighs as he licks my wetness from my lips.

He groans. "You taste so fucking good. Sweet and sexy. I want it all." His lips are back on mine, his tongue sliding into my mouth, searching for more as his fingers work faster and faster.

I gasp against his mouth as my pleasure mounts. I can barely breathe. He's making me feel...so much all at once.

If he doesn't stop, I'm going to come.

"Fuck," he says, pulling back from our kiss. "You feel fucking divine. I want all of your wetness wrapped around my cock."

In less than a second, he pulls his t-shirt off and kicks off his jeans. His cock is flat against his stomach, and I can't keep my eyes off it as it strains and bucks.

"Hold it," he says. "Coat it. In you."

I scan his face, looking for more direction, but he looks at me like I'm about to make all his dreams come true.

He steps forward and I pull in a breath. I reach down into my panties. I gasp at how wet I am. I'm not sure it's even normal. I bring my hand to his cock and slide it over his length.

He growls as I touch him. "I'm fucking shimmering with you."

Gaining confidence, I take him at the root and then with the other hand, guide his crown to my clit. My head falls back as the two connect and my skin scatters with goose bumps. All I can think of is him being inside me, stretching me, pulling all that feeling from me. But he wants something else first. A tease. A show.

I slide my knickers down a little so he can see my pussy, but only far enough to suggest I could pull them up at any moment and go back to my cheeseboard. It feels forbidden and dirty and oh so sexy.

I stand on tiptoes as I press his tip down so it slides

between my thighs and the cotton of my underwear. He's not going inside. Not from this angle. But I can get him almost as wet like this.

"Fuck, Eira."

I make a fist around him and he pushes into it, hitting my clit as he does, feeling my folds take his crown. He pulls back and slams against me again.

"Jesus, I think I'm close," he gasps.

I don't even know where the condoms are. I didn't expect to be at this point so quickly.

He pulls out and leans against me, pinning me to the kitchen counter, panting in my ear. I start to bring my hands to his chest.

"Don't move or I'll come," he says softly.

Finally he steps away.

"Jesus. It's like I'm sixteen and can't keep it together when I'm with you," he says.

I can't help but blush. A man who looks like Dax is bound to have a lot of sex in his lifetime. The fact that I can cause him to become so unraveled so quickly is a badge I'll wear with pride.

"It's the same for me," I say, doing my best to not breathe so I don't make him climax.

"Those fucking knickers."

I look down and then hook my thumbs through the sides and pull them up. The light pink has turned magenta.

Dax's growl gets my attention and as I look up, he's opening the condom packet. I hook my thumbs back into the sides of my underwear but he stops me.

"Leave them on." He lifts me onto the counter, rolls on the condom and before I can ask him if I'm sitting on the cheeseboard, he pulls my underwear to the side and plows into me like the world is about to end and I'm the last thing he's ever going to feel.

"Fuck, Eira," he hisses through his teeth.

I'm clinging onto consciousness, fighting every urge I have to cry out. Partly because I don't want to wake Guinevere and also because I don't know if I could put myself back together if I let myself feel everything right now. I may not be able to go back to being the old me if I allow Dax to take me over so completely.

My skin vibrates from my fingertips to my clit, but maybe it's not me. It could be that the entire world is shaking right now. Maybe we're in the middle of an earthquake and I'm just assuming it's down to the great sex. He pushes his hands over mine where they're gripping the counter and circles my wrists, pinning me in place. Keeping me in this exact spot because it feels so good. He slams into me again and again and again as he mutters a string of profanities into my ear.

So fucking sexy. So wet. So very, very tight.

He's so fucking hard and desperate and he's going to split me in two.

He's going to fuck me everywhere, come all over me and I'm going to beg him for more.

If feels so good to make a man like Dax wild. A man who's normally so exacting and logical, become so passionate and undone.

He releases one of my wrists and cups the back of my neck, hard, holding my head in place, not relinquishing his relentless rhythm.

"Look at me," he commands. "I want to watch you come."

I feel my orgasm start to rattle deep inside me as he

speaks, almost like he's coaxing my climax into the open, a charmer to the snake, a tamer to the lion.

"Dax," I choke out.

The vibrations across my entire body intensify, turning into shudders and involuntary shakes as my orgasm rips through me.

"That's right, Eira. Come for me." He pushes in again, his thrusts hard and perfect and *necessary*.

He cries out as I sink into the afterglow of my climax, my muscles contracting around him, milking him of the last of his.

And that's when I hear it.

The alarm on my phone.

"Shit," I say. "Shit, shit." I push him away. "My phone. The alarm. We were supposed to check on Guinevere."

I pull up my underwear and race out of the kitchen to the bedroom.

I get to her cot and Guinevere is sleeping soundly.

Guilt and confusion blanket me.

"She's okay, Eira." Dax appears behind me, puts his hand on my shoulder and hands me my phone.

"Yeah," I say. "She's okay."

How could I have been so distracted by Dax that I wouldn't hear my alarm? Who am I kidding? The house could have been on fire and I don't think I would have noticed. It feels strange to be so consumed by something that isn't about survival—to be so out of control. It feels uneasy.

Dax takes my hand and pulls me out of his bedroom.

"You have a missed call on your phone," he says as we go out into the hall. "From Eddie."

I look down at my phone. It's not just one missed call.

It's seven missed calls. What the actual fuck? I dial her number but she doesn't answer.

Shit. "She needs me," I reply. "I'm such a selfish idiot."

Dax tries to pull me toward him, but I push him away. "Eira, you're allowed to miss a call from your sister. That's not selfish."

I swipe up to see the notifications on my phone. Eddie called an hour ago. Right around the time Dax was kissing me.

I press on her number and the phone rings again. We stand in the corridor, Dax hovering over me like he's concerned I might lose it.

"She's not answering. What happens if something's wrong?"

I look up at him and then straight back down to my phone. I don't want to see the concern in his eyes.

"Bad things happen." I hit redial but I'm sent straight to voicemail.

Shit. Shit. Shit. Why won't she answer? She never cancels the call.

A message pings through and I open it quickly like it's the results of my lottery tickets.

Finally having a poo and then going to bed. Let's catch up tomorrow. I think I'm going to get a waitressing job.

"Why does she need a waitressing job?" I ask.

"I'm still focused on the bit where she's announcing her delayed bowel movement. Aside from possible constipation, she sounds completely fine."

He's right. It doesn't sound like she's knee-deep in serious trouble.

"Does she not have enough money?" I ask. I try to remember the last time I actually saw Eddie in person. "I haven't seen her since Christmas."

"Maybe you should visit."

"Yeah," I say. "I think I will. Tonight even." It might be good to get some space from Dax. He's so...consuming. All I see is him when he's around. Being with him is like being in a fantasy land where I don't have to worry about hard things or worries. But I need to keep my feet on the ground.

"Doesn't she live in Exeter?" he asks.

"Right, but—"

"You're not leaving to go to Exeter tonight," Dax says. "There will be no trains until tomorrow anyway. And you need to pack. Go tomorrow."

I nod. "Guinevere. You need to check on her. Through the night," I say.

"I have my alarms set up, Eira. You don't need to worry."

He says it like a person who's never needed to worry. But worrying is my job.

"I need to go to bed." I look up and meet his gaze finally. "Sorry. I'm just—"

He circles his arms around me and this time I let him pull me towards him. I can do nothing but sink into his chest.

"This is not a good idea," I say.

"What? Cuddling? Cuddling is the best idea ever."

I sigh but don't try to move. "You and me doing...the sex."

"Doing the sex?" He chuckles. "Are you having an issue with the English language?"

I shrug. "I'm having issues with everything."

"I can tell."

We stand in silence for a few minutes and I feel my heartbeat slow, my breathing return to normal. "I want to go see my sister," I say finally.

"I can drive you tomorrow."

"I won't let you. It's a five-hour drive and Guinevere needs to be at home."

He pulls me closer and presses a kiss to the top of my head. It feels so good, like this thing between us could be reality.

But it's not. At least, not for long.

TWENTY-NINE

Dax

I swear Guinevere just smiled at me. She kicked her leg and made her bouncer jig by herself for the first time ever, then looked up at me as if to say, "Hey Dad, see what I just did?".

"Are you so clever?" I ask her. "Of course you are. You're a Cove." I step out of the kitchen, the scene of the inaugural bounce, and call out, "Do you want me to get your bags?" I head through the open door into Eira's bedroom to see if she's in there. Her suitcase is standing at the end of the bed, her handbag balanced on top. "I can take it if you want." I go to grab it then wonder how I'm going to take it to the taxi with Guinevere at the same time. It's not like I can leave her in the bouncer.

My foot catches the wheels on the case, toppling the suitcase and upending the bag on top. I bend to scoop it up. Most of the contents have stayed in place because the bag was zipped up, but there's a folded piece of paper that I retrieve from the ground just as Eira comes into the bedroom.

"Oh," she says, taking the paper from me. "I can get the case. It's on wheels anyway." She glances at the piece of paper. "I was going to talk to you about this. I haven't made any decisions but...I have to consider it, given the circumstances."

I narrow my eyes, trying to figure out if I'm supposed to know what she's talking about.

"The circumstances?"

She rubs at her throat like something is lodged there. "You know. This. It's...I need to be looking out for other jobs."

My muscles tense and I glance back at the paper. "That's details of another job? You're leaving?"

She shakes her head. "No!"

Relief floods through me and I start to smile. She's not making any sense.

"Maybe," she amends, and my smile fades. "I don't know. This is complicated."

Is it? She's sweet and sexy and I feel different when I'm around her. More relaxed. More like a better version of myself. There doesn't seem to be anything complicated about that.

"But it doesn't have to be," I say.

"You're my boss," she says. "We live together. I know you just want us to deal with the here and now, but that's difficult for me. I support my family through my job, and if I get fired—"

"I'm not going to fire you."

"There are a thousand different scenarios that could result in this...arrangement not working for one of us. Even if we weren't sleeping together." She pauses, clearing her throat quietly.

I haven't screwed this up. I want her to stay. As Guinevere's nanny, but for me too. I can't imagine my life without Eira in it. It's only been a few weeks, but she fits. With me. With us.

"But even if we weren't, this job," she says, holding up the folded paper, "is a really good opportunity. It's for a Russian oligarch. I have responsibilities. Eddie is..."

"Almost finished university," I add.

"Right. And what if she meets someone in the next couple of years and wants to get married? She doesn't have parents to pay for a wedding."

"What if *you* want to get married?" I fire back before I think about what I'm saying.

She chokes out a laugh. "What? To who exactly?"

"Someone you spend time with and love and who loves you? Do you even have room for that in your life?" I ask. "Is there space for someone to care about you when you're so filled up with caring for everyone else?"

She goes to speak then closes her mouth.

"There are a thousand *what ifs*, Eira. There's always a reason to want more money. But if your sister wants to get married, that costs about a hundred pounds."

"You know what I mean." She sounds defeated. "It would be good to have more of a nest egg."

"For you?" I ask. "Or so you can look after everyone else?"

She blinks up at me.

"You're so good at caring for others. Me and Guinevere. Your brother and sister. But what about you? It would be different if you were going to take this new job because it was something you really wanted. Or you needed the money to set up your own business, go traveling, pursue a passion—or do *anything* for yourself."

"It makes me happy if Eddie and Dylan are happy."

"Of course it does. But it's not your *responsibility* to make them happy. Or it shouldn't be. I want my brothers to be happy, but I don't make career choices based on their happiness."

She fiddles with the handle of her case. "It's different. I'm all they have. They're all I have."

I want to scoop her up and tell her I'll give her the bloody nest egg. I want to make everything all right for her. But I don't want to railroad her into something she doesn't want. She needs to pick for herself. So instead, I just say, "I'm sorry." I can't make her see that she has more than just her brother and sister who care for her. She needs to feel that.

She doesn't respond, but I can tell there's so much she's not saying. "Anyway, I want to go and see Eddie. First she gets this mysterious scholarship. Now she wants to get a waitressing job. Something's off."

"What's off about winning a scholarship? Doesn't that make life easier?"

"Yes, but she didn't seem to know much about it when I asked her. I just want to check it out. Especially now she's got a job? It feels weird to me."

"Maybe she's growing up and wants to be independent. Maybe she doesn't want you making career choices based on her. Maybe—"

"I just want to go see my sister. I'm going to miss the train if I don't leave now."

I nod. "But you're coming back, right?"

She leans her head to the side like she doesn't appreciate the question. A faint flush climbs her cheeks. "Of course I'm coming back. Tomorrow in fact."

"We're still going to miss you," I say. I slip my hand around her waist and she leans into me.

"I'm only going to be gone one night," she says, "but same. Too much."

She's going to miss us, too. It's all the confirmation I need that I'll talk her out of leaving. Somehow. I don't want to lose her.

I press a kiss to the top of her head then release her. "Are you sure we can't take you to the station?" I ask.

"Absolutely not! It's way too much hassle and I can get a cab easily."

"What train are you on tomorrow?"

"I'll be back around eight." She must see something in my gaze, because she adds, "I'm booked on a train that gets in at seven forty-seven."

A knot of tension in my chest eases slightly. She's booked a return. She's not running away.

"Have fun," I say. "Just think about what I said. You need to start putting yourself first."

She forces a smile as if I've just asked her to do the impossible. But I know the only impossible thing is letting her go.

THIRTY

Eira

Sitting on Eddie's bed in her dorm room, I stare at the two mugs she's set on the desk. She's stuck white labels on both of them and written "Stay" on one and "Russians" on the other. She's making me write reasons to take the job from the Lebedev family and reasons to stay in the current job with Dax and Guinevere on strips of paper and put them in the corresponding mug.

But there's a twist—there's always a twist where Eddie's concerned. The only things I'm allowed to write are reasons that directly impact *me*. I'm not allowed to mention her or Dylan.

In return, she has to answer my prying questions honestly.

"I really can't think of anything else," I say. "Maybe I need more pizza." Truthfully, though I've only had one slice, the last thing I want is more pizza. My stomach lurches, not for the first time today. I've never experienced this much anxiety about leaving one of my charges for a short time, but I suppose Guinevere has been poorly. I tamp down the worry and focus on filling mugs.

"I wish I had some kind of equipment that could administer a mild electric shock," Eddie says.

"To stop me from eating the pizza?" I ask.

"To incentivize you to think about yourself more."

I groan. "Don't you start." I grab a slice of the vegetarian special. "Why does pizza always taste better with Coke?"

"A law of the universe. Just like why nannies always hook up with their single-dad bosses."

Something tells me I should never have confessed to Eddie about me and Dax. It was the first thing she asked me when she met me from the station. I've been so discombobulated about it, I told her right away. She was thrilled of course. She doesn't understand the complications it brings.

"The way I see it, these are not the choices I have," I say. "Whatever happens, I'm not going to be able to work for Dax for much longer. He's either going to get bored of me or..." My heart clenches at the thought of being dumped. I'll be devastated. Dax is so much more than gorgeous. He's got so much heart to go with that huge brain of his. He needs it coaxed out of him at times, but it's getting easier.

"Or?" Eddie asks.

I'm not following her. "Or?"

"You said he'll either get bored *or*. What's the 'or'?"

The *or* doesn't really exist. Things between Dax and I will end for whatever reason and then I'll be forced to leave. "There's no *or*."

"How could he ever get bored of you?" Eddie asks. "You're gorgeous and clever and resourceful and thoughtful and notice everything about everyone. And he clearly loves how you look after Guinevere. *Quelle surprise.*"

I wave her away and swallow my pizza, which seems to

drag down my throat like it's covered in nails. I throw the rest of my slice onto the inside lid of the box. I can't face any more. "Okay so he's not bored, but he ends things for whatever reason."

"Maybe he doesn't."

I roll my eyes.

"I'm serious. Maybe he doesn't. Maybe you're it for him and vice versa. Maybe he wants to marry you and have a thousand babies."

That's another reason we'll never work out. Even if we did get serious, I want my own children. Dax didn't want to be a father of one, let alone more.

"Okay, so say we live in Eddie's fantasy world. Dax and I live happily ever after. I'd still have to get myself a new job. I can't be his employee and his...partner."

Eddie fixes me with a look, grabs a slice of pizza and slumps back against the bed. "Maybe you're right. So what then? You still wouldn't take the Russian job because you'd be traveling."

"Right," I say, really trying to think of a solution to this ludicrous puzzle Eddie's created.

"But luckily for me, we don't live in Eddie's fantasy world. So I can take the Russian job." I scribble down *don't live in Eddie's fantasy* and stuff it in the mug.

"That doesn't count."

"It does too. I get to ask you a question now. Did you sleep with someone for money? Is that where the scholarship came from?"

"What?" she screams through her mouthful of half-chewed pizza.

She scoops up the sweetcorn that dropped out of her mouth and pops it back in. I try not to gag, unsure if it's because of the front-row view of Eddie's half-masticated food or because that last mouthful of pizza really didn't go down well.

When she's finished chewing, she says, "I should be furious at you, accusing me of being a prostitute because I got a scholarship, but I can't even be bothered. I just don't know how you jump to the worst-case scenario all the bloody time."

"Oh I don't know either, maybe it's the fact our parents died at the same time in a freak helicopter crash and then our uncle stole all our money."

"I've decided to only refer to him as Cuncle from now on," she says. "Because he's a cunty uncle."

"Good for you," I reply, rubbing my stomach.

"Honestly, if I could sleep with someone for money and get the best part of twenty grand, I'd probably do it."

"Eddie," I say, "*did* you do it?"

"Who's going to pay anyone twenty grand for a roll in the hay? I don't know what the going rate is for sex workers in Exeter, but I'd stake my life on it not reaching five figures, and maybe not even three." She pulls out her phone as if she's going to start researching sex worker salaries.

"A sugar daddy then. A rich older man paying for everything in return for regular...stuff."

"What stuff?" she asks. "Hand jobs or hoovering?"

"What the hell is hoovering?"

Eddie laughs. "As in vacuuming. It's not a sex position. Don't worry—you and Dax aren't missing out."

I can feel my cheeks catch fire. I've never discussed my boyfriends with Eddie, mainly because I haven't had a lot of them. Certainly none I've felt the physical need and mental pull I do with Dax.

"There's no rich man," she says, her smile fading. "Let me get the letter for you. I can tell you're not going to be convinced until you see the university logo."

She comes back with a piece of paper and thrusts it at me. "But what's even more exciting is the waitressing job. I think I'm going to be able to cope without your help. The restaurant is really nice, and I even get a meal when I'm on shift. I'll save even more money." Her eyes are shiny and bright. She looks genuinely excited at the prospect of serving people dinner.

"You need to focus on your studies. There's no point in being at university if you don't come out with a degree at the end."

She scoffs. "I won't be the first ever student to work a restaurant shift once a week. My degree is hardly in jeopardy. Working once a week isn't going to hurt my studies. I'd only be out with mates or in here eating pizza on Saturday nights anyway, so that's the shift I've taken."

"Maybe you need that time to decompress."

She laughs. "I'm twenty. I don't need to decompress. I'm fine."

"You don't need a job. I'm serious. What happens when they ask you to do another shift, and then another? Before you know it, you'll be a full-time waitress."

"If I promise you I won't ever take more than one shift a week, and I'll ditch the job if I feel it's impacting my studies, will that stop you worrying?"

"No." I shift awkwardly, closing the lid of the pizza box. The smell is really pungent. "It might help me stop worrying *so much*. But you've got to promise to be honest with me."

"When have I ever not been honest?" She rolls her eyes just as she finishes the sentence, because she knows what my reply will be. "I was eight years old," she says as if pleading for leniency. "You can't hold *that* against me for the rest of my life." Eddie snuck into my makeup bag when I was sixteen and tried out my brand-new liquid eyeliner. She dropped it all over my cream carpet, then proceeded to tell me and the housekeeper she'd seen the cat coming out of my room "looking guilty".

"What does a guilty cat look like again?" I ask, grinning at her.

"I only wish I'd tried the eyeliner out on him."

"Your lie might have been more convincing if you had."

"Pet makeup," Eddie says, narrowing her eyes and staring ahead. "You think that will ever be a thing?"

I groan. "I hope you don't think about this kind of thing in lectures."

She shrugs. "You say that now, but one of these days, I might hit on an idea with legs. That's what Dad did, right?"

Before they died, I didn't really know what my parents did. I knew it was something in finance. It was only afterwards that I discovered he'd managed funds for high-networth individuals, but in a way that gave them an element of control. Apparently it was revolutionary in its day.

"I guess," I reply.

"A degree's just a starting point. I've gotta keep thinking about what's next."

She's right. A degree isn't the end goal. I want Eddie happy, successful both personally and professionally. Getting to graduation is only a small step in a longer journey. My job as her big sister will never truly be done. That's why I have to maintain a stable career. The money provides me with the tools to help Eddie and Dylan, no matter where life takes them.

"That should really go in the mug," Eddie says.

Have I missed a couple of minutes? What is she talking about?

"*Eddie doesn't need your money.*" She scribbles it down and tosses it across the floor. "Another reason to stay with your sexy single dad."

"So just like that, I don't need to pay for anything for you?"

She shrugs. "Worst case, I can get a loan." She narrows her eyes. "Are you okay? You look a little...sweaty."

"Stop with the compliments. I'm blushing."

"You do look a little red in the face."

I roll my eyes and ignore how she's trying to deflect the conversation. "Owing people money is horrible. Especially if you don't have to. Which you don't."

"Don't you get it?" she asks. "I *want* to be independent. I want to do this on my own. And maybe I'll get myself in the shit, but if I do, I know you'll help me get out—not financially, but just by being there. I'm twenty years old. My uni fees are paid. I have a job. It's important I learn to do things on my own. The circumstances were awful and I'd never wish it on you, but what our...*cuncle* did...well, you've proven that however hard life gets, you can figure it out. That makes you powerful as fuck." She grabs my hand. "I want some of that for me, you know?"

"You want me to leave you in the shit?"

"Financially, I want to start figuring things out on my own. I'll never go through what you did, because you didn't have a safety net. You've given me that gift. But now I'm an adult. I think I should explore what I'm capable of. Frankly, I should have been applying for scholarships left and right, but I haven't because I knew you had it covered. I should have probably had a job by now too. Things are changing now, and that means you don't have to take the job with the Russians."

I can't help but smile at her. I'm so proud. Not just because she's choosing not to take the easy route, but because she's also managing to convince me that *not* making everything easy for her is actually the best thing I can do.

"Oh and by the way, I've spoken to Dylan. He and I are completely aligned. We're not taking your money anymore. We're both adults capable of making our own money. Neither of us wants you putting your life on hold just in case we need something. Not anymore."

"You two are conspiring?" I ask.

She grins like I've just given her the biggest compliment. "I said *aligned*. Not conspired."

It sounds like this is what she really wants. Perhaps it's even what she needs. I've always tried to protect Dylan and Eddie, but maybe there are disadvantages to being forever wrapped in a layer of cotton wool. "Maybe you're right," I say, trying to sound open to the possibility.

"Resilience is the most important thing I can learn."

How can I argue with that?

"Dylan and I don't need your help financially," she says as if she's summing up.

"Well, not now, but what if—"

"Then we'll figure it out. Whatever *it* is. And we'll figure it out together. We've got to stop acting like we're under siege and start living life, Eira. And when I say *we've* got to start living life, I mean *you*. You've taken care of us for so long. It's time for you to focus on yourself for once."

She threads her fingers through mine and leans her head on my shoulder.

"I love you," she says. "And I need you. *Always*. But not financially. Not anymore."

"I love you," I reply. "And I'll always need you, too." More than ever—though I don't say so. Because if Dylan and Eddie don't need me, I won't know who I am and how I fit into the world.

THIRTY-ONE

Eira

Is it me or can I smell vomit? I sniff once, then twice, before a metallic taste on my tongue and a churning in my stomach takes my attention. I reach out for I don't know what. I feel myself being pulled up, up, up. I don't know where I am—I just know I'm about to be sick.

Someone's holding my waist. Big hands. Strong hands. Not Eddie. Is it...? Where am I? "Eddie," I call out. Someone bends me at my waist. More hands on my hair. I wretch, my fingers finding the cold porcelain of a sink.

Everything is white and bright, a sharp contrast to the grainy, disgusting taste in my mouth.

"It's okay," someone says.

But it's not okay. I feel like my insides are on the most terrifying roller coaster ever and I'm standing, naked, having to endure a death-ride inside my own body. Everywhere hurts. Everything churns. I can't remember ever feeling this cold.

"Water," I reply.

Someone holds a cup to my mouth. I try to rinse the foul taste away.

And then black.

I'M VAGUELY aware of a bright light being turned on and then off again. I groan. This is the worst hangover of all time. Where am I? I might remember being bundled into the back of a car. Have I been kidnapped? What's the last thing I remember?

I must be dreaming. Or maybe I fell asleep in front of the TV and this is all a weirdly vivid dream?

"I'm just taking your temperature," a voice that sounds a lot like Dax says.

Yes, definitely dreaming.

"Dream Dax," I say, smiling as I feel the warmth of his fingers on my face. I try to open my eyes, but they seem sealed shut. "You're so dreamy, Dream Dax."

I feel something in my ear. It's cold and hard and hurts deep in my head. "Ow," I cry out.

"Sorry, baby. Just keeping an eye on how hot you are."

"Dax is hot," I say. "Sooo hot. And his bum..." I sigh at the thought of Dax's bum. "And I think he loves his daughter now. Which is..." I bring my bunched fingers to my lips and make a chef's kiss.

Back to black.

I WAKE UP INSIDE AN AVIARY. All I can hear is tweeting. Why on earth did I sleep with birds? I open my eyes and it's bright white and I don't know where I am. Is this a hospital? It's not Eddie's dorm. I start to push myself up on the bed, but arms encourage me back down.

"Just rest."

I turn my head and scream when I come face-to-face with Dax.

He smiles at me like I just kissed him on the mouth. "Hey. She's back."

I glance around and realize I'm back in my room in Dax's flat. Not in Exeter. Not in an aviary. I'm in London.

"What happened?" I shift on the mattress, trying to sit up.

"A vomiting bug?" he suggests. "The flu?" Then he shrugs, like he has no clue.

"Did you actually graduate from medical school?" I ask.

He chuckles, and I almost smile until the movement threatens to split my head in two.

"You need to drink water. You've been out of it for thirty-six hours, but—"

"Wait, how did I get here? I was in Exeter."

He laughs again. "You really don't remember any of that?"

I squint, trying to squeeze the memory from my mind.

"Eddie answered your phone when I called to check the train was on time. I was going to pick you up from the station, since Mum and Dad came over to see Guinevere and could watch her. Eddie explained you were sick. She sounded worried. Said you weren't making sense and she was considering calling an ambulance."

I shake my head. I don't remember any of this.

"I drove down to check on you."

I push up on the mattress, headache be damned. "You drove down? To Exeter? In the middle of the night?"

He holds my arms, encouraging me to lie down. "It wasn't the middle of the night. I was there by ten."

I lie flat on my back. "You drove down to Exeter? I could have got you an emergency nanny—"

Dax growls. "I didn't bring you back so you could work. I brought you back because...you're safe here. It's always best to be at home when you're not feeling well. It's more comfortable."

"You drove ten hours so I could be more comfortable?" I ask, confused and unsure what to make of such a kindness.

"Yes," he says, nodding as if he's working out a complex science question. "I guess I did. I didn't think much about it. I just wanted you to be comfortable. And I knew if you were here, I could make sure you were." He glances at me then looks away, as if I've caught him out doing something he shouldn't. "That, and I didn't want you to use being ill as an excuse to stay away."

I manage a half-laugh that turns into a half-yelp, the pain in my ribs stopping any fully formed expression of feeling. Images from the hours before flood my head, combining with the pain in my ribs. I cover my face with my hands. "I just remembered vomiting."

"But not in the car, thankfully," Dax says, smiling. "You waited until you were back here."

I groan. "Who was here? Who were you with? I remember someone."

"My mum was here in the beginning when you were sick, but only because she refused to leave. I packed her off to Norfolk. Dad too. It's just the three of us here now."

"Where's Guinevere? You can't have me here with a newborn. She'll get—"

"She's fine," he interrupts. "I'm a doctor. I know how to isolate a patient."

"But you're not a stethoscope doctor. You work with test tubes and data and stuff."

He chuckles. "Yup. That sums up my job pretty well. But I have a grasp of the basics. I just about remember how to use a thermometer and make a glass of water. The rest is...hazy." He shakes his head. "I can tell you're better. You're listing all sorts of reasons why you can't be taken care of. Seems like we're back to business as usual."

He pushes a few strands of hair off my face and it strikes me like a cartoon anvil on my foot—I'm not sure anyone has cared for me like this since I was a child.

Dax cares. Really cares.

About me.

But I'm not a child, and Dax is my boss. My boss who gives me butterflies whenever I hear his voice and goose bumps whenever I feel him close. A man who's made me feel more than any man before him. I'm pretty sure he's set the bar so high, no man will ever make me feel more.

It's clear to me what I have to do.

It feels tricky or inappropriate or just plain weird to be having this conversation while I'm lying in bed and he's kneeling at my bedside. I try to sit up.

He laughs. "You're not going anywhere."

I laugh too. "I'm just trying to sit up so we can talk."

"We're talking. I know a little about biology. Our voices work pretty well lying down."

"Wow, really, Doctor?"

He laughs. "Don't with the doctor. You're not strong enough for some of the things I want to do to you when you call me that."

My skin tingles like someone's sweeping feathers across my body. It's the most human I've felt in a while.

"Before I got sick, Eddie and I talked," I say. "For hours."

"What did you talk about?" he asks. "Us?" That one syllable means so much to me.

"Yes. And everything. How helping her might be hurting her. How her not needing my financial support doesn't mean she doesn't need me to be her sister. How she thinks I don't have the life I want—don't even know how to think about getting it."

He doesn't say anything, just nods like he's taking it all in.

"We talked about things I think you already know. About how I'm not going to take the job with the Russians."

He raises his eyebrows but doesn't smile. Just because I'm not choosing that job doesn't mean I'm choosing him. He knows that.

"And we talked a lot about how I feel when I'm with you...how different that is. How it's woken up a part of me I didn't know existed. All these things are mixed up in my mind, like my brain's a giant snow globe. I feel like I need some time for the storm to settle."

"In this analogy, am I Santa?"

I laugh. "You're definitely Santa." I reach for him and trail my fingers across his stubbled jaw. "It's the white beard." He pushes his face toward my fingers like a cat enjoying my attention.

"And what does the snow symbolize?" he asks on a sigh.

"I can't...see properly at the moment. There's too much to figure out. When things thaw, everything's going to be the same but different."

When he finally meets my gaze, I say, "I have to move out." I pause and suck in a shuddering breath. "I can't be your live-in nanny. This has gone too far."

He presses the heels of his hands to his eyes and sighs. "I know."

My chest deflates like a paddling pool at the end of summer. I know I have to go, but part of me wanted him to want me to stay.

"I'm not very good at this stuff," he says. "Fatherhood is...it's changing me. The physical closeness to another human..." He sucks in a breath. "I think it might have unlocked something in me. And then came you, and it's not just physical..."

"No," I agree. "It's not. For me anyway."

"For either of us. I don't take a ten-hour round trip for something that's just physical. My world is shifting. Before Guinevere, life was so simple. I had my work and that always came first. Everything else in my life was...not disposable exactly, but not a priority, either. Life was easy, for the most part. I knew what came first and what I wouldn't compromise." He sucks in a breath and shakes his head. "And now? Now I have all these competing priorities and I don't know how to make them fit together. I know I want Guinevere. And you. But I still want my research. I hope I can have all those things."

I want to promise him that he can have me, but I can't. Because I don't know who I am beyond caring for those I love. "I need to figure stuff out."

"Yeah, I get it. I want you to have the time you need to do just that. But the part of my brain that likes order and logic wants everything resolved."

"Life's not like that," I say. "Nothing's ever resolved. The best advice I can give a new parent is that everything's a phase, but it's advice for us all. Any certainty you had in your life before Guinevere was just an illusion. If it hadn't been, Guinevere would never have come along. We never know what's next."

He smiles at me, smoothing strands of hair off my face. "Of course you're right. And of course you've made me feel better. That's what you do."

But is that *all* I can do? Make others feel better? "I'll help you find a new nanny."

"You'll focus on getting well," he says, his tone warning.

"And then I'll find you another nanny."

"And after that?" he asks.

I pause and the silence thickens, descending like a fog.

"We live in the ambiguity for a little while," I say. "Is that okay?"

"Deep down, do you think we're done?" he asks, still reaching for certainty.

I try to swallow down whatever's stuck in my throat. "I'm not sure we're—"

"I don't want us to be done."

It feels like he just unzipped my heart and climbed inside.

"I don't want us to be done either. But let's figure out if this is about convenience because we live together or—"

"That's not what it is for me," he says.

"Then we'll find our way back to each other. But I need to figure out who I am when I'm not looking after people I care about. When I'm not giving all of myself away. I need the snow to settle."

"I get it," he says, his tone defeated.

"And you know what?" I ask. "This is good for you too. You can figure out how to be a father without me. It will be different with the new nanny. You'll feel more confident to do things your way. That will make you powerful. Or so Eddie tells me."

He gazes at me thoughtfully. "Maybe."

Maybe indeed. At the moment, nothing is definite. I can't see anything clearly at all. I have to trust that whatever happens, I'll be able to deal with it. History tells me that I'll figure it out. I just hope that when I do, Dax will still be here.

THIRTY-TWO

Eira

I carry the last of my boxes into our new rented flat and dump it in the middle of the living room floor. The pale gray and cream rug that came with the place is mostly obscured under the mountain of our belongings.

"I can't believe I'm moving you again so quickly," Callie says.

"But you're moving me *in* with you, so this is better, no?" Callie and I will be true flatmates for the first time.

"I thought you'd be a *live-in* for the rest of time," she says.

"I thought so too. It's certainly better financially," I say, grinning like I just won the lottery instead of taking a huge back step in my savings. I've never had to worry about my own bills before. Eddie's bills, Dylan's bills—they were my responsibility. Now, I have my own rent and electricity payments. It feels pretty exciting.

"You can stop that incessant smiling," Callie says. "Paying a gas bill isn't fun."

"It kind of is to me."

"Says the nanny with a load of savings."

Because of my complete fixation on the inevitability of stormy skies ahead, I have a comfortable safety net. Especially as Dylan and Eddie are both refusing to take my money and Eddie is insisting I take the scholarship money she got from the university. I still have to work, but Callie is right—I don't have to worry about this month's gas bill.

"Let's have some wine," Callie says. "I can't face unpacking any of this without alcohol."

We scurry about, hunting down Callie's wine glasses and corkscrew—there's so much I don't own that most people do at my age. It's a good job I have a flatmate who's done this living-on-her-own thing. We flop on the sofa that I used to sleep on before I moved in to Dax and Guinevere's place.

"Cheers," Callie says.

We clink glasses.

"Flatmates," she says. "Have you spoken to the agency?"

"Yeah. I'm going to do some temporary work."

"What, like maternity nursing?"

I shake my head. "Definitely not." It's hard to say no maternity nursing when the money is so good, but to earn it, you work around the clock.

"Good. Because that requires you giving yourself up for weeks at a time."

"Exactly. It's not what I want for myself."

A smile unfurls on Callie's face. "I'm so proud of you. I thought you were always going to be the girl who worked relentlessly for your employer and Dylan and Eddie. It's nice to see you thinking about yourself. For once."

"It still doesn't feel natural—"

I don't get to finish my sentence because Callie starts screaming. She spills wine as she leaps on the sofa.

"It's a fucking rat! Did you see that?"

I put my wine down on the floor and stand. "Where?"

She points at the floorboard over by the old sash window. "There. It went behind the box."

I creep forward. "Are you sure?" I ask. "You might just be dehydrated."

"You think I'm hallucinating because I haven't had enough Evian?" she asks. "I saw a bloody rat."

I peer behind the boxes stacked up in front of the curtain, but I can't see anything. I pull out my phone and put on the torch. "There's nothing here. Maybe it was your ex-boyfriend," I say. "He's a good enough reason to call the rat catcher." I abandon my investigations and head back to the sofa.

"I think outside of nursery rhymes, they call it pest control."

"I'll call them tomorrow," I say. "While you're at work."

"So, we just let the rats roam today?"

"We live in London. I heard you're never more than a meter away from a rat at any time."

I get a cushion in my face. "You're not helping."

"It's going to be fine." I learned that lesson before I realized I had. Eddie was right; I can figure out most things, and that makes me powerful as fuck. "At least they're our rats."

"We don't own this place, you know. We're renting."

"Okay, so the rats are on loan until we move out."

"I don't want them."

"So I'll have them. You'll come home tomorrow and I'll have trained an entire family of rodents to fold laundry and unpack boxes." I shrug. "You never know, I might take that show on the road and make millions."

"How much wine have you had?" she asks.

I ignore her question. "I feel free. Like I could do anything. I don't have to be a nanny anymore if I don't want to be."

"*Do* you want to be?" she asks.

"I don't know," I reply honestly. "I don't know if it's what I truly want to do. I think I need to try some other stuff as well. Maybe I'll take a night class. The idea of finishing at six and leaving the place I work is..."

"Let me tell you," Callie says. "It feels fucking fantastic. It's not healthy to live where you work. You're going to love it so much. Even with the rats."

"I am." Moving out of Dax and Guinevere's was definitely the right thing to do, but it doesn't mean I don't miss them. I do. Every day.

It's been two weeks and I go to bed every night thinking about them both. About how much Guinevere will have changed since I last saw her, whether she'd remember me now and if she smells the same. About how Dax's skin felt against mine, the hard smoothness of it. The comfort. The strength. How protected I felt by him.

I wake up every morning and think about how he cared for me while I was sick. Drove ten hours to bring me home. Pulled my hair back when I vomited. He's a caring, kind man. I'm sure Callie thinks I'm a fool to take a step back, but I need to be sure I don't want him because he needs me. I need to know I want him...just because.

My phone buzzes. "It's Eddie," I announce. She's sent me a link.

That's on the University Website. Just to remove any doubt.

I'm not clear what she means until I click through to find a page titled "Awards and Scholarships". I search for her name and it's listed just under the "GCC Scholarship Fund". I pause.

GCC.

Those letters mean something to me. I've seen them before.

I type back.

What's GCC?

The name of my scholarship.

"What does GCC mean to you?" I ask Callie as I type out the same question to Eddie. "Is it a corporation? I can't place it."

"*The* GC? Like Gemma Collins?" she asks.

"The reality woman?" I laugh. "I'm pretty sure she's not establishing scholarships at Exeter University. No, it's GCC. It's the name of Eddie's scholarship. The GCC Scholarship."

"No idea. Can we talk about getting a new sofa?" she asks.

Eddie doesn't respond, which is shorthand for *I haven't got a clue*. But I'm sure I've seen those letters before. I just can't remember where.

THIRTY-THREE

Dax

Vincent, Jacob and I loiter outside Jacob's gate in Holford Road, waiting for the agent.

"You think there's a problem?" Vincent asks.

"She's only fifteen minutes late," I say. "She's stuck in traffic. There's a road closure in St. John's Wood apparently."

"So you just bought it?" Vincent asks. "You only saw it once. How much did you pay?"

"Eight," I reply. "It works. Why would I need to see it more than once if I'd made up my mind?"

"I don't know. Fifteen minutes to make an eight-million-pound investment. That's quick decision-making." He slaps me on the back. "But less life-changing than the decision not to use a condom that one time." He nods at Guinevere, snuggled in the baby carrier strapped to my front.

"Apparently the best decisions are the quickest," I say.

"Coming from the guy who didn't want to be a father," Jacob says. "I'd say you've figured it out pretty quickly."

I don't say it, but I know I've got Eira to thank for how quickly I came round to the idea of being a father. She knew exactly how to encourage my interest in my daughter, how to bring us closer together. As usual, Eira went way beyond what was required to make sure Guinevere and I were as happy as humanly possible.

I miss her.

We exchange texts every few days. Each time I hear from her, I have to convince myself not to drive round to her flat, toss her over my shoulder and bring her home. To me and Guinevere.

I'm trying to be patient. To live in the ambiguity. It's not easy.

A green mini comes whizzing around the corner, screeching to a halt in the street and blocking the road. "Your keys!" Muriel sticks her hand out the window, a keychain dangling from her pinched fingers. "Congratulations! I'll park up and come and see you in."

"You know I can see into your living room," I say to Jacob as we climb the steps to the house.

"I'm having blinds installed tomorrow," he replies.

"Guinevere, this is your new house," I say. "Do you like it?" I know she's sleeping, but I ask her anyway. It's not like she'd answer me if she was awake, either—I just like chatting to her. "Your cousins are going to want to come in to use the pool, but we're not going to let them."

Jacob cups his ear. "What's that? Oh yes, the sound of the Uncle of the Year award going up in flames. You'll let us in, won't you, Guinevere?" he says, dipping to talk to her. "Kids have us all acting like fools." He laughs.

"And enjoying it," Vincent replies. "That's the part I'm looking forward to most. Being able to be an idiot and it being entirely acceptable. I can't wait for when they're old enough for water pistol fights and proper football practice."

"This generation is all going to be women," Jacob says. "We're going to have our hair in plaits and be made to wear eyeshadow."

"As long as we can do the water pistol fight after, I'm good with a little pink on my lids," Vincent replies. "Helps bring out the blue in my eyes."

"When do we start talking to them about periods and stuff?" I ask.

"Personally, I would give it a while," Jacob says. "Maybe wait until she's walking. Maybe even talking." He rolls his eyes.

I'm not laughing. Wouldn't it be best for someone who lives the experience of being a woman to talk to Guinevere about things like this?

Vincent rests his hand on my shoulder. "It's a long way off and who knows where you'll be? Your life might look very different when the time comes."

"I don't know if I'm enough for her," I confess.

"We all feel like that, mate," Vincent says. "And it's nothing to do with you being a single parent. We'll never be enough for our kids, because they deserve more than anyone could ever give."

He's right. Nothing will be enough for Guinevere as far as I'm concerned. There are plenty of women in my family I'm sure would be more than happy to talk to Guinevere about boys or periods or anything she doesn't want to talk to me about. But it won't be enough.

"I'm pretty sure we're going to feel like that for the rest of our lives," Jacob says.

"Like we're not enough?" I ask. "How depressing."

Vincent nudges me with his shoulder in a way that tells

me he's here for me. "I read somewhere—code for, *I saw something when scrolling on Instagram*—about how you can only ever be a *good enough* parent. I'm taking comfort from that. There's no 'perfect' as far as raising humans is concerned."

"The idea of being comfortable with imperfection is Dax's idea of hell." Jacob tips his head backs and laughs like a villain in a movie who's just exacted the perfect revenge on the hero.

Fact is, we're not at the end of this film.

"I'm sure some other men in your position would have just found themselves a stepmother for Guinevere," Vincent says. "They'd feel a need to fit into this mold society has created for us."

"I don't want a wife just so I can have a wife. The woman I marry will be a woman I can't *not* marry." All I can think about is Eira as I say the words. I'm standing here, about to move into our new house, wishing she was here. I'm trying to give her space, give her time to figure out what she wants and who she is, but it's torture. I'm sick of waiting. I'm tired of being patient. I want her. I want her to want me. And Guinevere.

"Wow, that's pretty poetic for a man of science like yourself," Vincent says. "You'll be taking up the violin next."

"Maybe," I say, really considering what he's saying. "It's not a terrible idea for Guinevere to see her father learn an instrument. To be bad at something and practice and get better—not overnight but bit by bit, because of the time investment I'd make."

"Who are you?" Jacob says. "You've always had such a black-and-white worldview. Now you're thinking about modeling failure?"

"I only ever needed to see the world one way," I reply. "Things are different now. Guinevere needs me to see things in shades of gray. Someone recently challenged me to live with ambiguity. I'm...doing my best."

There's a beat of silence before Jacob says, "If you tell anyone I'll deny it, but...I'm proud of you."

I nod. I get it. A lot can change in a few months. And I'm proud of the man and the father I'm becoming.

THIRTY-FOUR

Eira

We all sit side-by-side, facing the front, our canvasses propped on easels in front of us. Everyone seems to know what they're doing. Even Eddie.

"Did she say wet the paper before putting the color on?" I ask. "I'm totally confused."

"You can do either," Eddie replies. "It depends what effect you're going for."

"And what effect am I going for?"

Eddie laughs. "I don't know. I'm doing an abstract, blocky thing. So definitely paint on dry paper for me."

I guess I'll never know until I try. I dunk my clean paintbrush into water and start painting.

Next, I spray my paints with water, just like the instructor told us to. I'm hoping to mix a blue-green color reminiscent of the water of the Caribbean. "I always thought I'd end up going back to Antigua."

"You might still," Eddie says.

"It was nearly ten years ago. I thought I would have

gone back before now." When I started my first position straight out of Portland, I went on holiday with the family to Antigua. Of course, it wasn't much of a holiday for me. I was focused on a baby who didn't like the heat, had diarrhea, and wasn't eating or drinking. It was a hellish ten days. My only saving grace was Callie, who I spoke to three times a day. She reassured me I wasn't the worst nanny in the history of nannies and kept me sane for the duration of the trip.

I vowed that one day I'd go back, not as a nanny. When the day comes, I'll enjoy the sunsets and white beaches, the cocktails and clear blue-green water. I don't think I've thought about Antigua more than three or four times since that first trip. Other priorities always cropped up, and I focused on insuring against the bad times instead of looking forward to the good.

But here? Now? Trying an art class to see what it is I enjoy in life, it's the only thing I can think about. I want to bring those waters to life. I want to paint them, hang them on my wall and wake up to them every morning until I can take myself back to Antigua to enjoy them in real life.

Unfortunately, my ambition is circling a few thousand miles above my ability. "Why has my paint turned brown? I mixed blue and green and yellow. It's been a while since I left school. Has color mixing changed?"

Eddie laughs. "Everything's changed since you left school. It's been a while." She leans forward and studiously paints tiny strokes on the canvas.

I daub my paintbrush in the brown mess I just made and paint a circle on Eddie's cheek. I smile and sit back, admiring my work.

She freezes then turns her head very slowly to look at me. "Did you just paint me?"

I shrug like an unrepentant toddler caught trying on her mother's shoes. It's not that Eddie and I never have fun together—of course we do. We're sisters and we've always been friends. But something between us feels lighter since I visited her in Exeter. Maybe I've stopped trying to be her parent and I'm content to be her big sister.

Does this mean I'm capable of having a proper relationship with someone, not just be a caregiver? It gives me hope that Dax and I can have a happy ending where we give and take, and it's possible to be equal in that giving and taking.

"Paint on the canvas," she says, fixing me with a glare. "Or you'll get us thrown out." She shakes her head but can't suppress her smile. "Never thought it would be me telling you to follow the rules."

I clean the brown sludge from my palette, wash my brush and try again, picking up some of the lighter blues and greens and mixing them together. "Just so you know, it does look like there's a possibility you have poo on your face," I tell her. "I mean, obviously it could be paint, given where we are, but..." I reach over and daub green paint on her cheek, right next to the brown. "There. That's better. I think there's much less likelihood people will think someone shit on your cheek now."

This time she doesn't freeze. Slowly, she pushes her stool away from her easel, takes the biggest brush from the jam jar sitting on the small table between us and smashes it into the red paint.

I stand up. She wouldn't. There's no way she'd ever—

I try and dodge out of the way, but I'm too late and I feel the bristles of the brush against my nose. I squeal and back away. "Eddie! You— No."

She goes back to her paints. "Eira, careful—someone might thing you're Rudolph hemorrhaging from the nose."

She stalks after me with her brush, and I push against the glass of the window, trying to put some distance between us. "Better add some blue." I cover my face and crouch down.

"Ladies," the tutor's prim voice calls from behind us. "If we could refrain from painting each other, that would be my preference. The skin's oils mess with the bristles of the brushes."

Eddie and I lock gazes and break into grins before going back to our seats.

"I think I've finally found the perfect shade," I say, focusing on my palette and pretending I wasn't just paint-fighting with my sister in a roomful of adults who aren't renegotiating their relationships with siblings.

"Can't wait for the finished result," she says.

"Same with yours. It's coming on beautifully," I reply.

I sit, smiling at her, when I should be focused on the painting. "Love you, Eddie."

"Your phone is buzzing." She nods at the side table where I left my mobile.

I peer at the screen. "It's the lawyers," I say, a little surprised. "What on earth do they want?"

"They've probably forgotten to invoice you for something."

"Probably," I say and cancel the call. I want to focus on the future with my sister, not on the horrors of years gone by. I don't want to hear about how my uncle hasn't responded to our requests for explanations about x, y and z, or how he's delaying this and that. It's all I've heard since the day I turned twenty-five.

I want to paint the waters of Antigua and let myself imagine what it will be like to go back there one day.

THIRTY-FIVE

Eira

I trace the handwriting on the envelope I'm holding, imagining Dax's fingers around the pen as he crossed out his address and wrote my new one. Even though I knew what was inside wasn't from him, my hands still shook when I opened it, desperate to discover a trace of him inside.

All the envelope contained was yet another request from my lawyer to contact his office straight away.

I push the envelope back into my pocket and glance at the clock above the receptionist's head in Morgan & Co's law offices. Mr. Morgan has a lot of well-heeled clients, but from what I've seen over the last decade, his "& Co" is comprised of Judy, the receptionist, and a sandwich delivery service.

I wish Dax was here. I know I could turn up on his doorstep at any point and receive the warm welcome I crave. But I'm scared.

I don't want to go back to him until I'm sure I'm capable of being with him as an equal. We still text, although we haven't spoken on the phone or seen each other in person. I'm hoping that when I see him again, I see him as a man, not just someone I can take care of.

"Eira," Mr. Morgan says as he comes out of his office, his shirt sleeves rolled up. It's the first time I've ever seen him without a jacket.

"Mr. Morgan."

"Please call me Fred," he says.

We have this to-and-fro at the start of all our conversations. People introduced to me by my parents always felt slightly at arm's length, as if they were far more important than me and I should be honored just to be meeting them. I can't shake that feeling with Mr. Morgan.

I smile and follow him into his office, making a mental note not to refer to him by any name at all.

"So," he says, leaning over his desk from his chair behind it. I take the seat opposite. "We have a turn of events not even I could have predicted."

I try to conceal my sigh. I didn't want to come here today. There was a reason I hadn't given Mr. Morgan my new address. I wanted to move on from trying to chase after my dead parents' stolen estate. It's gone. I've lived years without it. I can live the rest of my life that way too.

Mr. Morgan's periodic summons over the last few years have always been precipitated by a small change in the law that made it easier to take my uncle to court. None of it did any good, because my uncle doesn't play by the rules. The law doesn't matter to him. The only reason I've come along today is to officially tell Mr. Morgan he should close the file.

"Your uncle is dead," Mr. Morgan announces.

"Dead?" I ask.

"Dead," he says again with a small nod. "As in not alive. Huge heart attack apparently. I was contacted by his lawyers a week or so ago." He says it like he's telling me a new cake shop has opened on the corner and I should try the lemon drizzle.

I feel numb—not because I'm sad about my uncle's death. How could I be? But because he was my last connection to my parents. It's not them I miss, but what they should have been. Who they should have been to me, and it's almost as if I miss the grief I should be feeling right now.

"Right," I say. "What about my parents' estate?"

He chuckles, which seems a little inappropriate, even though my uncle was a thief and a liar. "It means you get it all. Apparently, his investments since your parents' deaths have done quite well and the estate has grown during the time he's...been in control of it. It's now worth an estimated sixty million in total."

"So it's still...he didn't lose it all?" That had been a theory at one time—that he couldn't sign over the trust because he'd borrowed against my parents' assets and lost the money.

"Not from what I understand from his lawyers. There's no more fighting to get back what's yours. Even if there was a dispute around the ownership of assets, as he has alleged from time to time, he's left it to you in any event. The terms of his will mirror your parents', so Eddie's and Dylan's shares will be held on trust until they turn twenty-five. It doesn't matter if we say you're receiving what you should have done under your parents' will or what your uncle has left you. That means you can stop spending money on lawyers. Everything's settled."

"I don't understand," I say. "Why would he take everything from us and then give it back?"

"He obviously wanted the money while he was alive, but when he died, knew he should do the right thing."

I'm not sure handing back what you've stolen after you're dead counts as the right thing.

"Maybe he had a crisis of conscience. Or perhaps this was always his plan. I say, don't worry about the why and enjoy your new wealth. It's been a long time coming."

I zone out what Mr. Morgan is saying as he continues to talk. My brain is completely zeroed in on the bomb he just dropped. I'm about to inherit over twenty million pounds. And on top of that, my brother and sister are looked after.

"It can all be liquidized if that's what you choose," Mr. Morgan says as I tune back into him. "It will be up to the three of you to decide how to divide and hold it. I'll introduce you to some financial experts—wealth managers, if you will."

I nod. "Right, yes, that sounds good."

"Do you think the three of you will want to keep the family town house in Belgravia? I imagine that's deeply sentimental to you, given your parents' passing."

"Not at all," I reply.

It's not as if I was particularly unhappy there—my brother and sister brought me tremendous joy. Our nannies and housekeepers were kind. But there's no sentiment attached to that building for me, and I can't imagine Dylan and Eddie will feel differently.

"Unless it's a good investment, I think the three of us will be happy to sell." I scramble for my phone. "I should call Dylan and Eddie." I start to bring up our group chat and pause. "You're sure this is happening and you've not made a mistake?"

"I'm sure. Your uncle wasn't married, had no dependents. There's no one challenging the will. Finally, everything we've been trying to achieve is resolved. It's my pleasure to tell you that you are now a very wealthy woman."

I would happily trade it all to have had parents who spent time with me, knew me, loved me.

Maybe in another lifetime. But in this lifetime, this inheritance buys freedom for the three of us.

Even though both Dylan and Eddie told me of their desire to be independent and for me to focus on myself, this inheritance severs the last strand of doubt about their ability to support themselves financially. There's not a grain of uncertainty anymore. I definitely don't need a rainy day fund for any of us. All I can give my brother and sister now is my emotional support, my time, and my unending love.

Freedom. The word loops around my brain. I feel it all over my body, like I've shrugged off ten tons of weight and I'm floating. I have a sense of calm that I don't remember ever feeling before. And it's not about the money. Obviously, it makes life a lot easier.

It's about the resolution.

The past is now all firmly in the past. I no longer feel like a victim of history. I'm not my parents' daughter. I'm not my uncle's victim. I'm just me.

As I type out a message on the family group chat, all I can think about is Dax and how happy he'd be for me in this moment.

I'm *free* to have the exact future I want, even if I don't know precisely what it looks like yet. But suddenly, the storm in my mind settles, and at least part of the answer I've been searching for is crystal clear.

THIRTY-SIX

Dax

I open the front door of the Holford Road house that I'm still struggling to call home to find Zach and Ellie on my doorstep, holding up a bottle of champagne.

"Surprise!" Ellie says, beaming at me.

"Congrats, mate. You finally grew up and bought a house."

"Oh yes, that's the key signifier for me growing up—my real estate choices." I smooth my hands over Guinevere's back, sleeping peacefully in the baby carrier strapped to my chest.

"Oh and the baby thing—"

"Surprise!"

I nearly jump ten feet in the air as Mum and Dad appear at the door.

"Your father still can't park a car," Mum says.

I stand clear of the door while everyone files in. I've not had any visitors here yet. My family barely ever visited my place in Marylebone, which was too small to accommodate even a fraction of the Cove clan. That's not a problem anymore.

"You've got a pool I hear?" Dad asks. "Let's have a look."

"You want a tour before coffee?" I ask.

Everyone gives a resounding yes and so we head to the basement.

"The nanny has her room down here. It gives her some privacy." The new nanny is very...competent. Guinevere doesn't seem to have any complaints. Neither do I. She knows what she's doing and I leave her to it. When she's working, I'm working; when I come home, I want time on my own with Guinevere.

Daddy-daughter time.

Coming home is my favorite part of the day. I still love my work. I still believe the research I'm doing will change lives. Only now, I'm a little more aware of the importance of my own life and how Guinevere is the most important part of it.

"I haven't met her yet," Mum says. "Is she nice?"

"Perfectly," I reply.

"And what about Eira?" she asks. "Where's she?"

The hushed silence makes me think everyone wants the answer to that question.

"Eira is...living with a friend in Finchley."

My mum's eyebrows rise as if she's expecting me to elaborate.

I don't. Because I don't know if she's coming back. I don't know if she's still figuring out what she wants or who she is. All I can do is wait. That's what I said I would do, and I'm a man of my word.

"Shall we go and open that champagne?" I ask, turning and heading out of the pool room.

"How is the pool?" asks Dad. "Do you use it a lot?"

"Not yet. Guinevere is a bit little. I think when she gets to three months."

"But you've been in for a swim?" Mum asks.

"Not yet," I say. "I will when I get some time."

When we get up to the ground floor, my four visitors start to pace the place.

"This is the furniture from your flat in Marylebone?" Ellie asks.

"Yeah. I need to get new stuff, obviously."

"Yes, you do," Mum says. "You can't just have a two-seater sofa and a TV in this space." She looks around.

"It looks like you're squatting," Dad says.

"Sometimes you need to live in a space before you know what to do with it," Ellie says, ever the diplomat. "Oh and I brought you these." She pulls out a paper bag. "Just flapjacks."

I groan. "Thanks so much." Ellie's flapjacks aren't just flapjacks. There's a little piece of heaven in every bite.

"Is that what it is?" Mum asks. "Do you want to live in the space before you buy furniture? Doesn't sound much like you."

It's impossible to keep anything from my mother. She can read me like a book. "There are a lot of moving parts at the moment. I'm juggling work and Guinevere. I've only been in this house a couple of weeks. Give me a break."

"Has Eira seen it?" she asks.

Like a book.

"Yes. She came to view it with me."

She's nodding. "And she liked it?"

"Yes, she did." Every room I walk into, I see her here, even though she never lived here. Being here without her feels wrong. That's why I've not bought any furniture. That's why it looks like I haven't moved in properly.

Because I want Eira here first. I don't want this to be my place. I want it to be *our* place.

"And when's the last time you saw her?" Mum asks.

I groan. "Dad, can you distract Mum please? I feel a lecture coming on."

"Well, some of you boys need a little shove in the right direction now and then," Mum says.

"Quite right," Dad says. "That's our job. A little elbow to the ribs, a short, sharp kick to the shins." He grins like beating up his sons is at the top of the list of things he likes to do.

"I'm a single dad," I say. "I need your support and sympathy, not physical violence."

"You're just fine on the fatherhood thing. I'm not worried about that," Mum says. "That's just parenthood. But *Eira*, on the other hand—"

She's interrupted by the doorbell. I don't even try to disguise the pleasure I feel in walking away from the impending lecture.

"Get yourself drinks," I call over my shoulder. "Whoever it is will probably need me for at least an hour."

I'm still smiling as I open the door and find myself face-to-face with Eira. Emotions tangle in my stomach, and I have to stamp out the urge to pounce on her and pull her against my chest.

"Hi," she says and gives a little wave when I don't say anything. "I figured you would have moved in by now. I bought you a plant as a housewarming." She holds up a spider plant with a big red bow on it.

I've lost all words. I go to speak but nothing comes out. It's just so good to see her. I wasn't sure whether this day would ever come.

"Oh," she says, her gaze leaving my face for the first

time since I opened the door as she beams at my chest. "I didn't notice Guinevere. You're using the baby carrier we bought." She looks up at me as if I've made all her dreams come true. "That's wonderful, Dax." She reaches forward and pats Guinevere on her bottom. "She's such a good baby."

"I'm so glad you're here," I blurt.

Her face breaks into a huge smile and we both stand there, grinning like idiots at each other until someone shouts my name and the spell is broken.

I groan. "My mum and dad are here and—" I don't get a chance to explain more before Mum appears at my side.

"Eira, darling! Come in. How wonderful to see you. I was so disappointed when Dax said you'd resigned. I always knew Guinevere and Dax were in such good hands when they were with you."

Eira handles my mother like a champ and just changes the subject. "How is the house in Norfolk coming on?"

Mum takes the bait and starts complaining about how long it's taking. Much easier than explaining why Eira decided to leave and what's happening between us. Even though I really want to know the answer to the second question.

"Look who it is!" Mum says as she guides Eira into the kitchen.

I'm more than fucking happy she's here. I just wish my family wasn't. I know Eira didn't pop round to give me a potted plant. I want to hear everything she's got to say.

"Eira," Dad says, his gaze flitting from me to Eira and back again. "Good to see you, girl. How've you been? Couldn't put up with this one for long, I heard." He gestures in my direction.

"Who would?" Zach asks from where he and Ellie are

leaning on the rickety dining table where Eira and I played backgammon and ate pie. "Dax on his best day is bad enough, but with the added pressure of having a kid—"

Eira glances at me across the kitchen, and I don't hear what Zach and Dad are saying. It's so good to see her. She looks so beautiful. Her brown mane of hair looks less wild than usual, her smile brighter. I want to know everything that's happened to her since she walked out of the Marylebone house until the moment she stepped onto the doorstep.

"I heard your uncle died," Dad says, and it takes me by surprise. How did he know that? By the look on Eira's face, she wasn't expecting it, either. "I'm so sorry for your loss."

"Don't be," Eira says. "He wasn't a very nice man and his death has...uncomplicated my life. Substantially." She glances at me meaningfully. As much as I love my family, I really wish they weren't here right now. I want to know why her uncle dying has uncomplicated her life, and whether that newfound simplicity means she's here to restart—or start?—what's between us.

"Well, that's that," says Ellie. "Would you like a flapjack?"

"They look delicious, but I'm saving myself for dinner." She pauses. "In fact, I was hoping you might join me, Dax." She looks back at my family members. "But you have visitors so perhaps another day?"

"Oh we're not staying here," Dad says. "Apart from anything else, my son doesn't have any furniture. I don't know what you're waiting for. You seem to have plenty of money. Why don't you hire someone to help you?"

"Dax is taking his time," Mum says. "Nothing wrong with that."

"Nothing at all," I say, not taking my eyes from Eira. "I

don't have a sitter tonight, but if you wanted to come round—"

"Jacob and Sutton will babysit Guinevere," Mum says.

"I don't even know if they're in," I say.

"We're over there for dinner, along with Zach and Ellie, so there'll be six of us there. Guinevere will be in safe hands."

I'm not convinced about the people I share my gene pool with, but at least with Sutton and Ellie there, Guinevere might not go completely unnoticed.

"Sounds like I have a sitter," I say. "Or six."

She laughs. "Shall I pick you up at seven?" she asks. "For our first date?"

I laugh because a first date seems ludicrous, but I suppose technically she's right. We've never been out together. "I'll pick you up," I say. "I have your address, so—"

"It's okay," she says. "I'll pick you up."

I shrug. What else can I do? I don't know if there's a reason she wants to pick me up, but I'm not going to ask her, or even discuss it further, in front of my family.

"Good," she says. "So I'll see you later." She hands me the spider plant and says goodbye to everyone. I walk her to the front door.

"Thanks for coming," I say.

"Thanks for waiting." Her voice breaks on the last syllable.

How could she think I wouldn't wait? I reach for her and she takes my hand, and we stand on the doorstep for a few minutes, just holding hands, alternating between staring at each other and Guinevere.

"I don't want you to go," I say.

"I'll see you at seven," she says, then glides down the stairs and turns down the street. Every now and again, she looks back, sees me watching her, and her grin grows wider.

"Guinevere, this is a great day, my sweet girl," I say as she starts to stir from her nap. "A great day. Daddy has a date tonight. So you gotta go to Uncle Jacob and Auntie Sutton's place so I can have dinner with Eira. Is that okay?"

She started to make funny noises like a bird tweeting. I lift her out of the sling so I can hear them better. There's nothing sweeter than cuddling with my daughter, and the only thing that would make me miss an evening of it is an evening with Eira.

THIRTY-SEVEN

Dax

I could have messaged Eira to ask where we were going, but I haven't. I don't want to fuck this up, so I need to go at her pace, follow her rules. She said dinner and I'm assuming she would have said if she wanted me in black tie. After changing several times, I settle on a blue shirt and dark blue jeans and a jacket. I can't remember a time in my life when I was nervous. But I am now. Even when I flew to New York to pick up Guinevere, I didn't think about the repercussions long enough to be nervous.

Tonight there seems so much at stake.

The doorbell goes and as I stalk toward the entrance hall, I can't help but remember the first time I met Eira. She was covered in mud and, I thought, the very last person I was looking for.

How wrong I was.

I open the door, but there's no one there.

"Hello?" I call.

"Here!" She appears from behind the hedge in front of

my house. "I just found a bumble bee on your pathway and put him somewhere safer."

"Of course you did," I say. "Rescuer of animals and people."

She steps toward me in a long blue skirt and a white t-shirt, looking effortlessly cool and sexy in that way only she can. "Did I rescue someone?" she asks.

I can't do anything but smile at her. She looks so beautiful. Her hair hits her waist and her skin seems to shine.

"I bought something for Guinevere," she says, holding up a gift bag. "A towel. With her initials on it."

"Oh, thanks," I say, taking the bag from her. "Shall I open it?"

She shrugs. "Later. Let's walk."

I drop the bag into the house and lock the door. We head in the direction of Hampstead village.

"So, Guinevere's initials are GCC, right?" she asks.

"Right," I say, "Guinevere Carole Cove."

"And my sister's scholarship is the GCC scholarship. Turns out there are scant details about that scholarship, apart from the fact it's available for ten years and the criteria for consideration is that students have to have lost both their parents in order to be eligible."

There's no point in denying it. She's put all the pieces together. "It was a thank-you," I say. I knew Eira wouldn't have accepted money for Eddie's education if I offered it upfront. A scholarship for her sister seemed the easiest way to repay her in some way, and it had taken little effort from me. A phone call. A bank transfer. The university handled the rest.

The only sticking point had been timeframes. I wanted to make sure Eddie knew about her scholarship immediately and had the money within seven days. I wanted to relieve Eira's financial burden as soon as possible. Once the university realized I wouldn't change my mind, everything else slotted into place.

"For what?" she asks, pausing in the middle of the pavement.

"For taking Guinevere to the hospital. For taking such good care of her."

"That's my job. And it was viral meningitis anyway. She was fine."

"No one knew it was viral at the time. If it had been bacterial, she would have been in hospital before it progressed. You would have saved her life."

"It's a lot of money."

"Guinevere's health is priceless to me."

She reaches up and smooths her fingers over my brow. "I love hearing how much you love her."

She doesn't need to say what she's thinking: that it wasn't always like this. My bond with Guinevere has grown over the last weeks until it's the most secure, unbreakable thing in my life. It's as if she's been a part of me since forever.

"She'll be three months on Tuesday," I say.

"So big already."

"She's grown up so much. I'm not sure how I'm going to handle her getting bigger."

Eira slips her hand in mine and we keep walking. "You will," she says. "You will."

"Are you going to tell me about you? What you've been doing? Are you working?"

She smiles up at me. "Let's sit and talk."

We've arrived outside a restaurant with black and white awnings. Eira pulls me inside.

Once we're seated and have ordered some drinks, she

leans across the table. "I'm going to be honest with you," she says. "I think you're great."

It's like I feel cupid's arrow piercing my skin. She's so adorable.

"I think you're great too," I reply. "More than great." I don't want to scare her off, but I've never felt this way about anyone—never felt as if someone gets me like Eira does. The things my brothers tease me about are the same things she thinks are the best parts of me. It feels like no matter what I do, she'll look up at me with her hopeful eyes and I'll know that everything is going to be okay.

"You were right when you said I put everyone else first. My identity has been caught up in caring for others, so when that was stripped away, I didn't quite know who I was. Even though it's tiring, it's nice to be needed."

I need you, I think.

"I'm sorry if giving Eddie the scholarship took something away from you. That wasn't my intention."

She grabs my hand across the table and I revel in the softness of her. "It did quite the opposite. Eddie being independent of me and being able to stand on her own two feet is the best gift you could have given her. Or me." She lets out a small laugh. "And it happened at just the right time."

"It did?" I ask, intrigued by what's so funny.

"Eddie doesn't need the scholarship anymore. Please don't take it personally, but she's returned it to the university."

"What happened? Did she win the lottery or something? She's not dropped out?" I know that would be devastating to Eira.

"No, she's still studying for her degree. When my uncle died, Eddie, Dylan and I...we finally got our inheritance."

"Congratulations," I say. "You must be thrilled. I mean, I know it's sad your uncle died—"

"It's not sad. It means everything's resolved now. But things started to fit together before then. And you helped me with that. You helped me to see that I saw my value in the world as being dependent on helping others. I hadn't realized that before. And then when my uncle died, everything crystalized and it was as if I'd been set free from my past."

"Because of your inheritance?" I ask. "Does that mean you wouldn't have come back if your uncle hadn't died?" My heart clenches at the idea of Eira and I being so fragile.

"I needed to have a little space from you so I knew our relationship wasn't about my need to mother people. And then spending time with Eddie after she'd emancipated herself—financially I mean. It's different. Our relationship is evolving, and it gave me hope that I could be more to someone than a caregiver.

"Coming back to you isn't about the money. It's about being freed by the resolution of my past. I'm not an adjunct to anyone. Not my parents or to Dylan and Eddie. My uncle's death just speeded up all those feelings. Like I was on the precipice of feeling that freedom. His death just gave me a little shove." She laughs, and I feel it in my core. She's really happy.

"I want you to let me take care of you," I say, sweeping my thumb across her wrist. "And I want you to take care of me—but I don't need mothering. That's not...not what attracts me to you."

Our gazes lock, and I wish we were at home so I could pull her onto my lap and hold her against me.

"Good to know," she whispers.

There's a beat of silence, then another, and I feel as if

we're making up for lost time, like the bond between us is deepening, just by being here, holding hands.

"I know you're a new father and you have a new nanny—"

"You're not having your job back, by the way."

She gives me a look of feigned shock. "You've found someone better. I knew you would."

"Never," I say. "But I don't want you to be my employee."

"Good," she says with a decisive nod. "Because something I've learned about myself is that I can't sleep with my boss."

"Who else can't you sleep with?" I ask. "Because I need to make sure I don't fall into any of those categories."

She laughs. "It's going to be tough. I can't sleep with guys without a D in their name."

"Tick. What else?"

"Guys who don't love their daughters."

"Tick, tick. What else?"

"Guys without a dimple on their left cheek."

"Shit," I say. "Can I get a dimple implant?"

"What?" She pulls forward in her seat and releases my hand before reaching for my cheek. "You have one right here."

I catch her hand and kiss the inside of her wrist. "If you say so."

"What about you?" She looks up at me from under her lashes. "Priorities shift and change after becoming a parent. What do you want?"

Isn't it obvious? Doesn't she know?

"You," I say.

I enjoy the blush spreading across her throat.

"You," I say again. "It's that simple."

"Does that mean we're officially dating?" she asks.

"That means if I thought you wouldn't freak out and leave for another six weeks, I'd ask you to marry me."

She sucks in a breath, her eyelashes fluttering as she takes in what I've said. "Dax." Her voice is breathless.

"I'm not asking. But I will. In the meantime, we'll eat steak. Take Guinevere to the park. Decorate the house. Hang out with your brother and sister, my brothers, my parents. I'll go to work and try to change the world, you'll figure out what you're going to do, and we'll live our lives together. Just like we're married."

She laughs. "That sounds like a great plan, but there's one wrinkle in it."

I shake my head. I'm not worried. I started the evening off nervous, but seeing Eira, being with her, watching her watch me—I know. We are inextricably connected. There's no doubt we'll be together forever. "Tell me," I say.

"It may take a while to figure out what I want. I've decided I'm going to start at the beginning."

"Back to university?" I ask.

She nods. "Yup. I'm doing some night school, figuring out what's interesting, and then I'll apply. I don't have a plan beyond that. I hadn't thought past tonight and trying to win you back."

"You never lost me." And she never will.

THIRTY-EIGHT

Eira

As soon as I step inside Dax's place, even though I've never lived here, it feels like home.

"Wow," I say. "I like what you've done with the place." I sweep my hand around his waist and lean into him as I survey the few bits of furniture in the living room. All of it's come from the flat and looks pretty beaten-up in these new surroundings. "Have you been robbed?"

"You sound like my brothers." He chuckles. "Promise you won't freak out if I explain why it looks like it does?"

"Why would I freak out?"

He turns so we're facing each other. "I was waiting for you," he says in a tone I somehow know he only uses for me.

"Waiting?"

"I want a life with you, Eira. I want you to move in with us. And if you agree, I don't want this to be my home that you live in. I want it to be *our* place. A place we bought furniture for and decided how to decorate together."

My insides turn to liquid as he speaks. Dax isn't a love

bomber, he's just speaking from the heart and being authentic. That's the only way he knows how to be.

And that's just one of the reasons I love him.

"You are a good man, Dax. Thoughtful and sensitive, and I want us to live together too." A grin cracks across his face, but I hold a finger up. "On one condition."

"Just one? I was expecting a bigger list than that."

"I'm sure I can add to it if necessary, but the first one is the most important. For me anyway."

"Anything," he replies.

"I want to pay for half." It will be my second real estate investment, as I just bought the flat Callie and I are in. She's insisted that she's going to pay me half the rent, like I'm still living there.

"Half of the furniture?" he asks.

I nod enthusiastically. "Yes. And the house." I brace myself. I'm not sure what his response will be—I don't know how sure he is that we'll survive. Yes, he said he wanted to marry me, but does he want a partner? An equal?

"It's an expensive house," he says, cautiously.

"I understand that," I reply.

He shrugs. "If that's what you need, that's what we'll do. But you don't need to. It's a *really* expensive house."

I have a feeling Dax's entire philosophy of our relationship will be, *if that's what you need, that's what we'll do.* And I don't know how I managed to find a man with such confidence that he is happy for me just to do what I need.

"You're perfect," I say.

He shakes his head. "Far from. But I want to be the best man I can be for you. And Guinevere."

I shriek. "Oh my gosh, we should go and get her!"

He laughs. "Later. She's with Jacob and Sutton. I have a key. I'll go and collect her before her midnight feed."

I smooth my hand up his shirt, my body melting into his at the feel of him. How did I manage to stay away for so long? "Oh—one more condition."

He laughs. "I'll meet every single condition you come up with."

"I want a big tree. In the foyer, I think."

He looks at me like he's concerned I'm delusional. "A tree in the house."

"A Christmas tree."

He breaks into a grin. "Sounds good. Somewhere to put Guinevere's hand-and-footprints." He nods over at the decorations resting on the built-in bookshelves that have no books on them yet.

"Oh, Dax," I say.

He dips his head and presses his lips against my neck, the vibrations of his moan as he connects with my skin radiating across my body.

I push my fingers into his hair and enjoy the feel of him, savoring the knowledge of what's next. His fingers fumble at the hem of my t-shirt and I take a half step back to sweep it over my head. I reach for his buttons while he traces the lace of my bra around the upper swell of my breasts.

"I missed you," he says.

I use the palms of my hands to reach beneath his unbuttoned shirt, to feel as much of him as I can, before pushing the shirt off his shoulders. "Here?" I ask.

"Anywhere," he replies. "Everywhere." His eyebrows pulse and I shiver.

I sigh and he lifts my chin.

"Tell me," he says. "Tell me what you're thinking. I want to hear it all."

I hook my fingers into his waistband. "It feels big, that's

all. This moment. It's like we're crossing a line or something."

His hand cups the back of my neck. "You're right. Because it's one way from here. There's no going back. It's us, together, sharing our futures. It's the start of our forever."

I swallow. He's so earnest about it. So reverent. Intense.

"I like the idea of sex being a ceremony of sorts."

"Yes," he says, dipping his head and pressing his lips against my forehead. "Of commitment, of worship, of togetherness..."

"Dax," I say, tears gathering in my throat.

"If you're not ready," he says, "just say and we can wait. You don't have to move in, we don't have to do this. But I'm ready. You're all I want. Nothing has ever come close to how I feel when I'm with you. It feels like without knowing it, I've been waiting for you my entire life. You and Guinevere. I wasn't looking for anything, and in you two I found everything."

I stand on tiptoes, my fingers splayed on his face, and slide my lips over his—once, twice, and then he can't take the teasing. He pulls me toward him, deepening our kiss.

"You're all I want," I say as we part. "I'm ready for it all."

"Guinevere too?" he asks. "We're a package deal these days."

The way he loves her makes me love him more.

"I love you both," I say, my breath hitching as I speak.

"We love you too," he says, kissing me again. My lips, my neck, my face, my shoulders—he covers everything with this mouth.

And then he dips lower.

And lower.

And lower.

He takes my lace-covered nipple into his mouth, teasing with his teeth. I'd forgotten how good he feels. How good he makes *me* feel.

"I'm going to fuck you in every room, in every corner, against every wall." He kneels and strips off my skirt, then my underwear, before laying me down on the rug and shifting so he's between my thighs. "I've missed tasting you, feasting on you. I've missed your hot skin and your tight cunt."

My breaths come quicker as he speaks, and I cry out as he plunges his tongue over my clit. All at once I feel such a fool for staying away from this man for as long as I did. How I've missed him.

Missed.

This.

Bliss.

The stubble on his chin chafes against my thighs and I start to vibrate—my entire body shakes with desire. For him. For this moment. For Dax.

I'm vaguely aware of the sounds I'm making, but I'm powerless to stop them. The moaning, the pleading, the need for it all. It's impossible to hold back. Dax gets all of me, all the time, and I can only hope I get the same from him.

He slips a finger into me and his head falls forward as I clench. "Fuck, Eira." He works me with his fingers and mouth. I try to focus on something other than what I'm feel-ing, because otherwise it's going to be over too soon and I want this exact moment to last forever. But I'm not in control of my body. Dax is. And he has other ideas.

He presses on the delicate flesh between the bottom of my stomach and my mound with one hand and uses his fingers on the other, coaxing and cajoling me. His tongue is on me, and I'm lost in sensation. I have no power in this moment.

Dax owns me.

And that's exactly how I want it.

My orgasm explodes out of me like a long-confined tiger from its cage.

"You're a fucking goddess," he says, crawling over me. I'm throbbing all over, breathing like I just ran a marathon, my muscles atrophied, my sense of space and time erased.

I try to focus, watching as he slides a condom on. It's such a relief to see. To know that soon, I'll feel him inside me.

I gasp as he pushes into me, filling me right up to the hilt. Something tells me I'll never get used to how alive I feel when we're like this, our bodies as one, minds as one.

He moves over me, our gazes connected. I see every burst of pleasure in his eyes, feel his body tightening with every move closer to his summit. I hear each grunt of ecstasy and know it's all for me. In that moment, I understand that I'm *made* for him.

"You're fucking beautiful, Eira," he whispers, his voice thick as he moves into me. "So beautiful."

He hits the perfect spot, the perfect rhythm, the perfect drag. I lift my legs, locking them around his waist as he drives deeper and deeper into me. So deep that I wonder if I'll ever come back from this orgasm.

Sweat glistens around his hairline and by the tightness in his jaw, the strain of the tendons in his neck, I know he's close. I take a breath, feeling my climax thundering inside me, getting louder and louder and louder.

"I love you," I cry out as I tilt over the edge. Dax tenses —pressing, pushing, pulsing into me.

He collapses over me, and I wrap my arms around him and send a small prayer up to the universe.

"I love you," he whispers.

"Let's stay like this forever," I say on a sigh.

"Always." He rolls off me and lands with a splat on the rug-less wooden floor.

I laugh. "Are you okay?"

"Never been better."

I lean onto his chest. "Ever been to Antigua?"

"Erm, no. You?"

"How about we make it our first trip as a threesome?"

He narrows his eyes. "Okay. Is there a reason to go there?"

"I've always wanted to go back. It feels like a good place to start the rest of my life."

"I'll follow you wherever you want to go." His eyes are dark and soulful. The way he looks at me sends shivers down my spine.

I spot my phone, discarded next to me, and check the time. "It's eleven thirty," I say, hitching a leg over his and sitting astride him. I circle my hips and feel him jerk beneath me. I tip my head back, hoping he's ready for more. "I can't get enough of you."

"My alarm will go off at eleven fifty," he says.

I lift up and grab the base of his cock.

"Condom!" he shouts, and I freeze. The only thing we didn't talk about tonight was kids.

Our eyes catch, and he immediately knows what I'm thinking. "I'm going to get you pregnant," he says. "But not yet. Two kids under two sounds like it might be a lot of work."

I laugh, half-relieved, half-terrified, and grab a condom packet.

"You're completely right. But I do want—"

"As many as you want," he says. "I'll love each one of them."

Works for me.

He groans as I roll on the condom.

I hold my breath as I slide down onto him. His fingers dig into my hips like he's worried I might change my mind and move away.

As if.

"So deep like this," I mutter. I start to move and my limbs lose all coordination. My body goes loose and languid.

"It's too much, baby, isn't it? Too good." He chuckles and leans me forward slightly as he thrusts up. "Such good intentions of fucking me. I really appreciate the effort. But know that it's always going to be me fucking you. That's how we work best together."

I cry out at his words, at the feel of his cock pressing into me, his hands either side of my waist, holding me in place. The sound of thunder in the distance.

He slams into me over and over and over, and I can barely keep from collapsing on his chest.

"Fuck," he hisses, slamming into me again. His hands move to my elbows now, holding me up, trying to keep me in place so we can both get to where we're headed. "You're so fucking sexy," he says.

His words tip me over the edge.

Dax.

He's the only man who's ever made me completely vulnerable like this, and I love him for it.

THIRTY-NINE

Dax

The alarm screeching from my phone makes Eira jump in my arms. I press a kiss to her temple and release her from where we're lying boneless and exhausted.

"I won't be long." As I pull on my jeans, all I can think is, thank god she came back to me. Thank god she's here. I've never seen myself with a woman before, not for the long term. But Guinevere has shifted everything. My life is different to how it was, and so is what I want from it. My research was always at the core of my identity, but now it's like an orbiting moon—important, but it's not the sun. Guinevere and Eira are what set my world in motion. I need their pull, their warmth, their presence to exist.

All the lights are off in Jacob's place. As I peer into the crib, Guinevere is wide awake like she's been waiting for me. As if she's too excited to sleep because she wants to know if I managed to win Eira round.

"She's ours," I whisper. "She came back to us."

She kicks and gives me a goofy grin like she's just as relieved as I am. I scoop her up in a blanket.

"Hey," Jacob says, wandering into the hall. "Everything go okay?"

"Yup," I say. "Great."

"Good talk," Jacob says.

"It's nearly midnight and Guinevere is going to get crabby if I dawdle. I can catch up with you tomorrow, seeing as you're so invested."

"Sue me for wanting to know if my baby brother enjoyed a date with the woman he's been waiting for his whole life."

My gaze darts to his.

"What?" He shrugs. "Just telling the truth. Was obvious in Norfolk. I'm glad she's taken pity on you. Seems like she's more than you deserve."

I roll my eyes. "She is."

Jacob nods. "Good for you."

For a fleeting second, I wonder if Jacob has even a fraction of the need to protect me as Eira does for her brother and sister. "Thanks Jacob," I say, my voice softer. "You're a good brother."

"Yeah?" he asks. "That's because you're terrible, so I have to make up for it."

I grin at him and disappear over the road with Guinevere.

When I've finished locking the doors, I can hear the shower going. I settle Guinevere in her DockATot while I get her milk. As I turn, out of the corner of my eye, my gaze lands on the bottle right next to her.

I grin. Eira can't help but care. Fuck, how did I get so lucky?

I grab the latest *British Medical Journal* and sit, cradling

Guinevere in my arms, and give her the milk. I flip open the publication and start to read. "'Abstract Objectives To determine the extent and content of academic publishers' and scientific journals' guidance for authors on the use of generative artificial intelligence—" I break off. "This is going to be a good one," I say. "Might even be useful."

I feel Eira's hand on my shoulder before I hear her. "What are you doing?" she asks.

"Reading her the *British Medical Journal*. She loves it."

She laughs. "Of course she does."

"I'm serious."

She bends and gives Guinevere a kiss on the head. "Hey, sweet girl. I missed you."

Maybe I'm imagining it, but I swear there's a flicker of recognition in Guinevere's eyes.

"Can I get you anything?" she asks, heading to the kitchen. "I'm grabbing a water."

My jaw falls open as I see she's wearing my old Cambridge t-shirt. "No, but I'm going to enjoy the view."

Her head tilts to one side as if to tell me I'm incorrigible. "I'll have a drink and call a cab."

My body tenses and I frown. "A cab for who, exactly?"

She grins at me. "I'll head back to the flat and—"

"No, Eira. No, you won't. I'm not giving you up again."

She brings her glass over to the table and sits down opposite us. Just her being nearer calms me, like she's human propofol or something. "It's just one night. We haven't discussed logistics or what comes next and—"

"Do we need to?" I thought I'd made myself completely clear. "I want you. I want to be with you. I love you."

Even in this low light, I can see her blush.

"I love you too," she says. "And I want to be with you. But this is new and—"

"Then stay. There's no point in you going somewhere just because this feels fast. We both know this is it. That we're together from now on. Why delay the inevitable?"

She shrugs. "Okay, so I'll stay."

I don't even try to contain my grin. "Okay," I say.

"But I want some Guinevere snuggles. You're hogging her."

"I think we can arrange that," I reply. "You can burp her once she's done feeding. In the meantime, you want to tell me what kind of engagement ring you want?"

She narrows her eyes at me. "You're quite the romantic."

"Stop dodging the question. I'm not good with the creative stuff. I'm not like Zach. Unless you want to end up with something awful, you've got to give me some hints."

"I don't care about a ring," she replies. Before I get the chance to reply, she says, "You know something that I'd really love?"

"Name anything. If it's in my power, I'll get it for you."

"I want my brother and sister to get to know you. Sooner rather than later. Your brothers are... I've met them all. They all seem wonderful..."

"But they're overwhelming?" I suggest. "A pain in the neck? We can move so we're not opposite Jacob if you'd prefer and—"

She laughs. "I mean it—I really like your family, but I don't want to feel like I'm having to step away from mine to be with yours. Eddie is still young and needs me even if it's not in the way I thought. Dylan too, in his own way. I love them both and I want..." She clasps her hands together. "The Coves and the Cadogans to mesh well. I don't want my brother and sister to feel like I'm deserting them. It's been the three of us for a long time."

I groan. "Of course. I'm a selfish prick at times. Let's go and see them next weekend or invite them here. And then... maybe we should do what Nathan and Madison have done and buy our own place in Norfolk, so we have the base for the Cadogan-Coves."

"The Cadogan-Coves?" Eira asks.

"It's got a nice ring to it." I glance down at Guinevere. "Don't you think, Guinevere? You think we should all become Cadogan-Coves?"

Eira gasps. "You wouldn't mind changing your name?"

"I'd do anything for you," I reply. "If you want us all to be Cadogans, that's fine too."

"I think you might be a keeper, Dax Cadogan-Cove."

"Glad you think so, Eira Cadogan-Cove."

Guinevere turns her head and the teat of the bottle slips out of mouth. "Guess she's done," I say. "I think she wants snuggles with you."

I sit back in my chair as Eira puts Guinevere over her shoulder and gently pats her back.

Three months ago, I had no clue my life was about to change. And now it has, I can't believe this exact moment wasn't what I'd been aiming for my entire life. Everything in this second is perfect. I'm the luckiest guy in the world.

EPILOGUE

Eira

I shift from foot to foot, glancing at the side table and the footstool. "I think we need to move it back where it was."

Dax doesn't say anything, just puts Guinevere in her bouncer and picks up the footstool. I pick up the side table and we swap places. Again.

"It doesn't look like it did in the shop," I say. "It's bluer."

"Then we'll get a new one," Dax says. He's being so bloody patient with me it's annoying. I know I'm being irrational, it's just that I'm so nervous. I expected Dylan and Eddie to meet people and start families. I always saw myself as being the aunt who would visit each of them. I didn't expect them to be the ones visiting me and my new family. It's not that I don't think they'll accept Dax. I've spoken to them both by phone and they're delighted that I'm so happy. The reality is so different from what I've kept in my head all these years, I just need time to get used to it.

The doorbell rings and my stomach churns like I'm on a ship in the North Sea. "Shall I get it?" I ask.

Dax laughs. "Well one of us should."

I start toward the door. "Yes. I should."

Eddie's grinning at me as I open the door. "This is a bloody nice house," she says. "I've brought my swimming costume."

She catches sight of Dax behind me and barges in, thrusting her case at me.

"Dax!" Despite never having only met him once before, she wraps her hands around his waist and pulls him into a hug like he's her long-lost brother.

She steps back and looks him up and down. "Yes, as I remember, very good-looking," she says as if he can't hear her. "And you're definitely not after her money?"

I groan and shut the front door. "Stop with the inappropriate questions!"

"Absolutely never," she replies. "You might think you only have to look after us, but I'm here to tell you that we're here to look after you too. In fact, Dylan and I have put together a list of questions."

I put my face in my hands. It's only Guinevere letting out a squeal that stops the argument before it's started.

"Baby!" Eddie says as she follows the noise.

"Wash your hands before you pick her up," I call out, but she's already made the detour to the sink.

"She's super-cute." She flings the towel on the counter and bends to the bouncer. "I'm your auntie Eddie," she says, and my heart hooks onto my ribs.

Dax slides his arm around my waist. He asked me last night whether or not I wanted Guinevere to call me mummy and whether we should look into me adopting her. We had to park the issue because I couldn't stop the tears. Happy tears, but lots of tears nonetheless.

I'm thinking about it. I'm so used to being a nanny, I

need a little time to get my head round the possibility of being a mum. I won't love her any differently, whatever she calls me.

"Built-in babysitter," Dax says.

"We don't lack for those," I say.

"I hear you have four brothers and none of them are still single?" Eddie says. "I have to ask before Dylan gets here. He wouldn't allow it on our agreed list of questions. He said it was inappropriate."

"He wasn't wrong," I say.

"Your intelligence is correct," Dax says. "Five brothers, if you include my cousin Vincent, and we're all married or engaged or about to be."

Eddie groans. "Your timing is shitty," she says to me. "You could have found him a little earlier."

I glance up at Dax and then kiss him on the shoulder. I think I found him at the perfect time.

"Wait, what did you say?" Eddie asks. "Are you two engaged?"

"Not yet," I jump in to reassure her. "I wanted you and Dylan to meet Dax and then...we need to find a ring."

She turns to Dax. "So have you asked her or not?"

"Not officially," he replies.

Eddie nods. "Okay. And you're going to get pre-nups?" she says.

It's such a relief to hear her be so practical. So grown-up. When she turns twenty-five, she's going to be a very wealthy woman. She needs to be sensible.

"We went to see lawyers last week," Dax says. "Because Eira bought half the house and it's now also in her name."

"And you checked this with your own lawyer, Eira?" She uses the tone I've used with her a hundred times—the one that says, *Are you looking after yourself, are you protecting yourself, have you thought this through?*

"Yes. Everything's fine."

"So if I spill or break something, I'm in my sister's house, so I don't need to have a panic attack?"

Dax laughs. "You're in your family's house." He pats her on the shoulder. "So no, you don't need to have a panic attack."

"But try not to spill or break or set fire to anything," I say, rolling my eyes.

The doorbell goes again and I jump, even though I've been expecting it.

"That's your uncle Dylan," Eddie tells Guinevere. "Don't go near him. He stinks."

Dax starts to laugh. "This Cadogan dynamic feels very familiar."

"Do you have any hot friends?" Eddie asks Dax as I head to the door.

"I'll draw up a short-list."

As I open the door, Dylan's glassy eyes greet me, and instantly I feel the tears build in my own. "We did it," he says. I grab him and wrap my arms around him. It's the first time I've seen him in person since we got word of our uncle's death and our inheritance.

"I feel like a survivor," he says. "And it's not about the money. I mean we survived our parents' indifference and then their absence and then our uncle's betrayal. It's only now, as I pulled up in front of the house—the house that you're going to be living your best life in—that I can imagine a future where we can break free of the past."

He's right. Our uncle's death has cut the final tether of our history. We can look to our future now.

I release him and pull him over the threshold. "It's our

time to be happy."

Eddie walks toward us, Guinevere in her arms. "I've already told her you stink and she should stay away from you."

Dylan presses a kiss to Eddie's cheek. "I love you," he says, completely ignoring what she said.

"I mean, he's alright. And you can always count on him, trust him and all that. He's really loyal and kind and clever." She shrugs. "He just stinks. Can't help it."

Dylan doesn't even flinch at his sister's description. He spots Dax as he approaches and holds out his hand. "Dax. Good to meet you."

They shake and then hug. "Welcome to the family," Dylan says, nodding to Eddie. "You may live to regret the introduction."

Dax chuckles. "You haven't seen anything yet." He looks over at me. "I think the Cadogan-Coves were made for each other."

I think he might be right.

A FEW MONTHS *later*

Dax

We're all standing in wellies in a Norfolk field, looking across at our parents' new house two hundred meters away. The builders have finally left, and Mum and Dad moved back in last weekend.

"It looks great from here," Jacob says.

"It looks bloody expensive," Dad says and turns back to me. "Now, Dax, can you tell me why we're standing in the middle of next door's field?"

"The new house looks good. And it's big," I say. "But I'm not sure it's big enough."

"Big enough!?" Dad yells. "What are you talking about? It's the size of a small hotel. We have eight bedrooms! Four in the old house and four in the new house."

"Eight bedrooms is a lot of bedrooms," I say, trying to keep Dad calm. "But you have a lot of kids."

"Six," he says.

"Right. And we're reproducing at a rate of knots," Jacob says.

He's the only one I've told about my plans. We've become closer since I moved in opposite. Perhaps it's because we see each other more. Perhaps it's because we've both become fathers. Maybe it's because Sutton and Eira get on so well. Most likely it's a combination of all those things. And Eira. Because Eira makes me feel more connected to everything, including my family. Which is why we're all standing here.

Vincent chuckles. "That's true. Who's next to announce they're popping out another kid?"

Beau and Vivian exchange a look but keep quiet. I don't say anything but I can't help glancing at Eira, who's rocking a grumbly Guinevere. It's close to nap time. It's because of Eira that I even noticed my brother and his wife are keeping a secret. It's because of her I've got the connection to Guinevere I do. I literally owe her my life. My happiness. My future.

"Let's just enjoy baby Juliette for a few weeks, shall we?" Mum suggests, cooing at Sutton and Jacob's two-week-old daughter. "You rainbow babies get twice the love, did you know that, Juliette?" I don't think I even said anything to Jacob when he and Sutton lost their first baby. I guess I didn't understand how they would feel—what a light must have gone out in their world. I do now.

"So what's with the field? Are we going to have you

camp outside?" Dad asks.

"No, but we—Eira and I—bought the lot. I'm planning to build a place on it," I say. "As our families expand, even with Madison and Nathan having the place nearby, there just won't be enough space."

Mum lets out a sob, and I turn to her.

"You're upset?" I ask. I really hoped she'd be pleased.

Her eyes are filled with tears, and Dad takes her hand. "Told you," he mumbles to her, and she nods.

"What's going on?" Beau asks. "Did I miss something?"

"Your mother is happy, that's all," Dad says.

"Could have fooled me," I say.

Dad pats me on the shoulder, and I feel like I should know something I don't.

"What?" I ask. "What's going on?"

"I just thought you'd be the one I'd lose," Mum says. "Of all of you, you were always the most distant." She shakes her head. "I blame myself because—"

"No!" Dad bellows. "Not having that. He's both of ours. We both worked. If Dax was neglected, you're not taking the blame."

"We were all neglected," Beau says, laughing. "I could make a spaghetti bolognese at eleven years old."

Jacob rolls his eyes. "Boo-fucking-hoo. That's not such a big deal. We were just a busy, big family. We had to get resourceful at times. That's no bad thing."

"None of us were neglected," Zach says. He looks around as if he's expecting everyone to agree with him. Is he new? The only way to build consensus in this family is to target a common enemy. Or to have a baby.

"No one was neglected," Vincent says. "And that includes me."

"But Dax was always a little different," Dad says. "Your

mother always thought it was because he was the last of you. My theory was that he was just disdainful of us all."

"Oh he's definitely disdainful," Beau says with a chuckle.

"I still don't understand why Mum is crying," says Jacob.

"She's just relieved Dax isn't going anywhere," Dad says.

"Where would I go?" I ask, completely confused.

Dad pats my back, and I look at Mum, wondering if someone's going to answer me.

"I thought you'd just drift away, that's all," she says. "I didn't expect you to...be here." She clears her throat. "But I'm ever so grateful that you are. And Guinevere and Eira. And Eddie and Dylan too. You know you are now officially part of our family." She looks at Eddie as her voice cracks, and I pull her into a hug.

"We're like the Mafia," Dad says. "Once you're in, there's no getting out."

"You didn't neglect me." I speak low and directly into her ear. I want her to know I mean it. "I never felt neglected. I felt independent." Eira was neglected by her parents, but I never was. I pull back. "And now we're going to be neighbors. But not because I don't want to be with you. I'm just being practical."

"I'm delighted," she says. "You'll be a few yards away. The best of both worlds."

"There's room in this field for more than one house, isn't there?" Beau asks, and everyone laughs.

"It's going to be a compound," Kate says. "In the best way. And it will be great to have people's extended family up here. I know Granny's said she'll come up this summer."

"We'd love to have her," Mum says.

"We would," Dad agrees.

A grumble of thunder steals our attention and we all look to the sky.

"Let's head in," Dad says. "Don't want all these babies cold and wet. I'm talking about my sons of course." He laughs to himself. I catch myself smiling, too.

As we head back to the house, Jacob, Eddie, Eira and I find ourselves in a group at the back.

"So what's next for you, Eddie?" Jacob asks.

"That's the question of the day," Eddie says. She's been talking about nothing else since graduation. What to do until she has access to her inheritance and she can fund the startup she has an idea for.

"Can I make a suggestion?" Jacob says.

"Please! I just want someone to tell me what to do!"

Jacob laughs. "Just go and do life for a bit. Have some fun and create some memories. I have the best memories from when I was your age. That time I went to Paris and had to sleep on a bench and ended up in prison..."

"That doesn't sound ideal," Eira says.

"What about the time you poisoned everyone at the Michelin-starred restaurant where you worked as a bus boy?" I say. "Fun times."

Eira has a look of horror on her face.

"So, what? Go to Paris?" Eddie asks. "I don't want to stay in London and waitress. I want to do something exciting."

"Go backpacking around Europe. Go to Mexico and feed dolphins or turtles or whatever you feed there."

"I like the idea of an adventure," Eddie says. "But what? I don't just want to go backpacking. I need a plan."

"You could do a ski season?" Eira suggests.

"Yeah, except I hate skiing and the cold. Apart from

that, great idea."

"What about being a tour rep?" Jacob suggests.

"What are we talking about?" Nathan asks. He's broken off from the group in front of us.

"Eddie is trying to think of something to do before she gets her inheritance."

"First-world problems, right?" Eddie says. "I know I sound like a brat, but it feels like I have a window to have some fun."

"My previous PR director, Gretel, now runs an upscale hotel in New York," Nathan says. "It's meant to be a well-ness retreat in the city or something. She's always looking for staff. You could go and work for her."

"New York?" Eddie asks. "That sounds fun. What kind of staff does she want? I'm not a yoga teacher or anything."

"They always need waitstaff, housekeeping, that kind of thing," Nathan replies.

Eddie and Eira share a glance. They seem to know what each other is thinking without talking, but I'm sure Eira likes this idea. She'll hate that Eddie is so far away, but she'll live with it if it's in her sister's best interests.

"I've got waitressing experience," Eddie says. "And I like the idea of being in New York."

"Isn't that the place where no one talks?" Jacob says.

"Yeah, they run silent retreat days," Nathan says. "But not every day is like that."

"How do they keep children quiet?" Eira asks, probably already mentally planning our multiple trips to the resort to visit Eddie.

"Can you introduce me to your friend?" Eddie asks.

As we all line up at the door, Eira glances at me and I squeeze her hand. She smiles in the same way I do every time I'm reminded she's right by my side.

"I think I'm ready for the ring," she says.

I laugh. "Finally, you want to marry me."

"I always knew it would happen, but anytime from now would be okay by me."

Her timing is spot on because I have her engagement ring with me, and I'm planning on officially proposing at dinner tonight while we have all the Cadogan-Coves together.

"Anytime from now is okay by me, too," I reply.

"I was thinking Antigua via New York for the honeymoon," she says, half-laughing as she says it.

"Of course you were. Sounds perfect." I press a kiss to her lips.

I don't care where in the world I am, as long as I've got my two girls.

HAVE you missed any in the series?

- **Dr. Off Limits - Jacob & Sutton**
- **Dr. Perfect - Zach & Ellie**
- **Dr. CEO - Vincent & Kate**
- **Dr. Fake Fiancé - Beau & Vivian**
- **Private Player - Nathan & Madison**

Get my next book, Eddie's story in **The Boss + The Maid = Chemistry**

A bossy, alpha New York businessman who meets his match in the maid who makes his bed (in more ways than one)

The Boss + The Maid = Chemistry

BOOKS BY LOUISE BAY

All books are stand alone

The Boss + The Maid = Chemistry

The Doctors Series

Dr. Off Limits

Dr. Perfect

Dr. CEO

Dr. Fake Fiancé

Dr. Single Dad

The Mister Series

Mr. Mayfair

Mr. Knightsbridge

Mr. Smithfield

Mr. Park Lane

Mr. Bloomsbury

Mr. Notting Hill

The Christmas Collection

14 Days of Christmas

The Player Series

International Player

Private Player

Dr. Off Limits

<u>Standalones</u>

Hollywood Scandal

Love Unexpected

Hopeful

The Empire State Series

<u>The Gentleman Series</u>

The Ruthless Gentleman

The Wrong Gentleman

<u>The Royals Series</u>

King of Wall Street

Park Avenue Prince

Duke of Manhattan

The British Knight

The Earl of London

<u>The Nights Series</u>

Indigo Nights

Promised Nights

Parisian Nights

Faithful

What kind of books do you like?

Friends to lovers

Mr. Mayfair

Promised Nights

International Player

Fake relationship (marriage of convenience)

Duke of Manhattan

Mr. Mayfair

Mr. Notting Hill

Enemies to Lovers

King of Wall Street

The British Knight

The Earl of London

Hollywood Scandal

Parisian Nights

14 Days of Christmas

Mr. Bloomsbury

The Boss + The Maid = Chemistry

Office Romance / Workplace romance

Mr. Knightsbridge

King of Wall Street

The British Knight

The Ruthless Gentleman

Mr. Bloomsbury

Dr. Perfect

Dr. Off Limits

Dr. CEO

The Boss + The Maid = Chemistry

Second Chance

International Player

Hopeful

Best Friend's Brother

Promised Nights

Vacation/Holiday Romance

The Empire State Series

Indigo Nights

The Ruthless Gentleman

The Wrong Gentleman

Love Unexpected

14 Days of Christmas

Holiday/Christmas Romance

14 Days of Christmas

British Hero

Promised Nights (British heroine)

Indigo Nights (American heroine)

Hopeful (British heroine)

Duke of Manhattan (American heroine)

The British Knight (American heroine)

The Earl of London (British heroine)

The Wrong Gentleman (American heroine)

The Ruthless Gentleman (American heroine)

International Player (British heroine)

Mr. Mayfair (British heroine)

Mr. Knightsbridge (American heroine)

Mr. Smithfield (American heroine)

Private Player (British heroine)

Mr. Bloomsbury (American heroine)

14 Days of Christmas (British heroine)

Mr. Notting Hill (British heroine)

Dr. Off Limits (British heroine)

Dr. Perfect (British heroine)

Dr. Fake Fiancé (American heroine)

Dr. Single Dad (British heroine)

Single Dad

King of Wall Street

Mr. Smithfield

Sign up to the Louise Bay mailing list www.louisebay/newsletter

Read more at www.louisebay.com

Printed in Great Britain
by Amazon

41727817R00179